OTHER BOOKS AND AUDIOBOOKS
BY JENNIFER MOORE:

Becoming Lady Lockwood

Lady Emma's Campaign

Miss Burton Unmasks a Prince

Simply Anna

Lady Helen Finds Her Song

A Place for Miss Snow

Miss Whitaker Opens Her Heart

Miss Leslie's Secret

A NOVEL

My Dearest ENEMY

JENNIFER MOORE

Covenant Communications, Inc.

Published by Covenant Communications, Inc.
American Fork, Utah

Printed in the United States of America
First Printing: April 2018

10 9 8 7 6 5 4 3 2

ISBN: 978-1-52440-471-0

For Wayne and Eileen.
I love your son and being part of your family.
With you, I won the in-law jackpot.

ACKNOWLEDGMENTS

I AM SO GRATEFUL FOR all the people who helped me with this book.

Of course, Frank and my boys are my support system. They listen to my plot ideas, tiptoe around when I'm reading and writing, and endure hours of war documentaries. I'm the luckiest person in the world to have a family like mine.

Thank you to Laurie Lewis for your fabulous *Free Men and Dreamers* series. It inspired me, taught me, and touched my heart. I'm so glad we've become friends.

I'm grateful for my girls, Nancy Allen and Josi Kilpack, who helped me with this plot and encouraged me when I was nervous about switching from British history. You two are my anchors.

Thank you, Michelle Shaw, for sharing your pictures of winter in Detroit. Your kids are adorable.

I'm so grateful for a mother, Penny Lunt, who loves history and genealogy. She found an ancestor who fought at Frenchtown, Private William Tidwell. Knowing this battle is part of my personal history gave me a connection to the story and made it all the more special.

And of course, my dad, Ed Lunt, for the countless rock-hunting trips and for buying me my own little pickaxe so we could find fossils. Thanks for answering my questions about mineral compounds and geological phenomena. Your collection of rocks and bones and minerals and gems is a fixture of my childhood, and I loved including that bit of you in this story.

Thank you to the team at Covenant. Kami Hancock, for your sharp editing eye—thanks for smoothing out the rough edges. Thanks, Christina Marcano, for the beautiful cover.

CHAPTER 1

"Blast the United States of America." Abigail Tidwell spoke in a loud voice, feeling very self-satisfied at the echo the words produced in the empty woodbox. She smiled smugly and almost laughed imagining her father's or Isaac's reaction to her vulgarity, but thanks to the cursed United States of America, they were both away. And Abigail was left to manage the house alone. Including the outside chores.

Slamming down the lid, she huffed out a breath, though no one was around to see how inconvenienced she was, then wrapped a cloak around her shoulders and slipped through the door, bracing herself against the onslaught of frigid wind that blew the cold straight through layers of clothing, skin, and muscle, directly into her bones. Even after placing the last log onto the fire, she'd waited before going out to the woodshed to replenish the supply by the hearth, hoping the storm would end. But it hadn't let up all day, and if she delayed much longer, the fire would burn out completely, leaving her house cold and dark for the entire night.

She pulled her cloak tighter, noting how, in just a few seconds, the blowing snow had already nearly covered the blue wool in white flakes. Her cheeks stung from the cold. She trudged out toward the woodshed feeling put out. Neither her older brother nor her father would ever have let the woodbox become empty. But there was nothing for it now. If only James Madison hadn't declared war on Great Britain, then she and the rest of Upper Canada would not have to worry about brothers and fathers leaving home, gunships filling the Great Lakes, and battalions of troops marching through peaceful towns.

The American president was so far away in Washington City, and yet the war seemed so close to Abigail. Close enough that last summer, she'd heard the cannon blasts all the way across the river as the battle raged in Detroit. Luckily the British Army had taken the city and put a stop to the Americans' violence. And even more luckily, His Majesty's soldiers at Fort Detroit and Fort Malden had the services of the very best physician-surgeon in all of the empire: Abigail's father, Dr. William Tidwell.

Another burst of snowy wind nearly bowled her over, and Abigail thought of a few choice phrases she'd learned from Isaac and his military companions. Phrases she knew they would have been aghast to realize a young lady had overheard, but which seemed to perfectly fit as a description for the blue-coated enemy on the other side of the border. If not for the cursed Americans, Isaac—Major Isaac Tidwell, if one was to be particular—would be able to visit his family home on the outskirts of Amherstburg, Ontario, more often, instead of being assigned to train soldiers, guard prisoners, plan defenses, and endless matters of war-type business required for a man of his rank.

Abigail hadn't received a letter from Isaac in nearly a month. The true reason for the delay was merely winter. Ships couldn't sail over the frozen Lake Erie, and instead, letters and visiting brothers had to travel slowly and unreliably over the snow-covered land. Though she knew the truth, she found it much more gratifying to blame President Madison and his ridiculous declaration of war for all her inconveniences.

Though it cost his life, General Brock's well-trained British soldiers had already averted one American attack at Queenston Heights on the Niagara. *It serves those Americans right for trying to invade Upper Canada. With any luck, they won't try again.*

Abigail rounded the corner of the house, pulling her cloak even tighter against the wind. Although the chopped wood was kept in a small shed conveniently located beside the kitchen entrance, she couldn't open the kitchen door without brushing away the heap of snow blocking it. The snow had blown into high drifts against the east side of the house, and so instead of walking close to the outer wall and using it as a protection from the wind, she took a longer path, leaving her more exposed to the elements. And she grumbled the entire time.

The snow was deeper than it had been this morning when she'd gone out to the barn to feed and milk Maggie. She was glad her father and Isaac had patched up loose boards last summer and mended the leaking roof. Maggie's pen would be warm and snug and the feed dry.

Abigail glanced toward the barn then stopped. She looked more closely, squinting through flurries. But even in the waning daylight she could see the door was ajar. Surely she'd fastened it this morning. A coldness that had nothing to do with the weather clutched her heart. Had someone gone into the barn?

She turned and hurried back into the house, closing the door behind her and leaning against it. Of course it would be foolish for a young woman to investigate alone. No neighbors lived close enough for her to easily call on for help, especially not in this storm. The wisest course would be to wait until tomorrow when Mr. Kirby came by to fetch her milk and butter on his way into town. But she could hardly leave Maggie at the mercy of a thief or a wolf, or—she shuddered—a deserter. And what if she had simply forgotten to fasten the latch and raised an alarm for nothing?

Pulling her father's musket from the chimney pegs above the mantle, she opened the small box where he kept the lead balls and powder. Father had insisted she learn to handle the weapon, and Abigail had practiced loading and shooting numerous times. She was proud of her skill with the weapon that many would consider too heavy for her to even lift, but today her hands were shaking. Would she have to fire it at a person to protect her family's property?

She opened the door and reached for a lantern, hooking it over her arm and carrying it unlit as she stepped outside. She did not wish to give a possible intruder the advantage of remaining hidden in the shadows while illuminating herself.

She hardly noticed the chill or the wind as she approached the barn. Studying the ground outside, she saw no visible footprints, but if any had existed the wind would have erased them in any case. Her heart thumped as she clenched the weapon tightly and pushed open the barn door.

Peeking inside, she could see only shadows in the gloom. Maggie lowed from her pen in the far corner, likely displeased with the admittance of cold air. Looking toward the other side of the building, Abigail could see the outline of the wagon and the empty pen where Father stabled his horse, Magnus.

She stood still, listening for any other sound, but aside from the wind whistling outside and the whisper of a stray gust blowing straw over the ground, she heard nothing. But something wasn't right. She stood still, studying the inside of the barn as the obscure detail danced on the edge of her thoughts, just out of reach.

After a long moment, she recognized what was amiss. Blood. She smelled blood.

Abigail stepped back outside and lit the lantern, wishing she did not have to set down the musket in order to do so. Her hands were fumbling, and she feared someone might approach from behind while she'd set down the musket. What would she find when the interior of the barn was illuminated?

She held the lantern high and still managed to carry the musket—which was much heavier with one hand. Stepping quietly, she moved over the hard-packed dirt floor, and there, in the flickering halo of light, she saw him.

Abigail's first impulse was to run and barricade herself inside the house. But she stood frozen, fear stealing her ability to move. While she stared at the figure lying on the ground, two realizations occurred to her at the same time. First of all, the man was not moving, and based on the puddle of blood beneath him and the arrow sticking out of his side, he was injured very badly, if not dead. Secondly, and this realization was a matter of much graver concern: the man in her barn wore an American soldier's uniform.

Terror made her mouth taste like she'd licked a rusty nail. All of Abigail's muscles were clenched tight, and her mind first emptied then filled with a barrage of questions. None of which she knew the answer to. Where had the man come from? Was he alone? Was he a person meaning to do harm? He lay on his side as if he'd collapsed, blood covering his hands and clothes. Was it all his own?

She set the lantern on the ground and prodded his arm with the tip of the musket, but he did not move. Holding the weapon steadily aimed at him, she slid the lantern forward with her foot to get a better look and saw the rise and fall of his chest. He was alive then. But he did not shiver in his wet clothing, which was not a good sign, and blood continued to seep from his side. Though he was yet alive, he wouldn't remain so for long. She poked him again, this time harder, not trusting that he wasn't simply feigning insentience while waiting for her to move closer.

Her poke pushed him over so he rolled onto his back. The man made a noise so soft that it was less a groan than a sigh. The sound did something funny to Abigail's heart. A spot inside her grew warm, melting away some of the fear and opening a space that was filled by a swell of compassion. Though he was an enemy, he was still a man—someone's son, or perhaps a father. And Abigail was first and foremost a healer. And besides, she couldn't very well allow a cursed American to die in her barn, could she?

She lifted a coil of rope from a peg on the wall and tied one end around the soldier's wrist then threaded it through the spokes of a wagon wheel. Continuing along the side of the wagon, she threaded the rope though another wheel and tied it to the man's other wrist, quite proud of herself for the ingenious idea. Now, even if he did wake, he wouldn't be able to grab her while she worked on his wounds. And his hands were separated far enough so he couldn't untie himself, but he could still lie relatively comfortably on the ground.

She rushed back through the dark and returned with blankets, a bucket of water, and her small medical bag. The man still hadn't moved. In the flickering light, she could see he possessed strong cheekbones, and though his face was pale, it was well proportioned with a square jaw. If he wasn't a cursed American, he might be considered handsome. Now that he was bound, he seemed less menacing, and the feeling of compassion grew and with it, an urgency.

She removed the shako hat and felt his head. No fever. Well, that was good, although his skin was extremely cold. She checked the ends of his fingers, relieved to find no sign of frostbite, then turned her attention to the heavy woolen coat, trying to decide exactly how to remove it. It was wet and wouldn't slide off easily, and she'd already bound his wrists. The arrow had pierced straight through the wool, and she feared fibers would be inside the wound. But she imagined the thick material would have slowed the arrow down, possibly kept it from going too deep into the man's body. She decided she'd have to cut it off. Using scissors, she cut carefully around the arrow then cut along the length of the sleeves to pull out his arms, and finally drew the coat free, noticing the golden epaulets on the shoulders. She didn't imagine the captain would be pleased when he saw what had become of his uniform, but perhaps she could mend it later.

Next, she cut off his shirt, noticing it was made from soft cotton instead of the thicker homespun she was used to. A fine garment, but decidedly impractical for winter in Upper Canada. The man's chest and arms were muscled, his shoulders broad, and for some reason, this made Abigail blush. She was glad he was unconscious as she pulled away the shirt. She focused on her inspection. Aside from his arrow wound, he'd been cut on his upper arm. The wounds were clean. No swelling or discoloration on the torn flesh.

Abigail wasn't certain whether the soldier had fallen unconscious from the pain of his injuries or possibly exposure to the elements or even loss of blood. Perhaps a combination of all three.

She set to work, glad he wasn't awake to feel when she expanded his wound with a scalpel to extract the arrowhead. She moved the lantern close and checked the opening thoroughly to make sure no fibers or dirt had entered with the arrow then poured water over the wound. When she was satisfied that it was clean, she threaded the curved needle and sutured the lacerations closed. She used a mortar and pestle to crush herbs into a paste then wrapped thin cotton around the mixture to make a poultice that would hopefully keep away swelling and pain and draw out any infection. Holding the bundle against the wound, she tied bandages around the soldier's middle to keep it in place. Then she repeated the process with the wound on his arm. Luckily it was much shallower.

Abigail worked well into the night, hardly noticing the cold, doing everything in her power to ensure the soldier's survival. Once she was finished, she sat back, pushing away a lock of hair that had fallen over her forehead. So much was still uncertain. Would his body warm up? How much blood had he

CHAPTER 2

EMMETT WOKE AND WAS IMMEDIATELY struck by a flash of pain so strong that he gasped. He forced open his eyes, but his vision blurred, so he let them drift closed again. His head felt heavy, like it had been packed too full. And the pain. A burning flared in his side, just below his ribs, as if a searing iron was probing into him. He shifted, intending to touch the spot, but when he moved one arm down, the other lifted, stretching his side painfully. He groaned.

Water sated his parched throat, but he couldn't see where it had come from. He thought he heard kind words spoken in a woman's gentle voice, but that was obviously impossible. He must have fever madness. Time passed and he vacillated just on the edge of sleep, unable to force his mind to focus enough to fully wake.

An unknown amount of time passed, and finally, he felt a semblance of coherence. Cracking his eyes open, he saw he was in a dimly lit building with no furniture—a shed or a barn perhaps. The sound of a cow somewhere nearby made the second conjecture seem the most likely. He tried to move his arm again with the same result as before. *What the devil?* Turning his head inch by agonizing inch, he saw his wrists were bound. Though on an intellectual level he knew it would only cause more pain, his panic won out, and he pulled at the ropes, sending agony to his injuries. The knots were tight. His heart started pounding, and he tried to force his sluggish brain to make sense of what was happening to him.

His last memories were foggy. He was leading a company on a reconnaissance mission, hoping to gain information about Fort Malden's supply line for General Winchester. The regiment's trek north through Michigan Territory had been fraught with peril. The roads were nearly impassable, one day a swamp and the next, ice. Supplies were so far behind that the troops were in danger of starvation, and typhus fever spread through the camp, leaving three hundred men on the sick list at a time; an average of four daily died from the malady. And all this was in addition to the typical camp difficulties, such as blisters, leg sores, impetigo, and lice.

Emmett remembered crossing the frozen Detroit River with his small company and observing the fort from the woods, but something had happened . . . He tried to push through the murkiness, and suddenly the memory returned with sharp clarity. The Indian attack! Emmett jolted, trying to sit upright, but immediately wished he hadn't when the pain magnified and lights burst behind his eyes. What had happened to the men in his command? Were they injured as well? Captured? He must find out.

His burst of alarm exhausted him, and he lay his head back down . . . on a pillow? What kind of Indians wrapped their prisoners in quilts and provided feather pillows? His curiosity was overcoming the initial panic, and he tolerated the ache of moving his head again in order to have a better look at his surroundings. Nearby, he saw his hat and boots. And his uniform coat hung from a peg on the wall, the sleeve's gold decorations signifying his rank standing out against the dark-blue wool. What had happened to his gear? Had he lost his pack in the attack? As he became more aware, he felt that he was wearing a tight cap on his head, and on his hands—

The door creaked open, and Emmett's chest clenched when he saw the barrel of a musket poke through the opening.

A young woman entered, and he didn't know whether to be relieved or more afraid as she pointed the weapon at him. Did she have any idea how to use that old gun? He squinted, trying to make out her features in the gloom.

"Oh, you're awake," she said, and he couldn't tell whether her voice sounded surprised or relieved. The woman kept her distance, moving closer as she studied the bindings on his wrists, but not coming too close. Then, apparently confident that Emmett was still restrained, her demeanor relaxed. She leaned the musket against the wall near the door and brought in a lantern and a basket.

When the lantern light illuminated her, Emmett wondered for a moment if he was hallucinating. She was probably close to twenty years of age—making her around seven years his junior—and though he may later blame his opinion on blood loss addling his mind and giving the whole experience a dreamlike quality, he thought her unbelievably lovely. Her skin was a creamy white with a bit of pink on her nose and cheeks from the cold. Dark hair and dark eyes surrounded by long lashes contrasted against her skin in a way that was striking without being stark. He couldn't help but stare. Who was this woman? And what in the world was happening?

She moved toward him, crouching down and setting the lantern on the ground. "And your eyes are blue. I wondered—" She stopped talking, her cheeks turning pink as if she'd not meant to give voice to her thoughts. Clearing her throat, she adopted a more businesslike demeanor. "How do you feel, Captain?"

Though his officer training had included withstanding interrogation, negotiating with the enemy, and other procedures to follow if one was taken prisoner, nothing could have possibly prepared him for this scenario. He did not know how to respond.

At his silence, she wrinkled her brow. "Well, I imagine your injuries are still painful, and your head probably aches. You did lose quite a lot of blood." She squinted, peering closer at him. "It is normal to experience confusion. Not to worry, it will pass."

Confusion. That was putting it mildly. "Miss, am I your prisoner?"

"I prefer 'patient.' But yes, I suppose you are." She looked through the basket, drawing out some items. "I need to change your wrappings, if you don't mind."

"By all means."

She hesitated, and he saw a look of apprehension narrow her eyes and tighten the skin around her mouth. "I warn you not to try anything . . . malicious, sir. I am very adept with the musket."

"I would not dream of it, Miss . . . ?" He spoke the word as a question. Almost as much as his body needed healing, he needed information. If he could get her speaking, he might learn something useful; perhaps even discover a way to escape. It was imperative that he return to his men.

"Abigail Tidwell." She stood to give a small curtsy then knelt beside him, using scissors to cut the bandages from his arm. When she peeled away the wrappings, Emmett craned his neck to see the injury. The wound was close to three inches long and held together with sutures. He watched as she gently touched her fingertips to the gash and the area surrounding it and even leaned close to sniff it.

"How long have I been here?" he asked.

She didn't look up from her inspection. "I found you last night. It is nearly night again."

An entire day. The urgency returned. His men needed him. If they survived the attack, they could be wounded; at the very least, they were in hostile territory without a leader.

"The skin is red, but not overly so, and it does not feel hot, nor is there any discharge. It is healing nicely," she said, giving an encouraging smile. Then she reached for fresh bandages to rewrap it.

"Are you a doctor?" He meant the words to be teasing; of course a woman wasn't a doctor. The very idea was preposterous. But perhaps charm would work on this one, soften her defenses, and ease her fears about him.

"My father is a physician-surgeon, and I assist him."

The answer was a surprise. "And did he stitch my wound?" One thing he had encountered often during his career as a soldier was stitches, both on his own body and others', and he considered himself a sufficient authority on well-administered sutures. These were some of the best he'd seen.

"No. I did that." She tied off the bandage and then stopped, glancing up at him; her demeanor had suddenly turned less certain. He wondered at the reaction. Was she seeking his approval for a well-treated wound? He didn't imagine so. More likely she was worried that he did not believe she truly was the one to mend it.

"Where is your father now?"

The apprehensive expression remained on her face. "In the house. He should be here any moment." She turned back to the basket as she spoke, and he knew immediately that she was lying.

Now Emmett understood the reason for her worry. She was alone. After all, why would a doctor leave his daughter to tend to a patient when he was simply "in the house"? And there was also the matter of his restraints. They were the work of a person who was worried she might be overpowered. He kept his teasing expression. He could always count on winning a woman over with his flirting. He wasn't proud of it, but the skill had come in useful a time or two. "And does your father tie up all his patients?"

"No, of course not, but you are American. A person can't be too careful with an enemy soldier."

"I see." He smirked.

She still looked nervous, and he realized his charms weren't having the desired effect. Didn't she notice the roguish flick of his brow? Probably not. She was rather focused on his injuries.

"And are these socks, Miss Tidwell?" He wiggled his hands in their bindings, and colorful socks flopped back and forth off the tips of his fingers.

She gave a small nod. "I thought your hands might get cold."

"Blue and yellow stripes?"

"They were my grandmother's. She was nearly blind, so I would use the brightest yarn I could find to make her socks. She liked to see them."

He couldn't help but smile at the image of an old woman wearing the outrageously colored stockings. "And am I wearing Grandmother's hat, too?"

"My brother's." She pulled back the quilts to expose his other wound. The cocoon of warmth that had surrounded him was invaded by a burst of cold, and he shivered. But the invasion of chilly air brought with it another realization. Nearly *all* of his clothes had been removed. All that remained were his drawers.

"I'm sorry," she said, cutting the strips that bound his torso. "This one is much deeper. It will be tender." She brought the lantern even closer and laid her head nearly on the ground as she inspected the wound on his side.

"Miss Tidwell, where are my clothes?" He maintained a teasing tone, pretending to be shocked.

"They had to be removed to tend your wounds."

"Even the trousers?"

Red covered her cheeks and neck as she poked at his wound.

She was right—it *was* much more tender. Emmett sucked in a breath.

"They were wet, and you can't get warm in wet clothes. I needed to check your feet for frost burn, anyway." She rose to a kneeling position and set the backs of her fingers on the area around the wound, apparently checking his skin's temperature.

Her face, if possible, went even redder. Emmett laughed at her discomfort. And now he knew with utter certainty that she was alone.

She squinted and pointed at his side. "I know you cannot see it, but here is where the arrowhead was lodged. The wound is healing nicely, and there is no discharge." After a moment longer, Abigail retrieved fresh bandages, and he lifted up as well as he could while she reached under his back and across his torso a few times to fix the wrappings. "I saved the arrowhead for you, Captain Prescott," she said, pulling a sharp, triangular stone from her apron pocket.

"Why would you do that?"

She looked taken aback by the question, and rather offended. "I thought you might find it interesting. It's made from obsidian and has a rather unusual green tint."

"And how did you know my name?"

She glanced quickly toward his jacket.

"I imagine that you learned it from the letters in my coat." When she looked back, he held her gaze. "And you must have found the pouch of curious rocks in my pocket and assumed I'd want to add the arrowhead to the collection. I'm afraid you gave yourself away. You, Miss Tidwell, are a *snoop*."

She scowled and stood, tossing aside the arrowhead. Apparently teasing was not the way into this woman's favor. "Well, I had to know the character of the man in my barn, didn't I?"

"And what of *your* character, Miss Tidwell?" Emmett was growing tired of being polite. This was a matter of life or death, not a time for a young woman to play at doctor. There was a war happening this very moment, and he needed to return to his command. Though the position was excruciating, he shifted to the side to rest on one elbow. He was tired of Abigail Tidwell standing over him while he lay flat on his back, incapacitated. As if she were in charge here. He was a captain in the United States Army, for heaven's sake. "What kind of person ties up a bleeding man?" His voice came out angrier than he'd intended.

Abigail's eyes narrowed. "A person who is trying to save his life, thank you very much. And speaking of such, a little gratitude would be nice, but I suppose those common courtesies aren't of importance to cursed Americans." She snatched up the lantern and started toward the barn door, but then paused. She stood for a moment as Emmett blinked, momentarily shocked by her use of profanity. He'd certainly not charmed her.

She sighed and returned, fetching a cup and a teapot from the basket. "You need to drink."

She spoke as if giving him tea was the last thing she wanted to do, but she continued to tend him out of a sense of duty. Emmett held back a smile at the young woman's petulance. Duty was something he understood. She had a stubborn streak and was apparently used to getting her way, but he could see compassion overrode even her pride. Perhaps this failing was something he could use to his advantage. In time, her concern might prove useful. He must be patient, then, and above all not frighten her.

"I apologize," he said. "I suppose being injured hasn't improved my temper."

She knelt beside him and poured the tea, holding the cup as he took a sip.

Emmett grimaced. It tasted terrible.

"I know the flavor is bitter, but it helps with the pain." All traces of stubbornness were gone, and Abigail spoke in a gentler tone. "And you must sleep in order to heal."

"I do appreciate your excellent care," Emmett said. He could feel the ingredients in the tea beginning to take effect as his body grew heavy and his mind grew light. Laudanum, if he wasn't mistaken. A luxury seldom given to soldiers.

"Tomorrow I'll bring something to eat," she said, her voice sounding far away.

Emmett could feel his hold on awareness slipping away, and his final impressions were of his head being laid softly on a pillow and a quilt tucked around him.

CHAPTER 3

As ABIGAIL WENT ABOUT HER chores the next morning, Captain Prescott was never far from her mind. She was curious about him, which was to be expected. He was a stranger, after all. But in the time he'd been under her care, she'd peeked into the barn to check on him more often than necessary and knew she was being silly. Perhaps she could blame her excessive attentiveness on the lonely winter. Father and Isaac had been gone for months, and since the first snowfall, she'd ventured into town a very few times; usually only when she'd been sent for to assist with a birth. Most of the town didn't call for her when a resident took ill, not without her father. But occasionally she'd tended to a minor injury. She'd hardly even been able to go to church with the roads iced and buried in snow.

Her only visitor was Mr. Kirby when he came a few times a week with his sleigh to pick up the milk. And the older man wasn't much for conversation. Living more than a mile outside the small town had its drawbacks, so naturally she was glad to have someone to talk to, even if that someone was an American soldier who thought himself charming.

Once she'd dressed and set the kettle over the fire, she prepared a simple soup. Something to give her patient nutrition but not upset his stomach while he was still mending.

Abigail felt a rush of nerves as she packed bread and more bandages and medicines into the basket. What would Captain Prescott say today?

She couldn't help but wonder about the soldier's life. He spoke as a gentleman; obviously he was educated. And she liked the intonation to his speech. The blacksmith's wife, Mrs. Elliott, from South Carolina, spoke similarly. Both pronounced their words a bit differently, farther back in their mouths, it seemed. And the vowels were drawn out. Captain Prescott must be from the southern states, she reasoned. And she didn't like that at all. She knew what kind of people lived in the southern part of America. Wealthy landowners who profited off the labor of slaves. The very idea disgusted her. She'd heard tales of the cruelties of slave owners and considered anyone who could treat another soul with such brutality to be the worst type of creature. Nothing in Captain Prescott's letters had mentioned slavery, but she didn't consider that sufficient exoneration.

She threw on her cloak and stepped out into the frigid morning, wishing winter would end so she could see the sun for more than a few short hours per day.

Remembering how he'd called her a snoop yesterday made her stomach hot with embarrassment. Of course poking her nose into the man's correspondence and personal things hadn't been strictly necessary. But curiosity combined with loneliness had made her a meddler, she supposed. In any case, the letters had not been very interesting. One, that seemed rather cold, was from his father. But Abigail knew not everyone was as blessed with a father as affectionate as hers. Another was from a woman named Lydia and spoke mostly about mutual acquaintances, dresses, and parties. The other letters were military documents.

And his collection of rocks had captivated her. She'd not met anyone else who'd shared her fascination with geology. She wondered if he was interested in mineral compounds or just liked to pick up curious rocks.

Abigail paused outside the barn doors as her nervousness returned, making her insides squirm. She may have only imagined it, but there were a few moments the day before when she'd thought Captain Prescott was flirting with her. Of course, men had flirted with her before, but none of her suitors had lasted long. Men didn't like when a woman was interested in science or doctoring, which was considered a man's profession. Besides, not one of them could ever compare to her father. But Captain Prescott's flirting had made her feel shivery. And it unnerved her. She couldn't grow too fond of the man when she intended to turn him in to the soldiers at Fort Malden as soon as he was mended. And Captain Prescott was very difficult not to grow fond of. Abigail breathed in the cold morning air until she felt collected enough to enter the barn.

"Good morning, Miss Tidwell."

Abigail stopped in the doorway, surprised. Somehow Captain Prescott had pulled himself into a sitting position. He'd manipulated the rope, drawing it to one side so he could rest his back against a wagon wheel. One arm rested in his lap and the other hung, suspended in the air. The quilts were wrapped around his waist. He bowed his head forward and gave a smile showing a flash of white teeth.

She smiled back and gave a curtsy. "You look much better today, Captain." Maggie lowed loudly from her pen, and Abigail glanced toward her. "I have some food, but it will take me a little while to get milk. Would you like to eat breakfast now? Or wait?"

"I'll wait if you intend to join me." He rested his head back on the wheel's spokes.

The position didn't look at all comfortable, but Abigail was glad he was moving. Her father said patients recovered much quicker if they were able to get up and move about. She nodded and hurried to milk the cow.

A quarter of an hour later, Abigail returned. She took a pewter cup from the basket and scooped fresh milk into it. Removing a sock from one of his hands, she gave him the cup. She thought nothing tasted better than warm, creamy milk on a cold morning.

He took a drink and sighed, giving a nod. He must agree. Captain Prescott's hanging arm dipped when he lifted the other to drink. Rather like a marionette. The lack of control over his limbs must be extremely frustrating, but he did not act like it bothered him at all.

He lifted his chin, pointing at the bucket. "That's quite a lot of milk for one person."

"It is not all for me," she said, taking the lid off a larger can and pouring the milk inside. During the warm months, the family kept milk in the springhouse, a cool storage area built into a hill, but in the winter, the barn's temperature remained low enough. "My neighbor, Mr. Kirby, will take it into town to sell." She replaced the metal lid and moved the milk closer to the barn door. Laying a cloth on the ground, she knelt beside Captain Prescott. "How are your injuries feeling today?"

"Better."

"I am glad to hear it."

He set the cup on the floor. "If I say I am healed, will you let me go?"

His voice was light, but she did not think he was teasing. She poured warm soup into a mug and handed it to him. "I apologize, but I cannot. I must turn you in to General Procter at Fort Malden as soon as you are well enough."

His eyes tightened, but the rest of his face remained pleasant. "I see."

She took bread from the basket and sliced it, careful to keep the knife away from the captain. "You are an officer; I'm sure you will be treated well." A hot rush of guilt felt bitter inside, and she couldn't bring herself to look at him as she spoke. "Would you like butter and jam?"

"Yes. Thank you."

Abigail cut herself a slice as well, and for a moment they ate in silence. She was sorry to have ruined the pleasant mood and tried to think of things to say that might return the conversation to its earlier friendliness. "Your face is not as pale this morning." She cringed at the stupidity of the observation. She glanced up and saw he was studying her. He did not look angry that she was planning to turn him in, simply pensive.

Abigail tried again. "Where are you from, Captain Prescott?"

He brushed some breadcrumbs from the quilt. "I've lived in Baltimore for the past six years, stationed at Fort McHenry."

"Oh, my father told me about Baltimore. He said there is no city so culturally refined in all of the United States."

He nodded. "I suppose there are enough balls, concerts, and theatrical performances to please even the most genteel members of society. My father and stepmother have a home in the city, and they insist on going out every night to some sort of entertainment or another."

His lip curled the smallest bit, indicating that these pleasures were not to his liking. Abigail was rather jealous. She'd not traveled farther than the other side of Lake Erie, and while she enjoyed the gatherings in Upper Canada, they were not grand as she imagined an assembly in the elegant city of Baltimore to be.

He took another sip of the milk. "Did your father live in Baltimore?"

"No. He attended medical lectures from Dr. William Shippen at the College of Philadelphia. But he promised to take me one day to see a concert and the fine shops on Lexington Street."

"And the war has put a halt on your travel plans." Captain Prescott reached for a cloth, but his arm stopped. He winced at the pull in his side, and Abigail felt a renewal of the guilty sensation. She handed him the cloth, and he wiped jam from the corner of his mouth.

She nodded. "I suppose it has."

"My family is from Virginia," he said.

Abigail wrinkled her nose. "Slave owners."

His expression changed, a small smile pulling at his mouth, but his eyes didn't join in the smile, and she didn't know whether or not her words had made him angry. "Not everyone in Virginia owns slaves, Miss Tidwell."

She felt the reprimand, though she realized it wasn't a denial. She tried again to keep the conversation friendly. "And do you have other family, aside from your father and stepmother?"

"An elder brother and a younger sister."

Abigail smiled. "I've always wanted a sister. What's she like?"

"Not at all like you."

"Oh." She pulled back, feeling insulted and rather hurt by the bluntness of his reply.

He smirked at her reaction. "My sister does not tie up men in her barn. In fact, I don't think she has ever set foot in a barn in her life. She doesn't know how to identify igneous rocks, and at the first sight of blood, she'd have fainted dead away."

She softened, realizing he hadn't meant his words to be a slight. They were actually rather complimentary. "Well, it is fortunate that I found you, and she did not."

He raised his milk cup in a salute. "Fortunate indeed. Lydia would have needed more medical care than I if she'd discovered a wounded soldier."

"Lydia." She recognized the name from his papers.

"Yes, I believe you read her letter."

She nodded, not bothering to deny it when he already knew. "You're fond of her."

"I love my sister more than any person on this earth." Captain Prescott gave the first genuine smile she'd seen. And the effect was remarkable. His eyes brightened, sending wrinkles fanning from their corners. And his face lost its hardness, revealing a much more kindhearted man. "And I miss her dreadfully. Even though she is absolutely the most frivolous young lady who ever lived."

Abigail smiled in return, imagining the captain as a doting brother rolling his eyes at his younger sister's chattering. "And your brother. What is he like?"

The captain's smile dropped away and his eyes tightened. "According to my father, he is perfect."

She grimaced at the change in his demeanor, wishing she'd not asked the question that chased away his good humor.

He lifted a shoulder. "Surely you understand; you have a brother."

Abigail cleared away the remains of the meal and brought the basket of bandages around to his other side to check his injuries. "I think my brother is more like you, sir. He is kind and loving to me. But I haven't seen him for months. Not since the war began. He's stationed—" She snapped her mouth shut. "I probably shouldn't tell you."

Captain Prescott was watching her closely, and she realized she'd almost told something that could possibly endanger her brother, or His Majesty's Army. Although she wasn't sure what she could and couldn't say, remaining quiet on matters of troop movement when speaking to the enemy was likely the best policy.

She removed the bandage on his arm and found the cut was still healing exactly as it should. He leaned forward while she removed the bandages from around his torso, and she found the more serious wound to be in good shape as well. "Soon enough, you'll be back on your feet, Captain," she said as she rewrapped it. "I've only seen one other arrow wound, and it was shot by accident. The Oneida nation is typically very friendly."

"I doubt these Indians were Oneida. More likely Shawnee or Iroquois, or at least part of Tecumseh's Confederacy." His jaw was tight. "You, of course, know they are British allies. A small, lightly armed band must have been too tempting to pass up, especially with the prices the Crown pays for American scalps."

"That is not true." The very idea horrified her. "His Majesty's soldiers are gentlemen of honor." She was certain. One had only to meet Isaac to see the truth of that. The rumor must be American propaganda.

Captain Prescott remained silent and just watched as she finished wrapping his torso. His silence was actually more disconcerting than if he'd argued the point. She'd helped her father treat a man in Detroit who'd been scalped and, even though she did not cringe at the sight of blood, the absolute brutality of the act had sickened her.

"And what were you doing with your small, lightly armed band?" she asked, more to change the path of the conversation than out of actual curiosity.

He quirked a brow. "I probably shouldn't tell you."

Abigail felt acutely aware once again that they were on opposing sides of the war. For a short while, she'd almost forgotten. Getting acquainted with Captain Prescott was probably a poor idea. Realizing the war kept him away from Lydia just as it kept her away from Isaac had made her think they had more in common than not. And that just wouldn't do. Not when she was to turn him in as soon as he was healed.

Once she'd finished ministering to his injuries, he leaned back against the wagon wheel, pulling down his dangling arm and allowing the other to rise up. He rolled the stiffness from his shoulder, and Abigail thought again how uncomfortable the position must be. She took his hand and checked the skin on his wrists, glad to see the rope hadn't rubbed it raw.

He leaned his head back and regarded her. "What do you do with all your time, Miss Tidwell, since your father and brother are away? I mean, while you aren't tending to your barn prisoners."

She didn't deny that she was alone. Lying was becoming tiresome, especially when he could so clearly see the truth. "Well, as I said, I usually help my father. It seems someone is always ill in Amherstburg, though the residents don't call for me as often with him away. And I serve as the town's midwife."

He opened his mouth to reply but closed it, glancing toward the door.

A moment later, Abigail realized what had stopped him. She heard a horse. Had the entire morning passed already? "My neighbor, Mr. Kirby." She suddenly felt frantic. What if he entered the barn and found Captain Prescott? Would he take him to the fort? What if he looked into her windows and saw the captain's mended clothes hanging in front of the hearth? "Keep quiet," she whispered. She hurried to the door and carried the milk pail outside. "Hello," she called, closing the barn door behind her. "How are you today, Mr. Kirby?"

He climbed out of the conveyance, grumbling. At just over sixty years of age, Mr. Kirby was a perpetual grumbler. He lifted the pail into the sleigh and took out an empty one. "Heard there was a skirmish nearby."

"A skirmish?"

He nodded. "Met some redcoats in the forest." He jerked his head backward, indicating the road behind him. "Apparently a group of spies were attacked by Indians. Don't know if there were any casualties, but if I see one of those Americans nosing around here, heaven help me, I'll finish what the Shawnee started. Don't want those scoundrels threatening honest citizens. Need to keep my family and my property safe." He lifted a rifle from the sleigh's seat to prove his point.

Abigail grew cold.

He pointed at her. "You be careful, miss. No telling what those wild Kentuckians would do to a young lady, alone. I've half a mind to bring you home to stay with Mrs. Kirby and myself until your pa returns."

Abigail forced a smile. She waved her hand dismissively. "Don't worry yourself. I'll be fine. I have my father's musket."

He scowled and grumbled something under his breath while he returned to the seat in the sleigh. "You'll let me know if you see anything. Anything at all."

"Of course." Her smile felt painted on. "Good day, Mr. Kirby. Thank you again for delivering the milk for me."

He nodded and flicked the reins.

Abigail watched until the sleigh was out of sight behind the trees. Her legs felt like soft noodles. Knowing Captain Prescott had no doubt overheard the entire conversation, she didn't return to the barn. He'd know that she lied to protect him, and she felt confused and . . . ill. Her head hurt, and she needed to sit down and think. She didn't know exactly how to reconcile what she'd just done. Had she betrayed her country? What would Isaac say if he ever found out?

CHAPTER 4

EMMETT JERKED AWAKE. HE WAS angry with himself for falling asleep, but even though he'd assured Miss Tidwell he was much improved, the truth was, his body wasn't yet healed. It had taken an enormous effort to pull himself up to a sitting position and maintain it during the entire breakfast and medical examination.

The conversation he'd overheard between Miss Tidwell and her neighbor had left him tense. The redcoats not only knew about the attack, they were searching for his company. Had they found his men? Were his men even alive? He pulled on the ropes, frustration making his fists clench. He hated feeling so helpless. He saw his clothes in a folded pile beside his boots, and a basket sat close beside him. When he moved away the cloth, he found strips of ham and some cornbread, which he gratefully ate.

Laying back, he let his eyes close, and he thought of Miss Abigail Tidwell. He'd been almost certain she'd turn him in this morning. But she hadn't. Had his roguish smile worked after all? He discounted the idea immediately. Abigail didn't seem the type of person to be swayed by a bit of flirting. But she had been swayed. And he believed her worry for his well-being was the reason. He figured she considered him her patient and felt an obligation to care for him. Or perhaps it had nothing at all to do with him, and her stubbornness was to blame; she intended to turn him in on her own terms.

Whatever the rationale behind her action, Emmett's worry expanded to include her. If he was found in Abigail's barn, it would mean trouble for both of them. She'd taken a risk keeping him here and then concealing it.

A sound roused him, and he realized he'd fallen asleep again.

"Captain," a voice whispered.

Someone was shaking his shoulder.

Emmett woke completely and opened his eyes just as his bonds were cut free. He blinked, noticing shadows stretching across the floor. Was it already late in the afternoon? "Private Hopkins? Corporal Webb?"

The two men crouched over him. Jasper Webb's weather-worn face revealed none of his thoughts, as was typical for the Kentuckian. On his wiry frame, he wore buckskin clothing with tassels and moccasins instead of an army uniform. His hat was made from the head of a bear, giving him a fearsome look. The volunteer militia was an eclectic-looking group. Some dressed in their grandfather's old Revolutionary War uniforms, but most simply wore civilian clothing. Jasper was an excellent hunter and tracker and had spent years in the mountains of Kentucky. He didn't speak often, possibly because he was accustomed to time alone.

Barney Hopkins may have been Jasper's complete opposite. A large man from Ohio, and a bit slow-witted, he concealed nothing, his every sentiment showing in his words and expressions. Emmett had found him to be one of the most loyal men he'd ever known, and extremely honest. He could not have been any more relieved to see the two.

"Why don't you have any clothes on, Captain?" Barney Hopkins asked, helping Emmett into a sitting position. "Oh. You're wounded." He pointed to the bandages.

"I'm fine," Emmett said.

"And you're wearing a sock on your hand."

"How did you find me?" Emmett looked between the two. The buckskin-clad man had moved silently to the door and was peeking outside.

"Jasper," Barney said. "He found you. And all of us. After the Indian attack, we were scattered. We discovered your pack in the woods." He motioned to the side, and Emmett saw his rucksack.

"And is everyone . . . ?" He left the question hanging, not wanting to voice his fear.

Barney's expression fell. "Luke was hurt."

Emmett's heart grew heavy. Luke Hopkins was Barney's brother and, at seventeen, the youngest in their company. "Is he . . . ?" Emmett looked to Jasper.

"He's alive," Jasper said. His eyes narrowed slightly, telling Emmett the boy's condition was more serious than he wished to discuss in front of Barney. "Murphy is with him." All of the company had survived then.

Emmett pulled the sock from his hand and reached for the pile of clothing. He tried not to wince, not wanting his men to see how badly his injuries pained him. The shirt had a long seam where it had been mended. Abigail must have had to cut it off him. His coat was mended as well, and all of his clothes were clean. Once he was dressed, he started to put on his socks, but paused. Even though they'd been darned, they were still threadbare and worn.

He plucked the blue-and-yellow-striped socks from Barney's curious hands and put them on then his boots. The simple task of dressing had completely worn him out, and Emmett leaned back against the wagon. "They're searching for us, Corporal."

Jasper nodded. He looked back through the crack of the door.

"And we can't trust the locals, either." Emmett picked up the rope and wound it around his arm then hung it from a peg on the wall. He folded the quilt and pillows, setting them into the wagon with the basket that had held his lunch. "We must conceal all traces of my being here."

Jasper joined him, using a shovel to dig up the blood-stained dirt and spread it.

Emmett picked up the arrowhead and slipped it into the pouch in his pocket.

The three crept from the barn, and Emmett glanced back at the house. He felt a stab of remorse, leaving without seeing Abigail again. He owed his life to the woman, and he'd at least have liked to give his thanks and bid her farewell properly. But this was the best way. The longer he remained, the more danger he was putting her in.

They hurried across the open land and into the forest. Emmett couldn't help but shiver. He'd never known cold like that of Upper Canada. It bit at his skin, and he wished for a scarf or a pair of gloves. But he knew the only way to warm up was to keep his body moving.

Once they were beneath the shadow of the trees, they continued silently, heading north to where the river was narrow enough to cross. In a few hours, the night would be fully dark. Jasper fell back beside Emmett. "Luke is hurt bad." The man's whisper was barely audible. "Without a doctor . . ." He left the remainder of the thought unspoken.

Emmett halted. He hesitated but knew instinctively what they must do. Besides, there was not time to come up with another plan. "I know a doctor."

Emmett eased open the door, and the smell of warm bread greeted him. He slipped into the house with Jasper and Barney and followed the homey sound of a woman's humming until he stepped through a doorway into the kitchen.

Abigail spun, and when she saw him, her eyes grew wide. "Captain Prescott. You shouldn't be walking about. Your injuries." She started toward him and then drew back as if just now making a realization. "How did you get free?"

The other two men stepped into the doorway behind Emmett, and Abigail's face paled. She gasped and stumbled backward.

Emmett held up his hands. He should have approached this a bit more delicately. "Miss Tidwell—Abigail. Do not worry. These are my men. Corporal

Jasper Webb, Private Barnabus Hopkins." Emmett pointed at the others in turn. "They won't hurt you."

Her eyes darted back and forth. She moved to the other side of the kitchen, keeping the table between herself and the men.

"Block the door," Emmett said in a low voice, nodding toward the door in the outside wall.

Jasper moved to stand in front of it.

"Miss Tidwell, we need you to come with us," Emmett said.

Abigail watched Jasper with an uneasy expression. "Come with you where?"

"A camp on the other side of the river," Emmett said. "One of my men is injured. He needs a doctor."

She hesitated, her eyes moving between the three, and then she shook her head. She had, of course, traveled often enough across the river and all along the borders of Lake Ontario when the weather was warm, but that was before the southern side of the lake became enemy territory.

"Once you have seen to him, we will deliver you safely to Detroit," Emmett said.

"I cannot go with you."

Emmett's side burned, his head pounded, and his energy was nearly spent. They still needed to march through a cold forest filled with enemy soldiers and cross a frozen river tonight. He didn't have time to argue. "I apologize, miss, but I did not give you the option." He turned to Barney, glad to be giving orders again. Having a plan and knowing the steps to execute it is what he excelled at. "Gather anything that looks useful. There's a basket of bandages somewhere around here—"

Abigail bolted, trying to run past him, but he stepped in front of her. "You'll want to bring some warmer clothes and boots, miss. We have a long walk ahead."

She folded her arms and raised her chin. "I am not going anywhere."

Emmett stood straight, though his side protested. "Yes, you are."

Her eyes narrowed. "No. I will not."

Perhaps he'd been wrong in thinking Abigail was nothing like his sister. Her stubborn posture was exactly like that of Lydia's right before a tantrum. Emmett's temper rose. They were wasting time. "You are coming. If I have to carry you over my shoulder—"

"Miss." Barney pulled the leather hat from his head and held it by the brim. "Captain says you're a healer." His eyes were large beneath a furrowed brow and wrinkled forehead. He stepped forward, his earnest face open and pleading. "My brother Luke is hurt. He's only seventeen, and I told Ma I'd keep him safe. Please, will you help him?"

Abigail studied Barney closely. She was quiet for a long moment. She glanced at Emmett then at Jasper. Finally she nodded. "Yes. I will, Mr. Hopkins. If you will truly deliver me to Detroit. Thank you for asking politely." She shot a glare at Emmett.

He could have sworn Jasper's mouth twitched.

Abigail continued speaking to Barney. "I have a medical bag upstairs, but I should add a few more things. Can you describe for me your brother's injury?"

Barney grasped his arm above the wrist. "A tomahawk hit him here. The bone is broken, and Murphy tried to set it, but he said the arm is too inflamed."

"Is the wound bleeding?" Abigail asked. "Did the bone poke through the skin?"

He nodded. "Poked through, all right. It was bleeding at first, but we stopped the blood. Now there is just pus."

"And is his arm hot?"

"Hot and red," Barney said.

She nodded, and Emmett saw a wrinkle deepen between her brows. "We should hurry. Will you help me gather my things, Mr. Hopkins?"

Emmett stepped aside as Abigail and Barney left the kitchen. "Don't let her out of your sight, Private," he muttered as the man passed. The last thing he needed was for Abigail to run to a neighbor's house and raise an alarm. Making it through the forest and to the other side of the river without the redcoats or Indians spotting them was already a difficult enough task.

"Yes, sir," Barney said and then hurried to catch up with Abigail on the stairs. "Miss, I wondered if you have any more of those warm socks . . ." His voice trailed off, and Emmett turned to Jasper.

The man's gaze was fixed on the freshly baked loaves.

"Do Murphy and Luke have any food?" Emmett asked.

Jasper nodded. "I left them with a hare and some wild onions, but it will hardly be enough."

"Bring what you can find," Emmett said. He left Jasper to collect provisions and went to find Abigail and Barney. Hearing their voices, he followed the sound to a room on the upper floor. When he entered he saw Abigail packing small bottles and parcels into a bag. Barney sat on a chair, putting on a pair of red-and-green stockings. Based on the hat hanging on a peg, the room appeared to belong to a man, probably her father's. The bed was bare, and he wondered if it was her father's quilt that had kept him warm in the barn.

Guilt at invading this woman's personal space made Emmett's throat burn. He couldn't imagine how angry he would feel if strangers came into his home and demanded his compliance.

He left the room and continued along the hallway, entering another. He glanced around the small bedroom and saw a simple bed with a worn patchwork quilt. A child's doll sat on a dressing table with a woman's hairbrush and comb. Beside the bed were a collection of thick tomes about earth sciences and medicine. Hardly the type of reading material he expected to find in a cabin on the Ontario frontier, let alone in a young lady's bedchamber. On the windowsill, he noticed a row of colorful rocks: striped sandstone, a chunk of granite, and one with spectacular veins of turquoise were among the collection. He moved closer to study them.

"My collection is not as fine as yours, Captain." Abigail entered the room behind him. "I am a bit jealous of your quartz crystal."

Emmett pointed to one of the small rocks. "Yes, but you have a blue fluorite. I've only seen a specimen of this color when I was at university."

Abigail's face lit up in a smile, showing a dimple in her right cheek. "You know your minerals. I wondered. Now we shall have something interesting to discuss as we travel."

Emmett was taken aback by the change in her demeanor. None of the woman's former anger remained. She didn't seem to resent the imposition upon her or the intrusion into her home at all. Nor did she appear to hold a grudge. It seemed once her mind was made up, Abigail was the sort of person who did not alter her course, and he quite admired that about her.

She opened the wardrobe, and Emmett saw that inside hung two dresses. His sister had a closet larger than this entire room, filled with gowns, gloves, bonnets, slippers, ribbons, and who knew what else. Perhaps not all women required gowns and frippery to be happy.

Abigail pulled out one of the dresses and laid it on the bed. She stood for a moment, tapping her finger on her lip. "We should take food. I have root vegetables in the cellar."

"Jasper is gathering food," Emmett said.

"Good." She continued to tap her lip as if going through a mental checklist. "And dry clothes for Luke. Isaac should have some in his bedroom. And the quilt from the barn. The rest of my medical equipment is downstairs in the kitchen. I will fetch it on the way"—she drew in a breath—"Oh, Maggie. I will need to milk her before we leave. I'll leave a note for Mr. Kirby to care for her while I'm gone . . ." Abigail paused and looked toward the doorway at Barney.

"Mr. Hopkins, would you mind milking my cow for me? She will be quite miserable by the time my neighbor arrives the day after tomorrow."

Barney looked to Emmett for permission, and seeing his nod, he hurried away to take care of the cow.

Once he'd left, Abigail's expression became grave. "Captain Prescott." She spoke in a low voice and darted a glance toward the door as if making certain Barney was truly gone. "I do not know if I can save Luke." Her brows pulled tightly together, making furrows above her nose. "Broken bones are common enough, even when they've punctured the skin. I've tended to many of those. But from Mr. Hopkins's description, it sounds like there is already some infection. I will try, but days have passed and—"

"I understand."

"I will do everything I can, I promise."

"Thank you."

Her shoulders relaxed. "I'll find some clothes in my brother's room." She started past him, but Emmett hooked his hand on the inside of her elbow to stop her. He took the letter from her hand and nodded as he read Abigail's story about being summoned to Detroit by her father. He lifted his gaze. "Why didn't you turn me in, Miss Tidwell?"

She looked away, but not before he saw apprehension on her face. "You escaped before I had the chance."

He shook his head. Not good enough. "You had a chance, earlier today when the man came for the milk. But you didn't tell him about me. Why?"

"I don't know." She pushed her lips together tightly and puffed out a breath through her nose. "I just couldn't. I thought of Lydia and Isaac, and . . . you're still mending, and . . . I don't know why. But I couldn't. Not when I thought he might harm you." She pulled away her arm and started down the hallway.

He watched her go, feeling . . . something. Gratitude? Admiration? Curiosity? All of these, surely, but there was more. Abigail Tidwell was unlike any woman he knew, and his desire to know her better tugged at him until it was nearly an ache.

The sensation was unnerving, to say the least.

CHAPTER 5

ABIGAIL TRUDGED THROUGH THE SNOW on the forest floor, trying her best to keep pace with the men. Her breathing was heavy, and she felt as if she were practically running. How did they move so effortlessly when each step sank her in snow up to her knees? She supposed her shorter legs were part of the problem, as were her skirts. She wore both of her homespun dresses, leaving her finer gown behind, of course; the satin fabric wouldn't add any warmth. The two combined with her petticoats and cloak were heavy, especially with clumps of snow clinging to the hems. She wished she could just don trousers and march along like a regular person, but as it was, she fought her clothing each step of the way.

Jasper had brought the pot of lard from her pantry and insisted they all smear it over any exposed skin, especially ears and noses. She didn't like the slimy feel of it but was glad for the precaution. January nights in Upper Canada were cold enough that she'd not even complain about the blemishes that were sure to result from the practice.

One haversack, slung over her shoulder and across her chest, held her medicines and equipment, and the men carried the rest of the supplies, as well as their own weapons. Captain Prescott had brought her father's musket. Abigail's burden was the lightest, and yet she still lagged behind. A pity they couldn't walk on a road or a nice path, but of course the men needed to remain concealed from patrols.

As time had passed—nearly an hour, she estimated—she'd become accustomed to Jasper's disappearance and reappearance as he scouted ahead and returned to lead them on safe paths. The first few times she saw his shadow come out of the forest, she nearly screamed. The man's hat was crafted to appear as if Jasper's face was about to be chomped in a bear's mouth. The sight was disconcerting. He didn't speak often, and she was surprised how much a person could communicate with the smallest movements.

She assumed they were traveling north in order to cross the frozen river to Grosse Ile, a long island directly in the middle of the Detroit River, then continue across the river to the Michigan Territory on the other side.

Barney Hopkins moved between Abigail and Captain Prescott, walking beside each of them in turn. He also didn't say much, taking the captain's order to move in silence very seriously. But he did take Abigail's arm on occasion, helping her over fallen logs or through the thick underbrush with an encouraging smile.

Abigail liked Barney quite a lot. He was earnest and pleasant and eager to be of assistance. Truth be told, she liked all three of the men. And trusted them, as silly as it sounded. She should be afraid, following enemy soldiers across the border, but her fear wasn't *of* the Americans, but *for* them. She worried about the redcoats or the Shawnee finding them and fretted over what would happen if they did. The very thought was terrifying. Would a battle ensue? She supposed it would. And people would get killed or injured. She couldn't abide the idea of these soldiers not making it back to their camp where Luke waited. Barney worried for his brother, and she knew that worry—she worried constantly for her own brother.

These were men with families and homes who looked out for each other, and the one looking out for all of them was Captain Emmett Prescott. As for the captain, there was so much she wanted to know about him. He'd studied at the university, something Abigail wished more than anything she could do. How would it be to hear lectures from experts and study medicine with cadavers and wax models of individual organs?

Even men were looked down on for their curiosity about the inner workings of the human body. But for a woman, attending university was unheard of.

Captain Prescott was knowledgeable about earth sciences. Had he attended lectures from William Smith at Columbia College in New York City? Had he gone on actual digs to geological sites? What did he think of James Hutton's *Theory of the Earth* paper? She wished to ask him so many things but had found out often enough that men did not think such academic interest becoming of a young woman.

Was Captain Prescott of the same mind? She was curious about his life. He'd seen so much of the world, and she'd only seen a small part. What was Virginia like? And the grand city of Baltimore? And the Atlantic Ocean? She would likely only spend a few days in the captain's company before joining her father in Detroit and would probably not get the chance to ask all the things she wanted to know.

Captain Prescott marched steadily, but Abigail could tell from the occasional grunt and the way he favored his side that he was hurting. And she knew he would push on in spite of it. Finally, after they descended a particularly difficult hill, she stopped.

Barney looked over his shoulder and then turned and hurried back to her.

"Mr. Hopkins, we must wait." She gestured toward Captain Prescott with her chin. "He needs to rest."

Emmett noticed that they'd paused, and he moved back to join them. "Why the delay?"

"Miss Tidwell has called a halt," Barney said.

Emmett blinked, raising his brows. "Oh, has she?"

Barney nodded helpfully. "Says you need to rest, Captain."

"I don't need to rest."

Though he protested, she could see by moonlight that his face was pale and shone with sweat. "Captain, you are the one who insisted on a doctor." Abigail pulled on his arm. "And so I trust you will abide by my advice." She tugged him to a large rock, brushing off the snow before pushing him to sit. He didn't argue. She pulled off a mitten and felt his forehead. "You are very warm."

"We did just hike three miles through the forest." He started to rise, but Abigail put her hands on his shoulders, pushing him back down.

"If you continue in this way, you'll just make your injuries worse. I fear you are growing feverish."

He let out a frustrated breath. "I don't feel feverish."

"The feverish person cannot tell whether he is feverish," she said. "You really shouldn't be moving so much, or you'll impede your recovery." She realized her hands were still on his shoulders, and she dropped them to her sides.

Jasper emerged from the trees and joined them, his head tipping slightly in question.

"The longer we delay, the sicker Luke gets," Emmett said.

"Perhaps we should go ahead and you can come slower?" Abigail proposed. "Mr. Webb can show me the way."

Emmett shook his head and rose to his feet. "We stay together." He started forward, and Abigail took his arm, walking beside him.

Jasper moved silently ahead, and Barney followed behind them.

"What about your fever, Captain?" Abigail asked.

"I do not have a fever."

Abigail worried that the fever might even now be confusing him. "All right, sir. Prove it. Name the three elements that make up the mineral composition of granite."

He looked down at her, a small smile on his lips. "Feldspar, quartz, and mica."

"Well, that was too easy."

His smile grew. "Your turn, Miss Tidwell. What might cause amethyst to appear red instead of its typical violet color?"

"Hematite," she said. "Small spheres of hematite can exist just below the surface of the crystal, giving it the red color."

"I'm impressed," Emmett said.

Abigail shrugged as if the mineral structure of iron oxide were rudimentary knowledge as pride swelled like a bubble in her chest.

A cloud of fog loomed ahead, low to the ground, and the temperature of the air dropped. They must have reached the river.

As if answering her unasked question, Jasper stepped from the fog with a long, thick stick. He handed it to Abigail, indicating she should hold it horizontally with both hands. Abigail had used this precaution before; the ice could have pockets of air caused by irregular freezing. If she should step onto an unstable spot and fall into a crack, the stick would catch her. The men would use their guns in the same way.

She'd often skated on the ice, but walking across at night in the fog with British soldiers and Indians searching for them made her suddenly apprehensive. Abigail paused at the riverbank.

Emmett stood behind her. "Nothing to fear, Doctor."

His voice was warm with a hint of humor, which she knew was meant to be comforting. But she stood still. The river marked the border between Upper Canada and America. She was crossing into a territory where *she* would be the enemy.

He nudged her forward. "Come, I'll not allow you to fall."

Abigail nodded and walked the remainder of the way to the edge of the shore.

"Without any wind, our footprints on the ice will be visible all up and down the bank," Emmett said to Jasper. "A patrol will spot them immediately." They hadn't needed to worry about footprints in the irregular ground of the forest, Abigail assumed.

Jasper left and returned with a bushy branch.

"Just for fifty yards or so," Emmett said. "Farther out, the fog will cover our tracks."

Emmett started forward, and Abigail stepped onto the ice behind him, holding the stick in front of her in both hands as she walked. The snowfall had left a powdery covering over the frozen river that kept the ice from being too slick.

Without needing to be told, the group spread out, not wanting to put too much weight on any one section of the ice. Emmett led the way then Abigail.

Barney was next, and Jasper followed along behind the others, brushing away evidence of their crossing.

The distance from the Upper Canada side of the river to the island was quite far. Abigail thought she'd heard at one time that it was at least a mile and a half. As they walked, the fog got thicker, and cold rose from the frozen water beneath. Again Abigail cursed her skirts. They seemed to trap cold air around her legs. She was glad for her mittens and worried the others might develop frost burns on their fingers in spite of the lard. When they stopped again, she'd insist the men wear her grandmother's socks on their hands, though she was sure they'd complain about not being able to shoot with their fingers covered.

Time passed and she squinted ahead, but between the fog and the darkness, she couldn't see Captain Prescott or any of the others. She stopped, listening, but the night was silent. She didn't even see footprints. An eerie confusion came over her. Was she even moving in the right direction? Had she veered off course? If she had, they would never find her, and she would likely wander over the iced river in the wrong direction until she froze. Or until she fell through the ice. She clutched the stick and imagined the deep water, dark beneath her feet; she was separated from it by only a few inches of ice. She could feel apprehension building and tried to distract herself by thinking of a paper by John Dalton she'd read, on the composition of water. *One molecule of water has two hydrogen atoms covalently bonded to a single oxygen atom.* But it did nothing to calm her.

Panic took hold, and Abigail began to shake. She whirled around, looking for the others, but saw nothing. She kept turning until she was no longer sure which direction she'd been going. She started in the direction she thought was right but then turned, thinking she'd been mistaken. Dread filled her mind, and her heart started beating rapidly as she searched the darkness for . . . anything. Her impulse was to run, but a rational part of her mind knew that was not the answer. "Captain," she called out, her voice sounding small and hoarse. She coughed and tried again. "Captain Prescott! Where are you?"

"Abigail?" The relief at hearing his voice lasted merely for an instant. She couldn't tell which direction it came from.

"Captain, I'm lost." A sob choked in her throat as she tried to draw in a breath. "Captain?"

"Abigail, I'm coming. Stay where you are."

Another sob broke out, and the stick fell from her trembling hands, making a clattering sound on the ice.

An instant later, Captain Prescott ran out of the fog. Abigail's relief at seeing him was so overwhelming that her legs went soft, and she swayed.

He caught her in his arms and held her as she broke down into a bout of weeping.

Abigail felt utterly ridiculous sobbing against the man's chest. She was making wet, embarrassing noises and shaking uncontrollably but couldn't stop herself. The panic that had taken over her seemed to need to expel itself through blubbering and facial seepage.

"I'm sorry," she said with a hitching voice once she had enough control to speak. "I just . . ."

Captain Prescott rubbed her back and held her tighter. "No need to apologize."

She shook her head, drawing back and wiping her mittens over her wet cheeks. "I . . . I couldn't see . . . anything."

"I know."

Her face was cold as tears froze, making her eyelids and nose sting. Since her mittens were wet, she used the inside of her cloak to rub her eyes and the captain's wet coat.

Once her mind started to clear, she realized they were still standing together, their combined weight pressing down on the ice, increasing the weight-per-square-inch ratio.

She stepped back and crouched down to pick up the stick. Her hands were still shaking, and it slipped, hitting the ice and rolling away. "Oh, Captain Prescott, I am a terrible soldier."

He laughed and grabbed the stick, handing it to her. "You are a fine soldier." He held her hand, walking beside her. "I've heard no complaints from you this entire campaign, even though I'm certain marching through deep snow in skirts isn't easy." His hand tightened and he pulled her forward. "Come, we're nearly to the other side."

"How can you possibly know that?" Abigail said. "And how do you know which way to go?"

"I'm the captain, remember? It's my job to know."

His smile flashed again, and seeing it, Abigail's worries disappeared. She trusted this man, trusted him to keep her safe, to lead her through the darkness. Her relief was so welcome that she let her fear fall away and just concentrated on putting one foot in front of the other, fully confident that Captain Prescott would lead her to shore.

CHAPTER 6

EMMETT HELD ON TIGHTLY TO Abigail's mitten-covered hand. He could still feel her shaking, and he was anxious to get her to shore where she could sit and recover. And if he was to be honest, he'd not mind a minute to collect himself as well. Hearing her frantic cry through the dark fog had awakened a fear inside him that he hadn't felt before. His first thoughts were that she'd fallen through the ice or been attacked. He'd imagined wolves or fierce Indian braves assailing her, and in that instant, the only thing that had mattered was finding her and making certain she was unharmed.

And when he had, her weeping and shaking had nearly been his undoing. He wished to take her away from all of this, to put her somewhere warm and safe where fear and war and danger would never reach her. Her gasping breaths had made him worry that she might fall unconscious or grow hysterical, and he'd done the only thing he'd known to work when Lydia had been afraid: held her and waited for the episode to run its course. And surprisingly, it had worked.

The incident had left him shaken. He'd have run into any danger without preparation, and it was unlike him to forget years of training and sprint toward the unknown. Of course he would have risked his life to rescue any of his men. He worried for those in his command, took his charge seriously. He was responsible for them. But this was something more. Something that ran deeper, and he didn't know exactly what it meant or how he was to interpret it. Instead of dwelling on unfamiliar emotions, he focused on what he did know. Abigail needed to be kept safe. The idea that she could have been hurt or lost still had his nerves on edge.

He glanced back and saw that she was watching her feet, still holding onto the stick and following him blindly with something like childlike trust. He considered her reaction when she'd been lost in the dark. She hadn't called for help, she'd called for *him*. Although she'd only known him a few days, she had confidence in his ability to save her. The knowledge settled around his heart, warm and soft like one of Granny's striped stockings, and it also increased his feeling of responsibility when it came to her protection.

Miss Abigail Tidwell was the most complicated person he thought he'd ever known. The woman's leisure reading consisted of scientific analyses, yet her decisions were made out of compassion. She could suture a wound, bake bread, cure infection, milk a cow, knit socks, and recite the mineral composition of inorganic solids. But she'd become afraid in the dark fog.

A pity they would only spend a few days together. Emmett found Abigail to be fascinating. And he didn't think he could say that about many women of his acquaintance. Most of the young ladies his father and stepmother introduced him to were dull or insincere. Abigail was neither.

They reached the riverbank and found Jasper and Barney waiting. If either man thought it strange to see their captain holding hands with the doctor, they didn't show it. Jasper erased their footprints then led them into the forest. He motioned with a raised finger to his lips for them to remain silent. Apparently he'd spotted evidences of enemies on the island. Emmett would never fail to be impressed by the man's ability to track as well as keep them from being tracked in rough terrain.

Emmett motioned to him that they needed to halt, and Jasper nodded, scouting ahead until he found a darkly shadowed spot on a rocky hill where a sentry could watch as they rested. Barney brushed snow from a boulder and set the quilt he'd been carrying down, motioning for Abigail to sit.

She did so, slumping forward to rest her head in her hands and her elbows on her knees. Emmett wanted to sit beside her and put a comforting arm around her, but he refrained, knowing he needed to speak to Jasper.

He moved away from Barney and Abigail, climbing up the hill to where Jasper stood watch. "How far?"

"Maybe five miles," Jasper replied.

At the rate they were traveling, Emmett thought they would be walking at least two or three more hours. Their journey days earlier to reconnoiter the area around Fort Malden had been a slow one, with no roads to follow and with detours around any area that might have held enemy scouts. But this trip required speed. He was frustrated that his own energy was flagging and the pain in his side becoming more intense.

"Ten minutes more," Emmett said. "Then we press on."

Jasper nodded.

Emmett climbed back down the hill and found Abigail digging through her bag. She pulled out something that he couldn't see in the darkness and held it toward him. When he took it, he saw it was a rolled pair of stockings.

"For your hands," Abigail said. "Your fingers will get frost burn in this cold."

Emmett thought his hand had stayed plenty warm with hers wrapped in it. For a moment, he thought of arguing that he needed his hands free to shoot, but his cold fingers won out, and he pulled the socks on. He guessed he'd have to wait until daylight to see what colors they were.

"They're warm, aren't they, Captain?" Barney said, opening and closing his sock-clad fingers like he was animating a puppet.

Emmett nodded. "We'll continue in a few minutes."

"Here, Mr. Hopkins. Will you take these socks to Mr. Webb?" Abigail handed him another pair.

Once Barney left, Emmett sat on the quilt beside her. "How are you, Abigail?"

"Much better. I'm so sorry, Captain. The dark and the cold . . . I don't know why I went to pieces."

He clutched her hand with his, the grasp clumsy between sock and mitten, but under the circumstances it was the best he could do.

She responded by squeezing his fingers. "I know you are putting on a brave face, but you are in pain. I can give you something to ease it."

"We haven't time," he said. "And I need my senses alert."

She scooted around to face him, and her knees bumped his. "You must promise to rest once we reach the camp."

"I will rest."

"No. Promise it. You are still very seriously injured. All your healing will be undone if you don't take care of yourself."

"I promise to rest once we reach the camp."

The answer seemed to mollify her, and she relaxed.

Emmett knew she was right. He was pushing himself too hard, and he could feel his strength waning. But what other choice did he have? He needed to get these men and himself safely out of the enemy's territory and bring Miss Tidwell to Luke as soon as possible. They might even now be too late.

Once their reprieve was over, they continued through the heavy forest of Grosse Ile. The moonlight was completely blocked by fog, making the night nearly full dark. Emmett kept a firm hold on Abigail's hand the entire way. After an hour, they reached the west side of the island and started across the ice. They reached the bank of the Michigan Territory without incident, and he felt relief, like a clamp inside him had been let loose. The others seemed to move lighter as well. This close to Fort Detroit, Emmett knew the threat of an enemy attack wasn't fully alleviated, but it was much lower.

Abigail stumbled, and he glanced at her. In the dark, she was little more than a silhouette, but he could tell she was flagging.

"We're nearly there, Abigail."

She didn't respond but continued plodding along, her pace slowing until he was pulling instead of just walking beside her. She must be exhausted.

"Miss Tidwell, in what igneous rock compound might I find gem-quality tourmaline?"

She lifted her head. "Pegmatite."

"Ah, so you're awake. I wondered."

"Have you found gem-quality tourmaline?" she asked. Her voice sounded sleepy.

"Unfortunately, no."

"Pity, that."

Emmett decided to keep her talking. It was a distraction from his own pain and helped her to move faster. "So tell me, Miss Tidwell, how is it that you possess such vast scientific knowledge?"

"I wouldn't consider it vast. My pursuits are quite specific."

"Geology and medicine?"

"You saw my books."

"I did. And it makes me curious. I've never met a woman with such interests."

"You are the first person I've met who's shared my passion for geology," she said. "When I was a child, I gathered rocks that caught my attention, and I was lucky that my father indulged my hobby instead of discouraging it. He brought me books about mineral compositions from Edinburgh and Baltimore when he returned from attending medical lectures."

"I see. And how did you develop your interest and skill in medicine?"

"That is more complicated," she said slowly. "And more personal."

Though he couldn't see her, he could feel the caution in her words. And it fueled his curiosity. "Will you tell me?"

She was quiet for a long moment, and he wondered if he'd caused her offense. He was about to say something to change the topic when she spoke.

"When I was ten years old, my father accompanied my brother, Isaac, to England to purchase a commission at the Royal Military Academy. Mother and I stayed behind. She didn't like to be away from my grandmother."

"Because she was nearly blind?"

"Yes." She drew closer to him, and he wondered if she noticed. "While we were working in the garden, Mother scratched her leg on a broken piece of the fence. It bled a bit but didn't bother her at the time. However, a week later, it had developed into a festering wound. She took a fever and died within a few days."

"I'm sorry, Abigail."

She squeezed his hand. "When Father returned weeks later, he was heart-broken, as you can imagine. He loved her very much. But I was . . . inconsolable. I'd retreated to a dark place in my mind. I didn't eat or sleep, and I lost interest in everything—even my rocks. I felt guilty and angry with myself for not knowing how to help her." Her voice was unsteady. She cleared her throat.

"But you must have known it wasn't your fault," Emmett protested. "You were only a child."

"I know it now, but at the time . . ." She cleared her throat again. "So Father taught me. He brought me along when he attended patients and read to me from his medical books. Learning about medicine healed me, I suppose. It sounds silly to say it. But it gave me power where before I'd felt helpless."

"Your father sounds like a wise man," Emmett said, amazed by the man's insight into helping his grieving daughter. "My father behaved quite differently when my mother died."

"Do you want to tell me about it?" she asked.

Voices came from ahead, and Emmett pushed Abigail behind him, pulling the sock off his hand and lifting the musket.

Jasper stepped from the trees holding a torch. He was followed by Murphy.

"We've arrived," Emmett said, lowering the weapon. "Miss Tidwell, Private Thaddeus Murphy." He motioned with a tip of his head. "Miss Tidwell is a doctor."

Murphy's wrinkled face slacked in relief. By the flicker of torchlight, Emmett could see him run a hand through his gray hair.

Barney hurried past, and Emmett and Abigail followed. In a clearing, they found a fire between two small shelters made of branches. Emmett recognized Jasper's handiwork. The group hadn't brought tents on their reconnaissance mission but with Jasper's help had bivouacked comfortably in the forest. The man was unbelievably skilled in wilderness survival. Both of the lean-tos were open on one side, facing the fire to trap the heat. A pole, about four feet tall, separated the opening into two halves.

Barney pulled a branch from the fire, using it as a torch, and crouched down, illuminating the inside of one of the shelters.

Abigail released Emmett's hand and followed, kneeling on the frozen ground and pulling off her mittens. She scooted inside to examine the patient.

Emmett followed, crouching behind her, and watched as Abigail lifted up Luke's arm. "Bring the light closer if you please, Mr. Hopkins."

Barney complied and the flickering light showed the slender young man, looking pale and drenched in sweat. "Will you have to amputate, miss?"

"I hope not," Abigail said. "That solution is mandatory in a crowded field tent full of injured soldiers with only few surgeons to tend to them. But we have time to put all of our focus on one." She bent close and smelled the wound.

Even Emmett could see Luke's condition was grave. His clothes and hair were wet in the biting cold, yet he did not shiver. The skin of his arm was shiny, pulled tight by swelling, and red with infection. The wound was discolored, with thick pus crusted around it. He could tell the bone was broken by the way the arm above the wrist was bent at an odd angle.

When Abigail felt Luke's head, the boy's eyes flew wide, and he raved incoherently.

She brushed back his hair, placing a hand on his cheek. "Hush, Luke. Be calm, all will be well soon."

"Ma?" Luke's eyes were unfocused. He moaned and moved his head from side to side.

Emmett's instinct was to pull Abigail away before the boy unknowingly injured her.

She continued to stroke his cheek and hair, speaking in a gentle voice until Luke calmed.

"He will get well, won't he, Miss Tidwell?" Barney asked.

"I will do everything I can." She patted Barney's arm then twisted around to where Murphy stood behind Emmett. "How long has he had the fever?" she asked.

"A few hours," Murphy said. "He's been yelling out but doesn't know what he's saying. I put a damp cloth on his forehead to try to cool him."

"You did just right, sir." Abigail opened her medical bag and started rummaging around inside it. "His temperature is quite high, and the bones will have to be reset, but first, we must draw out the infection. That is the cause of the fever." She set a mortar and pestle on the ground, along with some vials and bottles. "I will prepare a poultice. And we must clean the injury. Scrape off the decayed tissue and discharge." She picked up a small dark-colored bottle. "It will be quite painful, but this will allow him to sleep through the worst of it."

She unstopped the bottle, and Emmett caught the unmistakable scent of alcohol and opium—laudanum. "Hold up his head, if you please, Mr. Hopkins."

Barney moved around her and lifted Luke's head so she could drip some laudanum into the boy's mouth.

"We have some time before it takes effect," she said. She rose and brushed off her skirts. She began to roll up her sleeves, glancing around the dark camp. Her eyes landed on a kettle beside the fire. "Mr. Murphy, please boil some water. And Mr. Hopkins, if you'd please help me remove Luke's wet clothes."

"And what shall I do?" Emmett asked.

She turned to him. "I did not forget your promise, Captain. You will rest." Seeing that he was opening his mouth to argue, she held up a hand, stopping him. "You'll not be in any condition to lead these men if you do not let yourself mend properly." She indicated the other lean-to shelter.

Abigail took his arm and stepped closer, her gaze capturing his. "Sleep. Please." Her voice was quiet, not calling orders as she'd done earlier but meant for his ears only, and pleading. He thought that voice could have convinced him to attack Fort Detroit alone, armed with only a child's slingshot.

She tugged him toward the lean-to and motioned for him to crawl inside. "I'll rewrap your wounds when you wake."

The thought of falling into a deep slumber and forgetting his pain was so tempting that Emmett didn't even argue. He assigned Murphy to take the first watch and Barney to assist Abigail, and within a moment of lying down, he slept.

CHAPTER 7

ONCE SHE WAS CERTAIN EMMETT was resting and the laudanum had taken effect on Luke, Abigail set to work. She'd tried to keep a reassuring demeanor, especially when she spoke to Barney, but in truth, she was worried that Luke would at the very least lose his arm. However, she resolved not to amputate until she'd put up a good fight to save the limb. Her true fear went much deeper. If the infection had moved into his blood, she didn't know if she'd be able to save him. Memories of her helplessness when her mother lay soaked in sweat, her leg swollen with red streaks shooting from the wound filled Abigail's mind, and she pushed them away, not letting the panic overtake her. She was no longer that powerless girl. She closed her eyes and took a calming breath, remembering her father's training and hours of study. She could do this.

She and Barney removed the sweat-soaked clothing and wrapped Luke in the quilt. Once they were finished, the boiled water in the kettle had cooled enough to use for cleaning the wound.

"Hold the torch closer," Abigail instructed. "But not so close that it will burn his skin—or mine." She could see by the nervous look on his face that Barney was worried, and so she did what her father had always done, and explained as she worked. *Knowledge dispels fear*, he'd said.

Taking out the bowl she used for bloodletting, she set it beneath Luke's arm to catch the fouled water then began to debride the wound. "I must make certain all the dried discharge and diseased tissue is removed and there is no foreign material inside, or when the wound is stitched up, it won't heal. See here, this bit of skin is decayed." She used a scalpel to slice off the dead flesh and poured water over the wound, working carefully until she was satisfied that only healthy tissue remained.

"And now, a poultice to draw out the infection." She pointed at the swollen skin and stood, returning the kettle to the fire. "If you would empty this bowl, please. And wash it very thoroughly." She handed the bowl of dirty water to Barney, who took it away. Beneath Barney's worried gaze, Abigail used the boiling water from the kettle to make a hot paste of wheat bran, which she set on the wound to draw out the pus, and then made a separate mixture of peppermint leaves, willow bark, and camphor to cool the skin. Once the poultices were bound in place, she rinsed the herbs from the mortar bowl.

She stepped out of the shelter and stood next to Barney by the fire, with Luke's soaked clothing and the dirty scalpel. "The wound needs to drain for a little while. Then we can set the fracture."

Barney nodded, his brows pulled close and raised, pushing up a stack of wrinkles on his forehead.

Abigail laid a hand on his arm. "I understand your concern. I have a brother too."

"What's his name?"

"Isaac. He's in the army. I worry about him all the time. What if he should be injured in a battle? My father and I wouldn't hear of it until weeks after it happened." Voicing her fear aloud caused a heavy feeling to settle on her shoulders. "Luke is fortunate to have you here with him."

"I promised Ma I'd watch out for him." Barney's shoulders sagged.

"And look at what you're doing right this moment," Abigail said. "Tending to him, just like you said." She crouched down and rubbed snow over the blood on Luke's shirtsleeve, knowing that remaining busy was the best way to keep from fretting.

Barney crouched beside her and did the same for Luke's coat, his large hands grabbing mounds of snow and clumsily grinding it into the bloodstains. Abigail's heart went out to him. He was such an earnest man, and she wished she could reassure him. Tell him Luke would recover and there was no cause for worry.

"I shouldn't have allowed him to come on this mission," he said. The fire-light flickered over his round face. "I thought keeping him with me was safer, but he'd have done better back at camp with the rest of the regiment."

Abigail filled the pot with snow and set it over the fire. "You did what you thought was best. Often we must choose between two uncertainties." She wiped her cold hands on her apron. "Mr. Hopkins, please don't punish yourself. You had no way of knowing your group would be attacked."

"Barney," he said. "You should call me Barney. Nobody ever calls me Mr. Hopkins. Even the muster rolls call me Private. But friends say Barney." He gave a small smile, though despondency remained in his eyes.

"Very well, Barney. And my friends call me Abigail." She smiled back and swished the shirt in the warm water.

Once the kettle steamed, she used the boiling water and carefully cleaned the scalpel. Father always stressed the importance of keeping her medical tools clean. She gratefully accepted coffee from Barney, knowing she needed to remain alert for hours yet. She hadn't even begun to address the bone fracture.

They hung the cleaned clothes near the fire and returned to their patient. When Abigail felt Luke's head, she found his fever still remained, although she thought it had dropped a bit. The skin around the wound was still swollen, but she decided the bones needed to be set while Luke was still sleeping and his muscles were relaxed.

"Now, do not worry, this looks rather alarming. I must enlarge the opening to remove any loose bone splinters," she told Barney as she sliced carefully into the skin. Fresh blood welled up, and she wiped it away with soft lint. Motioning the light closer, she studied the exposed bone. The damaged ends overlapped, pulled tight by contracting muscles. "If I manipulate the muscle, it will lengthen," she said, applying traction. "And the bones can be realigned."

The process took nearly a quarter of an hour until she felt the bones were arranged properly and the fracture was reduced so it could heal properly. She sat back, feeling a wave of exhaustion, but it was not time to rest, so she carried on. From her bag, she took the curved suture needle and waxed shoemaker's thread, and filled a small bowl with oil.

"Now, Barney, if you could hold the wound closed." She showed him where to put his fingers to pinch the edges of the torn skin together. Then she dipped the needle in the oil and painstakingly sewed the wound shut, tying off each ligature with a surgeon's knot, just how her father had shown her.

When they finished, she sent Barney with a hatchet to search for slabs of curved bark they could use to splint the arm. She wedged the torch between two rocks to provide light as she reheated the wheat poultice and wrapped both mixtures over the wound then cut a square strip of fabric the length of Luke's forearm. She sliced the edges of the bandage until each side had a strip that looked like tassels then folded them carefully over the arm, pair by pair, to hold the bone in place. Once Barney returned, they would splint it.

When she stepped back out to stand by the fire, she realized how dark the night was in the forest. A new fear arose, and her mind started to wander, wondering what might be just outside the circle of firelight. Where was Murphy? She knew he was standing guard somewhere but hadn't seen him. And Barney had been gone longer than she'd anticipated.

She cleaned her tools again and returned the scalpel to its case, checked that Luke was still sleeping, then tidied up the camp, though there was really nothing to do. She just felt nervous sitting still. She peeked in on Emmett but did not check his temperature, for fear she'd awaken him. She circled around the fire and then finally sat on a flat rock Murphy must have cleared of snow for this very purpose and tried to ignore the sinister feeling of the darkness surrounding the camp.

As if conjured by her fears, she heard a wolf howl, and it sounded very close. Her eyes darted around, trying to see into the trees as another wolf answered from a different direction. She wondered if the animals could smell blood from Luke's wound. Would they attack the camp? She darted a glance toward the branch shelter where Jasper and Emmett slept. Should she wake them? She found the musket and stood beside the fire, knowing she must protect Luke and the others.

A branch snapped, and she whirled around, pointing the weapon into the darkness.

"Easy there." Murphy stepped into the light, hands raised.

Abigail lowered the barrel of the musket. "Oh, I beg your pardon, Mr. Murphy."

"Heard the wolves, did ya?"

She nodded.

"Not to worry. They'll not approach the fire."

Another howl sounded.

"Barney is in the forest," she said, still feeling nervous.

Murphy nodded, and she saw exhaustion on his lined face. She wondered when he'd slept last. "I saw him. He's all right."

"Sir, perhaps you should sleep."

He yawned, as if her notice had given him permission to do so. "Aye, and that's why I've returned. Shift's over. Corporal Webb will keep watch for a few hours."

Abigail thought of Jasper's long hike and felt sorry for the man, being allotted such a small amount of sleep. "Barney will be tired, too. I'll convince him to sleep as well."

Murphy nodded wearily. He moved to the other shelter and bent down, shaking Jasper's shoulder. The buckskin-clad man rose silently, and Murphy took his place.

Abigail set down the musket and poured coffee for Jasper when he stepped around the fire. "Did you get enough sleep?"

He shrugged and spoke in a low gravely voice. "Haven't had a decent amount sleep since becoming a soldier."

Abigail grimaced. "I'm sorry."

He shrugged and drank the coffee.

"I'm surprised the wolves didn't wake you," Abigail said.

He glanced at the musket propped against the rock beside her. "You shooting at the wolves would have woken me." His mouth twitched, and she thought he might have been making a joke.

Before she could respond, Barney returned, stepping into the firelight. His arms were filled with slabs of curved bark. "Will these do, Abigail? I didn't know what size, so . . . "

She took the pile from him, smiling as she studied the various sizes. "I'm certain some of these will be exactly what we need."

Jasper set down the cup and started toward the trees.

"Enjoy your sentry duty," Abigail said then felt supremely foolish for the sentiment. But what farewell did one give a soldier headed out to stand guard?

He stopped and cocked his head, and from the rear, it appeared as if the bear he wore were considering what she'd said. Jasper lifted his hand as he disappeared into the woods.

Barney held his cold hands toward the fire.

Abigail set down the wood then took one of Barney's hands and studied it, looking for discoloration on his fingertips. "I wish you had a pair of gloves. It's not good for the skin to be constantly freezing and reheating."

He pulled the socks from his pocket and grinned, sliding them over his hands. "You remind me of my ma," he said. "Always taking care of people."

She smiled at the simple compliment. "Have you warmed enough to help me splint Luke's arm?"

Barney cut the wood to the size Abigail directed, using his knife to smooth the splinters on the ends. It would still be rough on Luke's skin, so she padded it with folded scraps of felt. The curvature of the bark fit around Luke's arm tightly, but when the swelling reduced, Abigail thought the fit would be right. Still snug so he couldn't move the bone, but not tight enough to restrict blood flow. They tied bandages around the wood splints, and Barney slipped a pair of blue and green socks over Luke's hands.

Abigail felt the young man's forehead. His temperature seemed almost to have returned to normal, which surprised her after so short a time. A spark of hope lit in her chest. The boy was possibly stronger than she'd imagined.

"You should sleep," Abigail said to Barney. "Luke's fever is down, and there's nothing more to do for now but wait."

He shook his head, looking ready to protest, but Abigail pointed toward the spot beside Luke. "You'll be close when he wakes."

Barney agreed and lay down beside his brother.

Abigail left the shelter. She knew the hours right before dawn were the coldest, and all she could think about was keeping close to the fire. The wolf howls sounded, but farther away, which was a relief. She put the unused scraps of bark onto the flames and pulled her cloak tight, arranging herself on the ground beside the rock. The ground was cold, but at least the snow had been cleared away. The exhaustion she'd kept at bay for hours was suddenly too strong to resist any longer. She leaned an arm on the rock, settled her head into the bend of her elbow, and slept.

CHAPTER 8

EMMETT DROPPED ANOTHER LOAD OF branches onto the growing pile beside the fire. He grunted at the pain that shot through his injuries. Though he'd slept through two watches, he was still exhausted. The morning air was cold, but the sun shone brightly on the snow, and he tipped his head back, enjoying the feel of it on his face.

He moved to the flat-topped rock and sat, glancing in both shelters. Barney and Luke slept in one and Abigail in the other.

Emmett had woken at dawn and found her shivering on the cold ground, curled up beside the rock and immediately berated himself for collapsing into a dead slumber without taking any thought to her comfort. Of course, she'd not lie down to sleep beside any of the men. He'd carefully untied the ribbons beneath her chin and pulled off the bonnet, thinking it would be uncomfortable to sleep in, and pulled her mittens onto her hands. Her fingers were freezing.

He was frustrated that he'd nothing better to offer the woman than a soldier's bivouac made of sticks and a few scratchy blankets. He'd asked Jasper this morning to construct another shelter for Abigail.

Allowing himself only a few more minutes to rest, he moved to Luke's shelter, crouching down and touching his fingers to the boy's head. He was surprised not to feel excessive heat. He touched his own forehead for a comparison. Based on his very limited medical experience, he thought Luke's fever had cooled. He hoped it was a good sign. The boy's color looked to be healthier, and he seemed to be sleeping deeply.

As Emmett placed a few more branches on the fire, his eyes fell on the old musket. He couldn't help but smile at the story Murphy had told him earlier about Abigail guarding the camp from wolves while the soldiers slept. Murphy and Jasper had spoken warmly about her, and he was pleased with how well the men had taken to her. Of course, it would be difficult not to enjoy a pretty woman's company after months of marching and drilling. But he thought they'd seemed to especially like Abigail. And in the most secret part of his heart, he admitted that in the few days he'd known her, he'd grown fonder of Abigail Tidwell than was sensible. If only circumstances were different, he thought he'd be in danger of falling in love with the woman.

He heard rustling from the shelter, and a moment later, Abigail crawled out. Her hair was mussed and her eyes sleepy. She pulled the government-issue gray woolen blanket tighter around her shoulders and blinked at the sunlight.

Emmett's heart flopped over. In that moment, Abigail Tidwell looked utterly enchanting.

Her gaze met his, and she smiled and walked toward him, yawning. "You shaved. Now you look like a captain."

"Are you saying I didn't before?"

"I should have said you look like a well-kept captain now." She pulled a pin from her hair, then another, and the loose knot unrolled, tumbling dark curls over her shoulders. She put the pins in her mouth then opened her pack and searched through it until she found a hairbrush. She sat on the rock and drew the brush through her curls. "Where is everyone?" Her words were a bit indistinct as she spoke around the pins.

Emmett was enthralled, watching her go about her morning routine. He thought how intimate it felt, to see someone performing the little tasks they did without thinking. Pulling his eyes away, he moved to the pot, taking off the lid and stirring the stew. "Jasper is setting snares, Murphy is on sentry duty, and Barney and Luke are still sleeping." He looked toward the shelter.

Abigail gathered her hair and twisted it around to make a knot at the base of her neck then stuck in the pins to hold it in place. "That smells wonderful," she nodded toward the stew.

He scooped some into a bowl and held it toward her. "Come, have breakfast with me. My table manners are much better when I'm not bound to a wagon." He winked as he scooped another bowl. "Although we don't exactly have a table."

She grinned and started toward the lean-to. "I should see to Luke first."

Emmett stepped in front of her, blocking her in the space between the flat rock and the fire. "I checked on him not half an hour ago. He's sleeping well, breathing deeply, and his fever is gone."

Abigail looked past him, but he didn't move.

"Even the doctor must take care of herself."

"But—"

"Eat."

She very prettily raised a brow. "That clean-shaved face has gone to your head, sir. Now you're barking orders."

"I *am* the captain, remember?" He raised his own brow and smiled to show her he was teasing.

She looked down at the stew and took the bowl from him, sitting on the rock. "I suppose it can wait a bit."

Emmett brought spoons and two slices of bread and sat beside her.

"And how are your wounds, Captain?"

"The sleep did wonders for my pain." He took a bite of the rabbit stew, delighted beyond belief at the turnips and potatoes they'd found in the Tidwells' root cellar. One thing a soldier's diet lacked was variety.

"This is very good," she said after a moment. "I didn't realize how hungry I am."

"There's plenty, so eat all you'd like."

"Thank you."

The pair ate in silence save for the songs of birds that Emmett couldn't identify. Finches, perhaps. He smiled at the cheerful noise. Only days earlier, he'd thought this forest to be cold and wearisome as his company trudged along. It was amazing what fresh bread, vegetables, and warm socks could do for the group's morale. He'd actually thought he heard Jasper whistling this morning, though the sound stopped as soon as Emmett got near.

He glanced to the side. Was it really the fresh provisions that caused such a change in his attitude? He doubted it. A warm breakfast in a snowy forest on a sunny morning was pleasant, but the company of a beautiful woman made the surroundings sparkle like a drawing in a picture book. He leaned back his head to feel the sun on his face.

"I don't believe I've ever eaten breakfast outside before," she said. "And I've certainly never slept in the forest."

Emmett glanced at her. "And now that you've done both, what is your conclusion?"

"I think food tastes better in the cold air. And people sleep deeper when they're physically wearied." She pulled her brows together as if she were contemplating. "But, I do not think many realize it."

"You are right about that. The amount of complaining I hear on a daily basis from the men in my company would lead a person to think there is nothing worse than sleeping out of doors or eating in the cool air."

Abigail set down her bowl and stood, moving around to his other side, motioning for him to remove his coat and lift his shirt. "And how many men are in your company?"

"When I left the regiment at Frenchtown, there were just over a hundred men in my command." He felt his expression grow grim. "Typhoid fever has significantly reduced the number, and I imagine there will be even less when I return."

Abigail reached around him, unwrapping the bandage. "I'm sorry, Captain. It must be dreadful to watch your men die."

He winced, both at her words and at the cold air hitting his skin. "More than I can say. I feel responsible for them. So many are volunteers, and of course all left behind a home and family. Murphy has a wife and daughter in Pennsylvania; Barney and Luke's aging parents are managing the farm in Ohio by themselves."

She inspected the arrow wound and the wound on his arm. "You're healing nicely. I think I will leave off the bandages. Soon we can remove the sutures." She sat back on the rock and wadded up the strips while he returned his shirt and coat. "What of *your* home and family, Captain Prescott? You were telling me about your father yesterday before we arrived."

"Ah yes, the Honorable Beauregard Emmett Prescott III." He heard the cynicism in his voice but didn't apologize for it.

Abigail looked surprised but didn't comment. She turned herself more fully toward him, waiting for him to continue. And so he did.

"You told me how your father helped you after your mother died. He praised you, showed you what you were capable of, loved you as you mourned. Upon my mother's death, my father did exactly the opposite."

The very edges of Abigail's eyes tightened. "How old were you?"

"My mother died when I was eight," Emmett said. "But her sickness began when I was born. Something happened during the birth, and she never recovered. You'd understand that better than I."

Abigail nodded.

"Mother was always ill. I hardly remember a time when she was not either in her bed or sitting in a chair covered in blankets. She didn't have the energy for parties or visitors and spent much of the time sleeping."

Abigail took his hand. "I'm sorry. It must have been very difficult."

He gave a small snort. "It wasn't difficult for *me*. Mother doted on me. She read to me, devised treasure hunts, watched me play. I was her entire world."

Abigail smiled. "She sounds lovely."

"She was. Of course, a boy thinks his mother the most beautiful woman in the world. But mine truly was. She was gentle, her voice soft and always kind . . ."

He allowed his voice to trail off as memories flowed through his thoughts.

Abigail squeezed his hand gently. Her expression was soft, and he found himself wanting to tell her everything. Perhaps he felt safe sharing with her because in a few days she'd be off to Detroit and he'd continue fighting. They'd likely never see one another again. His stomach felt heavy at the thought.

"Like I said," he continued. "Mother doted on me, and my father and brother resented it, though at the time I didn't realize it." Emmett let out a heavy breath. "Once she died, my father completely cut me off, focusing all of his attention on my perfect brother, Beau. He is, of course, in line to inherit the plantation.

"Father and Beau blamed me for Mother's death. Comments about how Beau performed so much better in school, remarks about my failings, disapproval, criticism, sarcasm, all of it turned my home into a place I couldn't bear to be. If it weren't for Lydia . . ."

"And what of your stepmother? What kind of person is she?" Abigail pulled his hand onto her own lap, holding onto it with both of hers.

"Emeline is pleasant and much younger than my father. She is never unkind, but she does not love me."

"Lydia loves you."

"She does." He forced himself to smile, feeling foolish for confessing so much. He sounded like a petulant child, whining about his upbringing. He wondered what Abigail was thinking. Did she think him resentful? Perhaps he should have left out some of the details. Especially the parts that sounded like complaining. "I realize now that Father was hurting, and he didn't know where to direct his frustration." He hoped that made him sound less sulky.

Abigail scowled. "But that is no excuse for treating a child as he did. Not when you were mourning, too. I am so sorry, Emmett. I wish . . ." Her voice trailed off.

He wondered what she'd meant to say. She wished she'd been there for him? She wished things had been different? And she'd called him Emmett. Did she realize it? Or had it just slipped out? He'd called her by her given name nearly since the day they'd met. But until now, she'd never done the same.

He was still turning over the implications of this new development when she gave a tug on his hand. "So after university, you joined the army to escape your home?"

"To some extent. I think there will always be a part of me that wants to impress my father. To be a hero and prove that I'm more than the spoiled child who was the cause of Mother's death."

"Emmett, you did not cause your mother's death. And you've no need to prove anything to anyone." She squeezed his fingers, holding his gaze with a serious expression. "You *are* a hero."

He gave a wry smile. "Well, so far I've spent five years stationed at Fort McHenry training, drilling, and performing sentry duty. Since the war began, I've marched for months through muddy mosquito-infested swamplands and frozen marshes, led my company into an Indian ambush, and was imprisoned in a young lady's barn. Not quite the honorable tour of duty I'd dreamed of."

"That is not it at all." Abigail's expression relaxed, and she scooted closer to him. "You honed your skills through five years of practice, led a hundred men on a campaign through the wilderness, enduring horrible conditions and sickness. You survived an Indian attack and kept your entire reconnaissance company alive." She pulled on his hand and leaned forward until he looked up at her. "You're a hero, Emmett. No matter what anyone tells you." Her eyes were intense, holding his gaze as if willing him to accept her words. After a moment she relaxed and a small smile pulled at her lips. "They don't give those gold shoulder decorations to just anyone, you know."

Emmett felt sheepish. Not only from her praise, but by the way he'd bared his soul, acting as if he'd been seeking admiration. He'd intended to simply tell the story, not whine and complain until she rewarded him with a compliment. "Abigail, I didn't mean to—"

"Captain! Abigail!" Barney's voice interrupted, and they both turned toward him.

He crawled out of the shelter, a smile on his round face. "Luke is awake."

That night, Emmett found himself ending the day in exactly the same way he'd begun it. He shifted on the rock, glancing between the three shelters and listening to the sounds of the forest over the crackling of the fire. Somewhere distant, a wolf howled. He heard an owl, and occasionally clumps of snow fell from trees. The chirping birds that had so gladly welcomed the sun were silent. The night was much colder than the previous had been.

He heard a rustle as Abigail shifted. She'd moved often during the hour he'd been awake, and he thought she must not be sleeping well.

His day had been one of the most enjoyable he could remember. The men were cheerful as they performed their tasks. Weapons had been cleaned and oiled, clothes washed, food prepared, and none had found reason to complain, which was a miracle in itself. They'd all been pleased to see Luke awake. The boy joined them for nearly an hour at the campfire and even ate some stew before Abigail insisted he return to the shelter and rest. While the others had been happy with his quick recovery, she was much more cautious, reminding him not to overexert himself lest his fever return.

The boy had been content to be fussed over and, truly, who could blame him?

The noise came again from Abigail's shelter, and after a moment she emerged. She held a blanket tightly around her shoulders and moved to the fire.

"Is something wrong?" he asked, keeping his voice low so he wouldn't wake the others.

"I am just so cold," she said. She shivered and buried her face in the blanket.

"Come along." Emmett took her arm and led her toward the flat rock. He sat on the earth before it, stretching his legs out toward the fire and pulled Abigail down beside him. Opening his own blanket wide, he wrapped it around both of them, nestling her beneath his arm. He should have been ashamed of his boldness, but under the circumstances, survival outweighed propriety.

Abigail continued to shiver, and he tightened his arm around her. Though he didn't particularly care for a soldier's close quarters when it came to sleeping space, being packed uncomfortably into a tent had one advantage. It had likely saved all of their lives by storing body heat.

"Better?" he asked once her shivering stopped.

She nodded against his chest then settled in more comfortably.

He leaned his cheek on her head, and after a bit, her breathing deepened. Emmett closed his eyes, enjoying the feel of the doctor nestled against him, and decided he didn't so much mind close quarters after all.

CHAPTER 9

ABIGAIL BLINKED HERSELF AWAKE, SURPRISED to see the sun had risen. She was still curled up with Emmett, and when she lifted her head, he smiled.

"Good morning."

Abigail could feel his chest rumble as he spoke. Her cheeks flamed red. Why she should be so embarrassed, she didn't know. Cozying so close with the captain had simply been a matter of sharing body heat. She sat up, drawing away. "Good morning."

"Good morning to you, miss." Murphy poured coffee into a mug and brought it to her.

"We worried you intended to sleep all day," Emmett said. He extracted his arm from behind her and stood, leaving the blankets draped over her shoulders. "Excuse me, but I need to take over for my corporal." He handed an empty mug to Murphy and stretched his shoulder. He smiled at Abigail, picked up a rifle, and left the camp.

Abigail thought his shoulder must be cramped from remaining in the same position for hours. Her embarrassment grew. "Jasper's still on sentry duty? He was on duty when I went to sleep."

Murphy nodded. "I relieved him, and so did Barney."

She'd slept longer than she'd realized. "He took an extra shift so Captain Prescott didn't wake me." Abigail felt foolish. "I'm sorry."

"He was glad to do it, miss."

"Abigail," she said.

Murphy dipped his head in assent. She liked this solemn man. He came around to sit on the rock, and she stood, brushed off her skirts, and sat beside him.

"You are all very kind to me, and to Captain Prescott. He acts like he's healed, but he needs to be careful not to overexert himself. Thank you for allowing him to rest."

"He's a fine man. The finest officer in the United States Army, and that's no exaggeration." Murphy's mouth was set in a line, and he gave a swift nod as if he'd just stated an irrefutable fact.

Abigail smiled at his devotion, blowing over the dark liquid before she took a sip. "I agree. He is a fine man. As are those in his command. You all do seem to get on very well."

"Miss—Abigail, did you wonder why the four of us were chosen to accompany Captain Prescott on this mission?"

Abigail hadn't even thought about it. She wasn't certain what exactly the mission was—some sort of scouting assignment, she assumed. But now that she considered, she realized that, aside from Jasper, the group was not exactly a stealthy band of reconnoiterers. "Why were you chosen? If you don't mind my asking."

"Our regiment falls under Brigadier-General James Winchester. We've been plagued for weeks by dysentery, typhoid fever, and a slew of other diseases while marching into Michigan Territory. Men are falling ill and dying every day. Luke there," he nodded toward where the boy slept. "He's the youngest in Captain Prescott's command, the smallest. And I'm the oldest. Captain knows I've a malady of the lungs. If I were to take ill in a soldier's camp . . ."

He shrugged as if the rest of the sentiment didn't need saying.

"Jasper, of course, has invaluable skills for a mission like this, and Barney won't leave his brother. But with the entire army to choose from, Captain selected the two weakest in his regiment, in hopes of keeping us from falling ill."

Abigail was touched by the man's words, and she wondered if Captain Prescott knew how highly his men thought of him. He may not think himself to be a hero, but Murphy certainly did. And she did as well.

Jasper entered the camp, and Abigail rose. She took a blanket from her shoulder and offered it to him. "Mr. Webb, I must thank you for your consideration for me. I know a soldier prefers his sleep to taking another shift on sentry duty."

Jasper shrugged. "I don't mind," he mumbled.

"Truly, I am grateful," she said.

"Jasper doesn't need sleep." Barney's voice interrupted them. He crawled out of his shelter, scratching his hair until it stuck up all around his head. "He's stronger than a regular man. He fought a bear, you know."

Abigail opened her eyes wide. "You *fought* a bear?"

"Wasn't by choice." Jasper shrugged again.

"Go on, show her the claw scars," Barney said.

"She doesn't want to see—"

"Actually, I would like to see them," Abigail broke in. "If you feel comfortable showing me." Of course she was interested in seeing the scars. What student of medicine wouldn't be?

Jasper gave her a curious look but turned around, removed his coat, and hitched up his shirt to reveal five long streaks crossing his back from his shoulder to his hip.

Abigail moved closer, fascinated. The gashes hadn't been treated or sutured, she could tell right away. Some parts bunched up, thick with scar tissue, and others had healed badly, stretched wide. She touched one gash that had gone particularly deep. "Oh, my. How did you ever survive this?"

Jasper dropped down his shirt and turned. "Wasn't as bad as it looks."

"It must have hurt terribly," Abigail said.

"Tell her what happened to the old bear, Jasper," Barney said.

Jasper darted a look at him then pulled the hat from his head and held it toward Abigail.

She took it, feeling the thick fur it was made from. "You killed *this* bear?" The head was enormous, even without its lower jaw.

A smile tugged at Jasper's mouth. "Yep."

"Killed it with a hunting knife," Murphy said from the other side of the fire.

Abigail didn't believe it was possible. She'd seen bears in Upper Canada. Luckily none had ever attacked, but she'd only ever heard of them being killed by a bullet, or several. Getting close enough to use a knife on a bear was suicide. Especially one of this size. "You are all teasing me, aren't you?"

"Nope." Jasper's twitching mouth resembled a near-smile.

"Corporal Webb, I've never heard of . . . I . . . ." She truly didn't know what to say. She wagged a finger at him, scolding. "You must be more careful in the future."

All three of the men laughed at this. "It's the bears that need to be careful," Murphy said.

Abigail joined in, her laughter mixing with the men's. "I believe you're right."

Jasper wrapped the blanket around his shoulders and started toward the structure. "I'll check the snares in a few hours," he said.

"Luke and I will check the snares," Barney said helpfully. "I remember where they are."

"And I'll assist them," Abigail said. "You sleep as long as you need to."

Jasper nodded and crawled inside the shelter.

Abigail realized she was still holding the furry hat. She brushed her fingers through it once more then set it on the flat rock. She moved to the small shelter and knelt beside Luke. "How do you feel this morning?" She laid her fingers on his forehead. His skin was warm but not hot. She was surprised not to feel any fever at all.

"Hungry," Luke said.

"I'll check your arm, and then you can have some stew."

"Thank you, ma'am." The color had returned to his cheeks.

"Please, call me Abigail," she said for the second time that day. She briefly wondered if she should just make a general announcement to the entire company that she would prefer to be called by her Christian name, instead of having to tell each man individually.

Abigail unwrapped the bandages, moving the splints and the inner wrappings. The arm was still swollen, hot, and very red, but there were no dark streaks and little seepage on the bandages. He appeared to be healing well, which surprised her. Of course, she was not disappointed to have Luke mend faster than she'd anticipated, but once he was well, she would depart for Detroit and Captain Prescott's company would return to its regiment.

And the thought was unexpectedly sad. She supposed it was because she'd spent the better part of the winter alone, but she liked these men, and she imagined if Isaac and her father weren't on the other side of the war, they'd like them as well. It was difficult to believe that only a few days earlier, she was practicing profanities to describe the American soldiers. An uncomfortable shame heated her belly when she remembered the words she'd used.

She thought the best way to make up for her unfounded judgments was to help these soldiers as much as she was able.

At least they would have a few days more together. And once they reached Detroit, she was sure they would be admitted under a flag of truce. They were, after all, peacefully accompanying her to see her father. And as an officer, Emmett would be treated especially well. Her father could inspect Luke's wound and Emmett's. He would know exactly what mixture of medicines the men needed, if they required further treatment, and when to remove the sutures. And he could listen to Murphy's lungs.

Abigail made sure they all ate a sufficient breakfast, saving the remainder for Jasper to eat when he woke.

Isaac's trousers were too large for Luke, so she gave them to Murphy. The knees of the older man's trousers were nearly worn through, and she didn't think they would hold another patch. Luke wore Isaac's shirt over his own, and, though it was quite large, Abigail thought it was a wise idea. He needed all the warmth he could get.

Luke was weak but still accompanied Barney and Abigail through the forest, inspecting the snares. They'd caught two large hares, and the three prepared them, building a spit over the fire to slow-cook the meat.

In the afternoon, clouds started to cover the sun, making her worry the night would bring snow. Jasper must have had the same thought because he and Barney set out to replenish their firewood stores.

Abigail had just finished cleaning the stewpot when Emmett returned.

His face lit up in a smile, and her earlier embarrassment returned. "Are you still cold, Abigail?"

She liked his look of concern. Up close she could see the light blue of his eyes surrounded by a darker blue at the edge of his irises. "I am, rather, but if I keep moving, it warms me a bit."

"Perhaps take a walk with me?" He offered his arm. "To keep moving."

The lightness of his voice set her at ease. "I'd love to," she said, clasping the inside of his elbow.

He led her away from the camp, and, after a moment, they climbed up a hill. They followed a path of tramped-down snow, and she decided this must be the route the men took to stand watch.

"How is your shoulder?" she asked.

"My shoulder?" He stepped high over a fallen log then reached for her hand, his fingers sliding beneath her elbow as he helped her over.

"You looked as though your shoulder was stiff this morning," Abigail said. "I'm sorry."

"Don't apologize, Abigail. That was by far the most pleasant night I've spent since . . . perhaps ever."

"But, your shoulder suffered for it, and so did your men."

He shook his head. "They didn't suffer at all." He tugged on her hand, leading her higher up the hill.

"They did extra duty to make sure I could sleep comfortably," Abigail protested. She was starting to get out of breath. Where exactly was he taking her?

"I didn't hear one complaint," Emmett said. He continued climbing but slowed his pace. "I don't think anything has ever made these soldiers as happy as fresh bread and your granny's socks."

She smiled. "They are good men."

He nodded. "That is very true."

"And they think highly of you, Emmett."

He turned his head and studied her for a moment then continued onward. A moment later, they came upon Murphy, standing where he could look down over the camp and the area around it. Abigail caught glimpses of the main road through the treetops. They greeted him and continued. The way became more difficult now that the trodden path was gone. Emmett slowed and held on to her hand, walking at a leisurely pace. "Abigail, when will Luke be strong enough to march to Detroit?"

Her stomach sank at the change in topic. This must be why he'd wanted to speak to her privately. "Soon, I think. In the next few days. He will need to move slowly and rest often, but he is mending rapidly."

"You seem surprised by his recovery," Emmett said.

"I am surprised. He must have more strength in that slender body than I gave him credit for. That and a strong will to carry on." She lifted her skirts as she stepped up onto a rock. "I did not imagine he would recover so quickly, if at all."

Emmett stopped and faced her. "I attribute it to his excellent doctor."

The praise brought a smile to her face. She stepped down, and they walked beneath the canopy of snowy branches. "I certainly cannot take all the credit. Jasper built a fine shelter that protected him from the elements, and Murphy took care of him. You knew where to find a doctor, and Barney helped bind his wounds. The entire company is responsible for his improvement."

He lifted his hand and inclined his head in a motion that seemed more suited to a fancy party than a snowy forest. "Well, on this, we will agree to disagree."

The way ahead was barred by thick undergrowth, so they stopped. "I'm glad you brought me to your camp, Emmett. I like your men very much." She lowered her lashes. "And their captain."

Emmett lifted her chin so their eyes met. He slipped a hand around her waist, pulling her toward him, and before she knew what had happened, his lips had captured hers.

Abigail thought her insides might melt. Her knees felt soft, and her heart beat wildly. She clutched the lapels of his jacket, eyes pressed closed, hoping the moment wouldn't come to an end. In the back of her mind, she remembered reading about the high concentration of nerve endings in the human lips and thought it was a very effective place for them. She felt the kiss throughout her entire body.

Emmett stepped back, his thumb brushing over her lower lip. His eyes had darkened, and the sight made a shiver move through her middle. He seemed to be waiting for her to say something, but her thoughts were a jumble. She just stared at him, her face heating. She should say something amorous, she knew, but she had no words.

After a moment, Emmett flashed the flirting smile he'd used on the first day they'd met. "I don't know if I've ever made a woman speechless before."

"Yes, I . . . That was . . . nice." Abigail decided saying nothing was better than idiotic babbling coming out of her mouth.

He laughed. "That it was, Abigail Tidwell."

She felt a bit indignant. Was he having a laugh at her expense? "I'm sorry, Captain. You caught me off guard, and I have never learned the proper thing to say after a kiss."

"Well." He slid a hand beneath her ear, his thumb stroking her cheek. "When you find yourself in such a quandary, another kiss will keep you from having to say anything."

Abigail was ready this time. When his lips touched hers, she slid her arms around him, careful of his wound, and held on to him tightly. She kissed him back instead of standing frozen like a statue, telling him wordlessly how her fondness for him had grown. And finally, gently, their lips parted. "Emmett, I don't want to go to Detroit," she said breathlessly, not opening her eyes. Along with her increased heart rate, an ache that was not explainable in medical terms grew in her chest.

He rested his forehead on hers, his hands dropping down to her shoulders. "I wish the situation were different. I wish we had a choice."

She nodded. The ache had spread to her throat, and she worried it had impaired her larynx.

Emmett's head jerked up suddenly, and Abigail looked around, fearing a wolf or some other danger was drawing close. A moment later she heard Murphy's voice.

"Captain, come quickly! The British Army. It's advancing toward Frenchtown."

CHAPTER 10

EMMETT CROUCHED DOWN AT THE sentry's position, peering over a cluster of snow-laden bushes. Murphy and Abigail crouched beside him.

The cold metal of the spyglass stung his fingers, but he did not take any notice, counting quietly under his breath as he estimated the number of troops based on the length of the column he could see in glimpses between the trees. "At least six hundred regulars," he muttered to Murphy. "Three cannons. One is a howitzer."

Murphy didn't respond. Emmett knew what the man was thinking, but neither of them said it aloud. The British Army was a threat in itself, but it was the large body of Indian warriors marching beside the red-coated soldiers that sent a cold spike of fear through his gut. His guess placed their number at more than eight hundred.

And they were all advancing toward the exhausted, untrained, and inexperienced men of his regiment. This army would slaughter them.

"How far to Frenchtown?" he asked.

"Ten, maybe twelve miles," Murphy responded.

Dawn, then, Emmett realized. The attack would come at dawn. "We have to warn them."

He rose to his feet but remained hunched down. He didn't imagine the army could see him among the trees and shadows with the heavy cloud cover, but a glint of his brass coat buttons was all it would take to give away their position. Not that the British soldiers would be surprised to know their progress was being watched. They'd expect it. No, it wasn't them he was worried about at all. The Indians were a different story altogether. In battle, they adhered to different rules. They were vicious and unpredictable, and . . . the cold feeling spread, energizing him to action. "Private Murphy, you, Corporal Webb, and I will leave immediately."

He felt a tug on his hand.

Abigail's eyes were wide. "Leave? You cannot leave."

He clasped his fingers around her mittened hand and started toward the camp after Murphy. She stumbled, trying to keep pace with him on the downward incline, but he did not slow. He could not. It was time for action, and if he didn't push away his own sentiments, his decision-making would be impaired. "I must," he said. "Barney and Luke will accompany you to Detroit. You'll be well-protected." He pushed away more fears. The thought of Abigail being taken by the fierce native warriors made him feel like a band of iron was compressing his chest. He pushed away that feeling as well, concentrating on action. He couldn't let his fondness for Abigail distract him from his duty.

"But it's nearly dark and you're still injured, Emmett. You mustn't overexert yourself."

A swell of affection rose inside him. Of course she was worried for his well-being over her own. He slowed his pace to walk alongside her and grasped her hand. "Abigail, that army is headed for my regiment. Men who look to me as their leader. Men who will fight and die tomorrow at dawn. I cannot neglect them. Not when they need me the most."

Abigail remained silent, and Emmett could only imagine her thoughts. She must be terrified knowing a battle was coming. When they stepped back into the clearing, Murphy and Jasper were packing their gear. Luke and Barney stood at attention, worry manifesting in similar expressions on their faces.

Emmett released Abigail's hand and stepped toward the brothers. "You two will deliver Miss Tidwell to Detroit. Be cautious; take suitable measures for her safety and Private Hopkins's health."

"Should we smother the fire, Captain?" Barney asked.

Emmett considered for a moment. The scouts had likely already seen the smoke. They may come to investigate, but he doubted it. Settlers lived throughout the forest, so chimney and hunting fires weren't uncommon. His gut told him the army would focus on their march, hoping to arrive in time to rest their men and prepare for an attack at dawn. And there was a chance, with the heavy clouds, that they'd not seen it at all. As night fell, Abigail, Luke, and Barney would need the fire for warmth and to repel predators. In his mind, the benefits outweighed the risk. "Leave the fire," he said.

He stepped closer to the two men, lowering his voice. He didn't want to worry Abigail. "If you are taken, surrender immediately. Do not fight. Insist on speaking with an officer. Tell the truth of the mission, your regiment, Luke's injury, how Miss Tidwell came to be with our company, all of it." Nothing they said could hurt the mission now, and the officer would know men of their rank weren't privy to any compromising information.

The brothers nodded their understanding.

Emmett turned and saw Jasper and Murphy wore their packs and haversacks. They held their weapons and were awaiting his order to move out. He grabbed his own pack.

Abigail stepped in front of him and grasped onto his forearm. "Emmett, wait."

Her voice shook, and the sound caused his heart to ache. He led her to the far side of the clearing where they could have a bit of privacy.

"What do I do?" Her voice rose in tone as her panic grew. "Should we hide? I think it will snow. What about the wolves? The Indians? Luke is still very weak. What if the army finds us?"

Emmett dropped his gear and placed his hands on her shoulders, hoping to reassure her as he would any of his men, with a calm voice and logical discourse. "If you're discovered, you'll be taken safely to your father in Fort Detroit."

"But Barney and Luke . . ."

"They are militia, not regulars. They'll be quickly released." Being captured would actually be a good situation for Abigail, he thought.

She shook her head as if unable to speak, and tears coursed from her eyes. A sob shook her and Abigail clamped her hand over her mouth. The sight made something inside of Emmett crack, and the feelings he'd kept at bay rushed out. It was with great effort that he pushed them back where they belonged. "Please don't be afraid. Barney and Luke will keep you safe, Abigail." He was surprised to hear the softer timbre of his voice as he tried to speak through a constricting throat.

He pulled her toward him, holding her tightly. When he glanced at the camp, he saw the other men had become suddenly attentive to their packs or the pile of firewood.

"We should all go together or stay," Abigail said.

He drew back but didn't release the embrace. He held her gaze as he spoke. "Abigail, I'm sorry. If I'd known . . . I'd never have brought you here. It wasn't my intention to leave you like this."

"I'm scared." Her voice was hardly more than a whisper.

"You'll be safe. The wolves won't come near the fire, and by tomorrow or the next day at the very latest, you'll be with your father."

Abigail's brows furrowed and she shook her head, reminding him again of Lydia in a stubborn bout. "I do not fear for myself." She darted her eyes to the side, swallowing, and then looked back at him. "You are going to fight that army. Those cannons are going to be aimed at you and Jasper and Murphy. You're walking directly into danger, and I won't ever know . . ." Her voice choked off, and she put her hand back over her mouth.

Emmett's body felt heavy like it was filled with lead canister shot. "Do not fear for me."

She turned her head to the side, crossing her arms, somehow managing to look defeated and petulant at the same time.

He caught her chin and touched his lips to hers. This time, the kiss wasn't hopeful, there was no questioning either of their affection for the other. This was a farewell kiss, and Emmett was taken by surprise at how badly it hurt.

"Miss Abigail Tidwell, you are a black opal." She blinked and wrinkled her nose, and Emmett smiled at the confused look on her face. "Beautiful, rare, interesting, and just when I believe I know you, I am surprised to find there is more depth than I imagined."

Abigail's eyes softened into an expression that warmed him from head to toe. Her brown eyes, still wet with tears, shone with pleasure at his words. Her mouth curved into a soft smile, and Emmett knew he would remember how she looked at this very moment for as long as he lived.

"Thank you, Emmett. I do not think anyone has ever paid me a more thoughtful compliment."

"Goodbye, Abigail." He brushed the backs of his fingers down her cheek then turned quickly, forcing himself to step away. "Murphy, Webb—move out."

He marched into the forest without looking back, knowing if he did, there was a very real possibility that he'd not have the strength to leave.

Emmett led the men through the thick Michigan Territory woodland. Although they would move much faster on the flat road, he knew there would be a risk of meeting advance scouts and picket guards. They couldn't take the chance. The columns of attackers would move slowly. They had supplies and weapons and fifteen hundred men to move. Even dodging around trees and rocks, Emmett's small band would outpace them easily.

The snow began just as night fell. He turned up his collar and wished he had a pair of granny's striped socks on his hands. He hefted the pack on his shoulders and wondered what was happening back at the bivouac camp. Was Abigail cold? She would certainly seek shelter in one of the lean-tos, wouldn't she? They'd left the two blankets and Abigail's quilt. Would it be enough? Were they keeping dry? As the snow fell thicker, he hoped it hadn't put out the fire. Almost without thinking, he paused, glancing back over his shoulder.

"She'll be all right," Jasper said, coming up beside him.

Emmett kept walking. "Of course, I wasn't . . ."

Jasper's furry hat was covered in white flakes. And with the way the sides of the hat fell, Emmett couldn't make out his face. Not that he'd be able to read much in the man's expression anyway. "You made the best choice, Captain," Jasper said.

Emmett thought if anyone else had spoken so bluntly about his orders, he'd have reprimanded them for insubordination. But coming from a man of so few words, a person who observed and seldom offered an opinion, the statement was reassuring.

He nodded his thanks to Jasper, knowing the buckskin-clad Kentuckian would see the movement through the dark and falling snow and understand his meaning.

They continued on. The snow stuck to the ground in thick drifts, slowing their steps. Hours passed, and Emmett was frustrated that he'd still not fully regained his strength. He tired much sooner than he should have. But lives depended on them, so he pushed through the pain, ignored the fatigue, and maintained a steady march through the dark and uneven terrain. It was almost a relief to hear Murphy's labored breathing and have an excuse to rest.

Jasper left to scout the army's position, and when he returned, he reported the British had set up camp at Stony Creek, just a few miles north of Frenchtown. Knowing the redcoats and their Indian allies would be well-rested and their principal officers were very likely right this moment using their scouts' reports on the Americans' positions to strategize their attack gave Emmett a resurgence of energy. He nearly ran the remaining miles, and was relieved at last to hear the warning shout of a sentry.

"Who goes there?"

"Captain Emmett Prescott. I must speak to General Winchester immediately."

The sentry stepped closer, studying Emmett by moonlight as thick flakes fell around them. "General Winchester is at his headquarters."

Emmett's side ached. He was exhausted, cold, and now furious. The general's headquarters were in a farmhouse on the other side of the Raisin River, three miles away. Why was the commander not with his troops? "Surely he's been warned about the British and Indian army bearing down on us at this very moment."

The sentry looked past Emmett as if he might see the army looming behind him. "I don't know, Captain. Because of the weather, no pickets have been sent out along the roads."

"Who's the field officer in charge?"

"Colonel Wells, sir."

Emmett stormed past the sentry. They'd less than an hour before dawn, and for all he knew, the enemy was setting into position at this very moment.

He left Jasper and Murphy with orders to find their regiments and warn their commanders.

Striding into the open field to the east of town, Emmett stuck his head into the first tent he came to. "Where is Colonel Wells?" he demanded in a yell.

A man sprang from his bedroll and stood at attention, blinking himself awake.

Emmett's frustration was nearly tangible. The man had been in a deep, unbothered sleep, just like the rest of the camp. How had they not been warned? "Where is Colonel Wells?" he repeated.

"The colonel and Captain Lanham rode away a few hours ago. Left Major McClanahan in charge."

Emmett spun and left the tent. It wasn't difficult to find the major. He sat beneath a tree with two other men, smoking. When Emmett approached, they all rose and saluted.

"My regards, Major McClanahan," Emmett said. "Sir, we are soon to be under attack. An army of over fifteen hundred redcoats and Indians is even now marching toward us armed with heavy artillery."

The major ordered the others to raise the alarm.

Cries of, "To arms!" sounded, and the peaceful camp came alive as men poured out of tents and shouted orders. Emmett was relieved that the major at least recognized the truthfulness of the warning.

"It's just as the colonel feared," Major McClanahan said as he and Emmett strode quickly through the confusion of men. "The general didn't . . . uh . . . trust the information about an approaching army, but Colonel Wells assumed it was true. He rode off last night for reinforcements." He must have gone for General Harrison's army at the Rapids. Emmett vaguely wondered if he would make it back in time but did not dwell on it. He couldn't place his hopes on what may happen but must focus on what he should do now.

"Where are the ammunition stores?" Emmett asked.

"With the general at his headquarters." The major's tone conveyed a world of meaning. He'd not speak out against his commanding officer, but both of them knew General Winchester's unwillingness to take the warnings seriously and prepare the soldiers had very likely doomed them all.

Emmett lifted his chin and kept a calm expression. Despair and fear spread like a plague among soldiers. He'd not allow his men to see his apprehension, or the battle would be finished before it even began. He saluted Major McClanahan. "I must join my—"

The crack of the sentries' muskets fired, sounding an alarm. Immediately afterward, bombshells and cannon shot rained down, exploding throughout the still-unorganized camp.

Major McClanahan screamed over the artillery fire, calling out orders and urging his men to remember their training, load their weapons, and form a line. The cannons continued to fire on the unprotected soldiers, and their return fire was ineffective, as they couldn't see their enemy through the darkness.

Emmett fired the musket into the night then ran into Frenchtown, finding his men behind the fence that surrounded two sides of the town. They were shooting at the soldiers attacking from the north and west. Jasper stood with the First Kentucky Rifles and Murphy with the Pittsburg Blues. Emmett felt proud as he looked over the Second U.S. Dragoon Squadron and the Nineteenth Infantry Regiment and made a note to commend his lieutenants for forming ranks so efficiently. He exchanged Abigail's father's musket for a proper rifle and joined the battle.

As daylight dawned, the scene became clear. The exposed soldiers in the open field were being driven back through their camp. From the surrounding forest came the sound of war cries as Indian warriors ran through the trees and flanked the retreating Americans. They attacked with guns, tomahawks, and knives, snatching off the "scalp locks" from their enemies' heads and sending the army into a disordered panic as the commanders yelled and tried to reestablish order.

The cannon shot continued to explode, sending blasts of snow, dirt, and blood into the air in the midst of the chaos.

Emmett ordered the Kentuckians to concentrate their fire on the gun crews, and a few moments later, the cannon's blasts were silenced.

He caught Jasper's gaze and saw a glint of satisfaction in the man's eye. "Well done, Corporal," Emmett said.

The British were not discouraged by their loss of cannon power. "Fix bayonets," came the commander's cry, and the sharp blades were attached to the redcoats' Brown Bess muskets.

Emmett called out orders of his own, which were repeated by the lieutenants. They must hold steady.

The Americans who'd managed to retreat into the town turned, and at Emmett's orders formed a line, protecting Frenchtown on three sides. The other side was bordered by the river. Lieutenants moved back and forth delivering orders. Injured men were pulled out of the line and laid between homes and in yards to wait for medical care. The snow was churned dirty with blood and mud as the British infantry charged and were met with a volley of bullets. Emmett fired and then used his weapon to deliver a blow to a redcoat. He pulled back to reload, commanding the men to take up the weapons of their fallen comrades.

And so it continued. The British and Indians mustered again for an attack, but the Americans held the line, driving them back again and again.

Ammunition was running low, as was morale, but the soldiers kept firing, turning back the British charge. At this latest withdrawal, a cheer went up from the line, and Emmett couldn't help but grin.

CHAPTER 11

ABIGAIL SHIVERED IN THE LEAN-TO. She was both trying to take up as little space as possible so she didn't crowd the men and keep herself away from the cold air at the edge of the shelter. The snow fell so thickly that it was filling the opening and spilling inside. The fire had long since gone out, making the night darker and colder than she could have believed.

She and the others had agreed that remaining together was a better option than sending away one of the men to stand as sentry. He'd not be able to see farther than a few feet anyway, and they were safer as a group.

In spite of his protests, Luke lay between the two of them, wrapped in the quilt. With the amount of blood he'd lost, as well as his body still mending from the fever, he should be kept the warmest. But he still shivered, and from the sound of their breathing, neither of the men was able to sleep. The ground was simply too cold.

Finally, Abigail rose up onto her knees, holding the blanket tightly around her. "We must move about or our body temperatures will drop too low."

She heard the sounds of the other two moving.

"I think we should start walking," she said.

"Might as well freeze going somewhere as lying here." Luke's voice was shaking.

"Shall we start for Detroit?" Barney asked.

Abigail had considered this very question for hours as they'd huddled in the cold. She had an idea but worried the men wouldn't go along with her plan. She was determined to try. "I think we should go to Frenchtown." She held still, waiting to see how they'd react.

Both men were silent, and she could feel their discomfort as if they'd spoken it aloud. They were caught between the options of obeying their captain's orders and obliging a lady's request.

Finally Barney spoke. "But Captain Prescott said——"

"Captain Prescott gave his command out of worry for my well-being. And Luke's. We are closer to Frenchtown than Detroit, are we not?"

"Suppose so," Barney said.

"Luke cannot stay here in the cold," she said. "He will be cared for in Frenchtown. And the army will return me to my father more quickly and safely than if the three of us spend the next few days tromping through the forest."

She thought her argument was sound. And her points were truthful. Luke's care was foremost in her mind. In Frenchtown, the regiment was bound to have a surgeon, and certainly there was a house where he could be kept warm as he recovered. Or at the very least, the British would take him in a wagon to Detroit, where her father would care for him.

But she had another reason for wanting to go to Frenchtown, one she didn't say aloud. She must know what happened to Emmett and the others. If there was truly to be a battle at dawn, she wished to be there to provide medical care, and though she knew it was silly, she felt like being near was important. Not that she'd be able to protect anyone in battle, but she couldn't just sit here in the cold forest or set off for Detroit without knowing how they'd fared. She simply could not.

The men didn't speak, so Abigail continued. "At any rate, we must move, or we will freeze. We may as well move in the direction that will be most beneficial to the others as well as Luke."

"Captain did say 'take suitable measures for Abigail's safety and Private Hopkins's health'," Barney said. "Can you travel, Luke?"

"If we move slowly."

"Very well, then it is decided." Abigail crawled out of the shelter and put on her bonnet, pulling her cloak and the woolen blanket tightly around her shoulders.

The men followed, grabbing the packs they'd prepared for travel the next morning.

"Here, Abigail," Luke said. "Take the quilt."

She shook her head, though she knew he could not see it in the darkness. "You need it more than I." Hearing his intake of breath as he prepared to protest, she touched his arm. "We can trade soon, once you are warm."

They set off, trusting Barney's sense of direction to get them to the road. Moving through the thick snow in the dark forest would slow them so much as to be pointless if they hoped to reach Frenchtown the next day. And besides being easier for travel, there was a good chance they'd be found on the road by soldiers—from either army—and taken to the town.

They walked in silence, with only the sounds of Abigail's rustling skirts and an occasional grunt from one of the men, until they finally emerged from the tree line. Abigail could only see shadows, but she could hear by the change in acoustics that they were in an open space. After the security of the forest, she felt exposed and vulnerable. And seeing the way Barney and Luke held their guns and looked from side to side, she imagined they felt the same.

She supposed conversation might set them at ease. "Barney," she said. Her voice was much louder than she was used to with the trees muffling the sound. She spoke softer. "Tell me about your family in Ohio. You mentioned your mother, and there's Luke, of course. Have you other siblings?"

"Two sisters," he said. "Younger than me, older than Luke. Both married."

"And do they live near you?"

"Within a few miles. Close enough to help Pa and Ma with the farm while we're gone. Not much to do in the winter, anyway."

"And when will your militia contract be served?"

"We've a month more," Barney said.

They paused, brushing off the snow from a stump for Luke to sit on. Resting when Luke was tired had become so natural that they did not even discuss it—just paused in their walking, waited a few moments, and carried on. Marching on the tramped-down snow of the road was so much easier than trudging through the thick drifts that he rested less frequently.

The two sat on either side of him.

"What do you intend to do when you return home?" Abigail asked.

"Barney has a sweetheart," Luke said with the teasing inflection of a pestering brother.

Abigail was glad to hear it. If Luke had the energy to tease, he must not be suffering too badly.

"What is her name?" she asked.

"Winnifred Morgan." Both men replied at the same time, one sounding playful and the other affectionate.

"I think Winnifred Morgan is a lucky woman," Abigail said.

They rose and continued along the road.

"I hope to marry her," Barney spoke in a low voice, meant for her ears only.

"I am happy to hear it," Abigail said. "You will make a fine husband, Barney."

She couldn't see his expression, but she thought he held his head taller. Slowing her pace, she walked beside Luke.

"And what do you plan to do when you return home?"

"I hope to go to school. Perhaps attend a university."

"What will you study?"

"I'd like to do doctoring, like you." He sounded nervous as if worried she'd disparage his idea.

"I hope you do, Luke. And I hope you write me letters and tell me all about it." Abigail felt the familiar longing to attend a university, but of course for a woman, wishing for such a thing was useless.

"I will," Luke said. He sounded much more animated than he had the entire journey. "Do you know, Pa met a man in Cincinnati who said the outer settlements are desperate for doctors? Some will even pay the university fees." He was quiet for a moment. "I wish I'd been awake to see you tend to my arm, Abigail. I was certain it would have to be amputated."

"I'm glad it didn't." She realized the young man would have no hope of a career in medicine with only one arm. She was once again grateful that Emmett had brought her to the camp and the men had entrusted her with Luke's care.

After another rest, they continued on. She imagined each in the party was caught up in his own thoughts. Barney was thinking of the woman he'd left behind, Luke of his future plans, and Abigail could not keep herself from remembering Emmett's parting kiss. Her heart was heavy with worry about Emmett, Jasper, and Murphy. Had they made it to Frenchtown? Or had they been captured before they were able to deliver their warning? Her mind turned over different scenarios, each causing more worry than the previous, until she finally had to stop. She distracted herself by mentally reconstructing the chemical compositions of all the sheet silicates she could think of.

More hours passed, and Abigail thought it must be near dawn. She wondered how far they'd gone. Surely they'd covered close to seven or eight miles, maybe more.

The thought had no sooner entered her mind than she was startled by the sound of gunfire followed by explosions. She gasped and looked around as her body started to shake. Barney took her arm, and she could barely see his face in the dim predawn. His mouth was drawn into a grim line, his brows furrowed. The battle had begun.

Once the initial terror passed, Abigail felt frantic to reach the town. Emmett could at this moment be lying on the ground, the victim of one of the blasts.

They hurried along, stopping less often in their impatience to reach Frenchtown. The sun rose, and though they still could not see the town with the forest on either side of the road, a cloud of brown smoke floated in the sky ahead.

The cannon discharges became so loud that Abigail could feel them shaking the air. And in between blasts were the noises of gunfire and the indistinctive sound of turmoil. She could not see the battle, but she could smell it. Gunpowder stung her eyes and made her cough, and even though it was likely her imagination, she was certain she could smell blood.

The cannon blasts stopped, but the gunfire continued, and now she could hear shouts and the roars of hundreds of men locked in battle. But eventually this stopped as well, and only the smoky smell remained, becoming thicker as they neared the town.

Shapes and movements appeared between the trees, and suddenly the way ahead was cleared and Frenchtown and the aftermath of the battle came into view.

In spite of herself, Abigail drew back and took Barney's arm. In the eerie silence, evidence of fighting was everywhere. The ground was a mess of dirty snow. Clumps of material that she realized were injured or dead men were strewn about as if a giant had dropped his collection of wooden soldiers haphazardly around the clearing.

People moved about, carrying wounded men toward the town. Some simply sat and stared; others helped comrades. The chaos still existed, but it was subdued and a feeling of misery hung heavy like the cloud of gun smoke.

Abigail could not make any sense of what she was seeing. Which side had won the battle? She started to ask Barney but felt him stiffen. Looking up, she saw a group of Indian warriors approaching.

The men were muscular and bare-chested with painted skin and sharp weapons, but it was the scalp patches they carried that snatched the air from Abigail's lungs and made cold terror spike through her veins.

She clung to Barney's large arm, her mind feeling sluggish and alert at the same time as utter fear covered her, cold and heavy.

The Indians reached them and grinned menacingly, motioning for Luke and Barney to drop their weapons.

The men complied. Barney stepped forward, moving himself to stand in front of both Abigail and Luke. Abigail could see his fists were tight, but he still shook.

Two of the warriors aimed their guns at Barney, and the man who appeared to be the leader of the Indians drew a knife and started toward him, an evil expression curling his lip and making his dark eyes glint. Abigail put her hands over her face and closed her eyes, bracing herself for her friends' pain nearly as much as her own. Her breathing was jagged, and all of her muscles tensed.

"Hold, there!" a voice called from behind them. "You, stop immediately!"

Abigail peeked through her fingers and saw a man in a British uniform approaching with hurried steps. He waved his hands in a shooing motion, and the Indian warriors moved away, looking back with disappointed glares.

Realizing the man had saved them, Abigail let her breath out, and her body slacked with relief. The man caught her arm, perhaps fearing she would swoon. At this point, it wasn't out of the question, Abigail thought. She'd never in her life felt such all-encompassing dread, and the utter relief that followed it made her light-headed.

"Thank you,"—she noted the chevrons on his jacket—"Lieutenant."

"Lieutenant Sebastian Fox at your service, miss." He gave Barney and Luke a quick glance then called a pair of soldiers over, instructing the two Americans to be taken to join the other prisoners.

The soldiers took their weapons, and Luke handed the quilt to Abigail.

"This man is in need of medical care," Abigail said to the redcoats, but they gave her hardly a glance before her friends were marched away.

So the British were the victors, Abigail realized. A week ago, this would have been her preferred outcome, but today, knowing Emmett and his men had been defeated wrenched her heart with anguish. She had to find them.

Still holding on to her arm, the lieutenant studied Abigail. "Now, if you please, miss, explain who you are and what you were doing."

Abigail didn't like the man's demanding tone, but she figured he had a right to be suspicious of anyone during wartime.

"My name is Abigail Tidwell, sir. Perhaps you know my father, William Tidwell. He is a physician-surgeon in Fort Detroit."

"Yes, I am acquainted with the doctor. And if I remember rightly, his home is in Amherstburg. So, that begs the question, 'What is his daughter doing on a battlefield more than twenty miles away, with two American soldiers?'"

Abigail definitely didn't like the lieutenant's tone now. And the way he looked at her made her wary, as if he were trying to discern the best way to use any information she might give against her. The man was very handsome. His speech was that of an aristocrat and his uniform impeccable, which she thought strange after a battle in the dirty snow.

"I am a healer, Lieutenant. I have come to assist with the wounded in hopes that I might travel safely with the army back to my father."

His eyes narrowed. "That is not an explanation." He took the bag off her shoulder and opened it, poking through her medical equipment with a bored expression.

"It is rather a long story, and I think now my time would be better spent tending to the injured, if you don't mind, Lieutenant."

"Perhaps I do mind." His lip curled into a sneer. "I find your presence as well as your behavior highly suspicious, Miss Tidwell. And as you are no doubt aware, His Majesty's army has no mercy for spies, nor traitors."

He leaned toward her, perhaps meaning to intimidate her, but Abigail had just survived an encounter with scalp-collecting Indian warriors. She'd slept in a cold forest surrounded by wolves and walked miles through the darkness and falling snow. She wasn't about to let one snooty British officer frighten her.

The impasse lasted only a moment before a young man approached. He saluted and stood to attention. "If you please, Lieutenant Fox, General Procter sends his regards and requests your presence, sir."

Lieutenant Fox's eyes narrowed, but he nodded, his gaze still boring into Abigail. "Corporal, please take this woman to the field hospital."

CHAPTER 12

EMMETT STOOD AGAINST THE WALL in the small upper-floor bedroom the British were using as a prison for the officers. He glanced around at the other men. Some paced or sat on the floor. A few held their heads in their hands or stared vacantly. Colonel Lewis was wounded and laid on the bed, his head wrapped and his face pale. All felt the heavy weight of their defeat.

Emmett was very aware of the men missing from their company and what their absence meant. They were either dead or in the hospital tent. He approached Major McClanahan. "Do you know what's become of Colonel Allen?"

The major looked up and sighed heavily. "Shot in the head by the Indians after he surrendered. Saw it with my own eyes."

Emmett bowed his head. He'd admired the colonel, had trained beneath him, and considered him a friend. "We lost good men today," he said, mostly to himself.

Major McClanahan pressed his lips together. His jaw was tight. He gave no answer, but what answer was there to give?

A group of lieutenants stood close together, their voices lowered as they lamented the casualties and combat errors. He heard them talking about Major Graves's Kentuckians, who ignored their commander's orders and fled in panic at the sight of the attacking Indian warriors.

"Over a hundred cut down and scalped by the whooping savages . . . ," one man was saying. Emmett turned away, not wanting to hear more.

Another of the young lieutenants—Lieutenant Devon, if Emmett remembered correctly—stood alone, gazing at a miniature portrait that Emmett assumed was a rendering of his fiancée, or at least a woman he hoped would one day assume the role.

Emmett thought of Abigail. Of her stricken face when he'd left her in the forest, of the softness of her lips, her mittened hand finding his, her intelligence and peculiar interests. Coming face to face with one's mortality changed a man's perspective, Emmett thought. He supposed in a way it robbed a person of the ability to lie to himself, and Emmett found that, even though it was foolish after so short a time, he could no longer deny that he was in love with Abigail Tidwell.

His worry for her was so overwhelming he thought he might be crushed under its weight. Unanswerable questions pounded in his head. How had the small band fared through the cold night? Abigail knew to keep moving to prevent their bodies from becoming too cold. But what if she'd fallen asleep? He trusted Barney and Luke, but the forest was full of predators, not to mention fierce Indians. There were so many factors, so many unknowns. Thinking about something horrendous befalling Abigail was more than he could bear. He should never have involved her in this war.

It was selfishness on his part; he realized that now. He'd hoped to help Luke, but the longer he was with Abigail, the more difficult it became to imagine not being with her.

He pushed away from the wall and paced, patting the lovesick lieutenant on the shoulder as he passed.

Near the window, General Winchester sat on the room's one chair. His elbows rested on his legs, hands hanging between his knees. The man looked despondent. Emmett found it difficult to feel sorry for him. It was because of his poor planning and refusal to listen to the scouts' warnings that their force had been defeated so thoroughly. Men had died, men that Emmett knew and served with and shared a bond as close as any brothers; men that had depended on him to keep them alive, and men he looked up to. At least the general had managed to get his uniform coat back from the Indian chief, he thought cynically.

He found a new spot on the wall and leaned his head back, closing his eyes, thinking what he could have done differently. If he'd only run faster or left camp earlier. If there had been time to plan, to distribute the ammunition storages, to set up defenses . . .

If only.

Guilt, hot and bitter-tasting, filled his throat.

Maybe his father was right and Emmett *was* worthless. He couldn't even lead his men through a battle. Images filled his mind, visions of his comrades falling, memories of their voices crying out in pain, looking to him for help that he couldn't offer. He opened his eyes, pacing toward the window in hopes of distracting himself.

He looked toward the field hospital tent. The British surgeons would obviously care for their own soldiers first, but he prayed the Americans were being treated as well. Before he'd been taken prisoner, he'd tried to see to the worst of the injuries. Tying tourniquets and using anything he could find to press against a wound and stop the bleeding until a surgeon was available was the extent of his medical assistance. Mostly he'd only been able to offer comfort.

He'd found Murphy leaning against a fence holding his chest and felt a rush of relief to find the man hadn't been injured. The gun smoke had burned his lungs. Emmett had sent him to the field tent. Hopefully a surgeon would know how to treat him.

He didn't realize he was staring at the hospital tent until something caught his eye. A patient with his arm in a sling was being led toward a group of sleds. Emmett guessed they would take the injured men to Fort Detroit. But it wasn't the man with the wrappings that made Emmett stop and stare. It was the small woman leading him.

It couldn't be her. Was his mind deceiving him? But no, it was most certainly Abigail. What on earth was she doing here? Her hair had come loose, strands falling around her face, and the apron she wore was covered with blood. She'd been working for some time, he guessed. And for her to be in Frenchtown, she must have walked all night, as he had. What had happened? Had she and the Hopkins brothers been captured?

He closely watched the tent opening, and a few moments later, a man was carried through on a stretcher. He recognized Abigail's quilt covering the patient and, sure enough, she emerged again, helping another man.

Emmett willed her to look up. The house he was in was on the very edge of town. If she would only lift her gaze, she'd see him. But she returned to the tent and emerged two more times before stopping and rubbing the back of her neck. She rolled her shoulders as if they'd become stiff and bent her head from side to side. She started back inside but stopped as if she'd heard something or realized she was being watched.

She turned, looking curiously around until she glanced into the upstairs window, and her gaze locked with Emmett's.

He touched his fingers to the glass.

Abigail pressed her hand to her breastbone and closed her eyes. Her shoulders dropped, and her head fell forward, her entire body displaying a powerful relief.

Emmett's apprehension lessened, and a warm feeling of comfort came over him.

Abigail raised her eyes again, giving a small smile, and then she cocked her head as if she'd heard something from within the tent. She waved then hurried back inside.

The entire exchange had lasted less than a few seconds, but the change it brought in Emmett's spirits was profound. Abigail was safe—not only safe, she was tending to the wounded, and he could not imagine a better person for the job. And she'd been worried about him. He wasn't surprised by it, but her relief at seeing him had touched him. It gave him courage and strengthened his will to go on, where before he'd felt naught but despair.

Abigail was a gift. Her feelings for him were a reassurance that no matter where he went, what prison he'd be sent to, or how alone he might find himself, there was a young woman with brown eyes, long curling lashes, and an astonishing knowledge of elemental minerals who cared what became of him.

It was late afternoon when the door finally opened and the officers were ordered to descend the stairs. The British soldiers and their prisoners would begin their march toward Fort Detroit immediately.

Emmett followed the others but paused on the front doorstep as a conversation from inside the house caught his attention.

A group of British soldiers were arguing.

". . . reinforcements are on their way from the south," one man, who Emmett recognized as the army's leader, General Henry Procter, was saying. "We cannot delay any longer."

"But if we take all the prisoners and leave no guards for the American wounded . . ." another man said, leaving the rest of the statement hanging.

Emmett stepped to the side of the doorframe so as not to be seen by the men inside the house.

"They will have to fend for themselves," another man said, and Emmett assumed the nasally voice belonged to the young lieutenant with the handsome face and nicely pressed uniform.

"Sir, you must know what will happen. The Indians are difficult enough to restrain with our force present. If the wounded prisoners are left with no protection . . ."

"A pity, isn't it?" the pretentious lieutenant said with a sniff.

Emmett heard their footsteps approaching and moved from the doorway. His mind turned over the conversation. Would General Procter truly leave the wounded Americans to the mercy of angry Indian warriors? Somehow, he must get word to them.

The officers were ordered to march with their regiment, and when Emmett arrived, he found more than half of the troops missing. Most, he knew, had been killed, but others must be in the hospital tent. How could he warn them? Once the army left, they would be helpless.

The column began moving, and he organized his men into rows, waiting for their turn to join the procession. They started to march, and ahead he saw Abigail tending to a man near the side of the road. Here was his chance.

"Excuse me, miss," Emmett called to her. He stepped out of the line.

Abigail spun. And he prayed she wouldn't reveal that they knew one another.

"You dropped this," he said, holding out his pouch of rocks.

Her eyes squinted, but that was the only indication she gave that she was uncertain about his motives. She reached for the pouch.

"Abigail, send all the men with the British tonight." Emmett spoke quickly, keeping his voice low. "Even the wounded. Don't allow them to stay behind."

"But so many are hurt," she said.

"They must all leave—as many as you can send."

"You there, get back in line!" The lieutenant Emmett had seen earlier started toward them.

"And you must leave as well. Today. Do you understand?"

Abigail nodded. She took the pouch and turned away. "Lieutenant Fox, how nice to see you again." She dipped in a curtsy.

"What is the meaning of this, Captain?" Lieutenant Fox asked, his shrewd eyes darting between the two of them.

Abigail smiled prettily at the man. "The soldier was simply returning my pouch. I must have dropped it."

"Move along, Captain," Lieutenant Fox growled. He snatched away the pouch from Abigail's hands and poured out the rocks into his palm. "What is this?"

Emmett moved away but continued to watch the interaction from the corner of his eye. He didn't like the lieutenant, and he especially didn't like the lieutenant speaking to Abigail.

"It is just my collection, sir." She took the pouch from him and started picking the stones from his hand and dropping them back inside.

The lieutenant's eyes narrowed. He turned over his hand, dumping the rocks onto the ground and stormed away.

Abigail crouched down and picked them up, returning them carefully to the pouch. She glanced up once and met Emmett's eye before he turned and marched away with the rest of the prisoners. He had full confidence that Abigail would do all she was able to get the wounded out of Frenchtown. He could do nothing more than pray for those left behind.

CHAPTER 13

THE JOURNEY TO FORT DETROIT took two days. Abigail rode in a horse-pulled wagon with patients who were unable to march. Different surgeons were assigned to other wagons or sledges, so she found herself with only injured soldiers to talk to. Since none of them seemed disposed to conversation, she settled into the corner of the wagon box, blankets around her in a spot that felt like her own nest. The wagon swayed as it moved along the road; the noise of the horses' hooves crunching on the packed snow repeated in a pattern that lulled her to sleep often over the course of the journey, and when the wagon rolled over a rock or into a dip, it woke her with a start. The British Army had brought plenty of blankets, and for the first time in nearly a week, she was warm and had time to herself to ponder.

As per Emmett's request, she'd done all she was able to convince injured men to march with the British Army whether they felt well enough or not. She'd also insisted that many of the wounded Americans be transported with the British. The proposal was met with quite a bit of resistance from the surgeons. They assured her transportation would be sent back for the Americans once they reached the fort, but she argued and pleaded and, in the end, assigned men to empty spots among the other patients. But there was simply not enough room for all of them.

Leaving men behind, either because they refused to leave or they were simply too incapacitated to be moved had made her feel like a failure. She'd have liked to remain in Frenchtown to ensure they were properly treated but remembered Emmett's admonition and left them with the townspeople who graciously took the soldiers into their homes to care for them.

She watched the departing soldiers, ensuring that all five of her friends were among them. They had all left the town safely and each looked healthy. Luke gave her a bit of worry, as did Murphy, but if they'd fallen behind or been unable to continue, she'd have found them along the road. And that gave her some comfort.

Along the twenty-mile journey, the wagon stopped quite often to care for troops who'd fallen out of line because of one ailment or another. With all the stops, and moving at a slower rate, the infirmary detachment fell farther behind the main body of soldiers and prisoners, so Abigail did not see Emmett or any of the others during the journey.

On her lap, she made a hollow in the folds of the blanket and poured out the pouch of Emmett's rocks into it. She'd done this often over the hours, studying each mineral and element in turn. When she'd originally looked through the pouch, the clear quartz crystal had seemed the finest piece in the collection. But her opinion on the matter changed with each study.

This time, she was drawn to a nugget of native copper. Common enough in the Michigan territory, but this particular specimen had oxidized in an interesting pattern. Patches of deep jade color covered nearly an entire side of the nugget. The other side was a very pure copper, its color a shiny pinkish brown. She turned over the nugget in her fingers, wondering what Emmett had thought about this particular bit of metal. Where had he acquired it? Had it been part of a trade with a native tribe? Or had he found it on the ground? What made him decide to add it to his pouch?

She thought about Emmett's warning as he'd marched away from Frenchtown. She'd never seen his expression so serious, or so worried. What had he thought would happen to the prisoners left behind? Did he know something? Or did he simply want to make sure the men stayed together?

The copper was cold in her hand. Abigail ran her fingertip over a rough edge and down along the smooth opening of a cavity. She wondered what would happen to Emmett now as a prisoner of war. Would he be given parole and sent home? Or would General Procter send him to a prison camp? She thought of the others and hoped they were being treated well. She prayed Luke and Murphy were not pushing themselves too hard. And Barney—she hoped he was able to remain with his brother. Would the British guards think Jasper was a person to be feared because he wore a bear's head and seldom smiled?

She worried for all of them.

The wagons finally arrived at the fort, passing through the heavy gates and beyond the high picketed fence with its sharp points running along the top. Abigail climbed out of the wagon, and she and the other surgeons supervised the relocation of the patients into the hospital buildings.

She assisted a man with a broken ankle from one of the wagons. His injury must have pained him quite a lot, and she thought traveling over the bumpy road would have been agony.

She held him around his waist, and he leaned his arm heavily across her shoulders as he hopped into the building. Once she settled him onto a hospital cot, she heard her name, and the voice in which it was spoken brought a smile to her face.

"Father!"

Abigail's father pulled her to him and then held her at arm's length. His spectacles slid down his nose, and he pushed them back up in a familiar motion. "What in the world are you doing here, my daughter? And how did you come to be with the army?" He shook his head as if answering his own questions. "No, there will be time enough for explanations later. We have much to do, and I am grateful for your help."

With the other surgeons, Abigail and her father spent the remainder of the day seeing to the wounded and ill. She quickly realized there were more men in the hospital buildings than just those injured in the battle. The march to and from Frenchtown had produced frost burn on cheeks, fingers, and toes, as well as blisters. Typhoid fever had stricken men and women inside the fort, as well as those coming from the battleground. Sutures were applied, bandages changed, poultices mixed, medicines administered.

By the time her father found her for supper, Abigail was exhausted. She followed him along the streets of the fort, hardly noticing which direction they were traveling, until at last, he led her inside and up a set of stairs to a stone room with a small bed.

"Rest yourself, Abigail, and I will return soon with supper."

She lay on the bed, and did not wake until she felt her father shaking her shoulder.

"Come on, now, Abigail. That is plenty of sleep for a person," he said in a voice that was both practical and loving. Hearing it brought more comfort than she could have imagined.

She sat up and rubbed her eyes, noticing a tray of bread, cheese, and slices of venison on the table beside the bed. Her father sat down in a straight-backed chair and crossed one leg over the other.

"Is it suppertime already?" Her mouth felt sticky and her head heavy.

"You slept through suppertime, my dear." He pushed up his spectacles and smiled affectionately. "And breakfast. I've brought your luncheon."

"Oh. I suppose I was more tired than I realized." Abigail spoke through a yawn.

"I've arranged for a bath," he said. Then drawing out a bundle, he handed it to her. "And your clothes will need to be washed as well."

She spread out the bundle and smiled at the dress he'd found. She rarely had new clothes, and this blue cotton was beautiful. "Thank you, Father."

He smiled, the familiar creases forming in his cheeks, and stood. "I will return in an hour. I believe I've a story to hear."

The door had scarcely closed behind him when a knock sounded.

A servant girl who introduced herself as Mae showed Abigail to a bathing chamber on the lower floor and took away her clothing to wash. A tub of hot water was already prepared, and it felt heavenly. Once she was cleaned and dressed, she made her way back to her father's chamber and found him writing in the large leather-bound book where he logged the names of patients, their ages, diagnoses, and treatments. He was convinced that only through keeping thorough records would a doctor improve his ability to treat patients.

She sat on the edge of the bed and ate, knowing better than to disturb him while he worked.

Finally he dabbed off his quill and corked the ink bottle.

Abigail stood and held her arms away from her sides. "What do you think of the dress?" She'd been delighted by the style of the gown. It was undoubtedly one brought from England by demand of the officers' wives. The high waist and ribbons were elegant and the cotton softer than the coarse homespun fabric she was used to.

"You are always the loveliest young lady in any room, no matter what you might happen to be wearing."

Abigail smiled at her father's hyperbolic compliment and sat back down, holding the tray toward him.

He shook his head at the offered food and settled back in the chair, moving his shoulders back and forth, and crossed one leg over the other, clasping his hands around one knee. "Now, my dear. Tell me everything."

And so she did. Abigail's story lasted longer than an hour. She described Captain Prescott's wounds, her treatment, the men appearing in their kitchen and taking the musket. She told about crossing the river, repairing Luke's arm, and how Jasper fought a bear. She described the lean-to shelters and the horrifying Indian warriors. Her throat was becoming scratchy as she told about the battle's aftermath and Emmett's warning.

The only thing she did not tell him about was the kiss. Well, two kisses. *Three*, if one wanted to be precise. It wasn't that she didn't trust her father, but the moments felt private, and it seemed like sharing them would lessen their significance. Besides, that information wasn't crucial to his understanding of the story anyway.

Her father remained silent during the entire narration without interrupting. If there was one thing her father was known for, it was listening.

When he saw that she was finished, he released his knee, setting both feet onto the floor, and steepled his fingers in front of his lips. Abigail knew this meant he was considering. Her father did not speak without first thinking through all angles of something. Neither she nor her brother had inherited this trait, she'd often thought.

After a moment, he pushed up his spectacles. "Abigail, I am so proud of you."

She had not anticipated that reaction. Abigail hadn't thought her father would be angry with her—he rarely was. But she had expected some reprimand.

"Your decisions were very understandable, my daughter—very unselfish," he said. "An indication of your caring nature. You can be headstrong at times, and I cannot say I am pleased that you placed yourself in danger, but I cannot fault you for wanting to help others." He smiled. "And I believe your medical skill to be equal, if not superior, to that of any of my associates."

Dr. Tidwell was generous with praise, but Abigail knew he did not distribute it undeserved. Her heart glowed at his words. "Thank you, Father." She felt a blush heat her cheeks. "There is one matter on which I hoped for your advice."

He inclined his head. "Of course."

Abigail brushed her hands over her skirts, loving the soft fabric beneath her fingers. She did not quite know how to put her thoughts into words and so took a moment to think it through. He waited patiently.

"I know I should not have helped the Americans, Father. They are the enemy. But once I came to know them as people, I simply could not consider them as such."

He steepled his fingers again, his brows pulling together as he thought about what she said. He was quiet for a long time then finally lowered his arms. "Abigail, if you had left Captain Prescott to bleed to death, or let Luke's arm fester, I believe you would have been the wicked one." He leaned forward in the chair, his face very serious, as it was when he was teaching her something important. "Each of these armies contains noble men. And each contains men with evil hearts. Let a person's character be the indicator of a real enemy, not the color of his uniform."

His words filled her with reassurance, even if they did border on treason. She felt in her heart that they were true. "Thank you, Father."

He smiled and stood, stretching out his back by pressing his fists against it and leaning back his shoulders. Abigail noticed that he'd grown thinner. Very likely he was working long hours and not taking the time to eat properly.

Dr. Tidwell reached out a hand and assisted Abigail to her feet. "There is a small inn in town that serves flaky buttermilk biscuits with the supper selection. Perhaps you and your new dress would like to join me?"

She grinned at his awkward attempt to be charming and took his arm, squeezing it as she laid her head on his shoulder. Soon enough, she'd have to return home, but she was determined to treasure this time with her father.

The pair walked through the streets of the fort, and Abigail tried to orient herself. She'd not paid attention when they walked to her father's quarters the day before. They walked past buildings that appeared to be barracks and others that must serve administrative functions. As they passed the stables, she looked beyond and saw soldiers guarding a courtyard full of tents. This must be where the prisoners were housed. Abigail slowed her steps and looked among the men moving between the tents, hoping to see one of her friends. She felt a sting of disappointment when she couldn't but knew she shouldn't pay too much attention to the prisoners. Her friendship with the enemy soldiers could be damaging to her reputation as well as to her father's. She did wish she'd caught a glimpse of a particular captain with blue eyes, though.

The inn was only a short walk from the fort. When they stepped inside, the smells of warm food and the sounds of laughter encircled them.

Abigail looked around the room, noting that the majority of patrons wore the redcoats of British soldiers. As they moved toward a table, a familiar face caught her attention. Lieutenant Sebastian Fox. He and a few men whose clothes were also impeccably pressed were laughing at something a woman sitting at their table had said. Hearing her brash laughter joining with the others, Abigail didn't think she was the type of woman she would want her brother to be dining with.

They moved to a quieter part of the inn's dining room and enjoyed a meal of roasted whitefish and potatoes, of course accompanied by flaky buttermilk biscuits. As they ate, they were interrupted several times by soldiers asking for medical advice. Abigail was irritated that the men would bother her father during his supper, but he did not act disturbed at all. He listened thoughtfully to their symptoms and gave advice or promised a treatment to be delivered that evening.

"Really," Abigail huffed after a man with impetigo on his knuckles had finally taken his leave. "Can people not allow you to eat in peace?"

Her father bit into a biscuit and a drip of honey slipped onto his chin. He dabbed it off with a napkin. "I am not too busy to relieve a person's discomfort, Abigail."

She was just about to deliver a counterargument when another shadow spread across their table.

"Pardon me, Doctor."

Abigail lifted her gaze to see a naval captain standing beside her father's chair. He stood with hands clasped behind his back and legs spread apart. She imagined this must be how he stood on the deck of a rocking ship.

"Captain Lovell," her father said. "What a pleasure to see you. May I introduce my daughter, Abigail?"

The captain inclined his head. "How do you do, miss?"

"Very well, Captain. A pleasure to make your acquaintance. I believe I saw your ship as we walked through the town." She'd noticed the large brig sitting perfectly still in the frozen river and the men standing on the surrounding ice guarding it.

He nodded. "One of the curses of a lake appointment—immobility." He smiled. "But if we can't sail, the American's can't either, so I try to enjoy the winter months."

Abigail smiled since she was unsure quite how to respond.

"And how is Mrs. Lovell?" Dr. Tidwell said.

The captain suddenly became fidgety, scratching behind his ear and shifting his weight. "She is feeling very . . . ah . . . uncomfortable."

Her father nodded, his face pleasant. "Perfectly normal," he said. "She is very near to term."

Ah. Abigail understood now. The captain's wife was close to delivering a baby. She thought it strange that men became so ill at ease when discussing these matters. Well, excepting her father of course.

Her father glanced at her and then back to the captain. "Sir, if I might offer a suggestion. Abigail has served as a midwife in Amherstburg. She is quite skilled, if I might say so without sounding boastful. Perhaps Mrs. Lovell would prefer to be under a woman's care, as my experience is much more suited to tending bullet wounds and fractures."

Captain Lovell's face relaxed into a relieved smile. "I believe she would like that very much. Might I send for you soon, Miss Tidwell?"

She nodded, feeling the familiar warmth that filled her when her father spoke so proudly of her. "I am staying in the fort with my father."

"With the injuries and prisoners from Frenchtown, the surgeons and I are fortunate to have extra assistance," her father said, making it sound as if he'd sent for her to help with the influx of new patients. Abigail had been worried that the strange circumstance that had brought her to Fort Detroit might have unwanted effects on her father's reputation or her own. In just a few sentences, her father had both explained away any perceived wrongdoing on her part, as well as made her feel invaluable.

"Yes, very well. I thank you, Miss Tidwell, Dr. Tidwell."

He gave a crisp bow and left.

"Well, you shall be busy for a few weeks at least," Dr. Tidwell said. "That is, of course, unless you are eager to return home sooner."

"Not at all," Abigail said as she bit into a flaky buttermilk biscuit.

CHAPTER 14

EMMETT PACED ALONG THE LINE of men as he inspected his regiment in Fort Detroit's prison yard. He'd hired a woman to wash his uniform and a barber to cut his hair and give him a shave. And ordered the officers below him to do the same. He knew it was good for the men's morale to see their commanders looking respectable, especially in these circumstances.

The prison camp was in an empty section of the fort Emmett believed had previously been used as a training ground. The men slept in tents, and the officers were housed in the nearby barracks. In the three days since arriving at the fort, Emmett found that nearly every moment of his time was occupied making certain the mess distributed sufficient food for those in his command, organizing committees to see to basic camp duties, seeing to the ill and injured, and more than anything, he felt it his responsibility to keep the men's spirits up. His eyes rose to the British flag waving over the fort, and he felt dismayed as he had every time he'd chanced to look at it. The sight of that standard upon American soil was demoralizing. And he could feel the effect on his men.

Once the inspection was over, he dismissed the men. The sounds of voices and of feet crunching in the snow began as soldiers returned to their tents, performed their daily duties, or milled around the prison yard under the watchful eye of the guards. Emmett stepped into Murphy's tent and sat on a stool beside his friend's bedroll. "How do you feel today?" he asked.

Over the long march, Murphy's cough had gone from occasional to long fits of hacking. His breathing was labored and sounded as if dry leaves were caught in his throat. He smiled weakly, his face appearing gray. "Same as yesterday, sir."

"I insist you go to the hospital tent." Sick and injured prisoners were cared for separately from the British soldiers in a tent on the very edge of the prison yard, near the stables. "Come with me." Emmett helped Murphy stand and slid an arm below his friend's shoulders.

They walked slowly across the yard, pausing a few times as Murphy succumbed to a fit of coughing. A man wearing a surgeon's apron met them at the door, and he and Emmett helped Murphy to a cot.

"The physician-surgeon will be here in a few hours," the man said, not unkindly. "Rest until then."

Emmett made certain Murphy was comfortable then left the tent. He started back toward the barracks but stopped when he saw a man walking in the shadows along the inside of the high picket fence. Lieutenant Fox. The way the lieutenant glanced back, as if making certain nobody was following put Emmett's instincts on alert. As did the man himself. Lieutenant Fox gave the impression of a person who would happily involve himself in underhanded dealings if he deemed the reward worth the risk.

His curiosity was piqued. Looking around quickly, Emmett spotted a barrel and hefted it, carrying it on his shoulder. He walked straight ahead without glancing back, knowing men who appeared to be engaged in a task were less likely to be stopped than those creeping along in the shadows. He nodded to the prison guards as he passed. They gave him a strange look but didn't stop him, apparently assuming he was carrying out orders from someone. Even though he was a prisoner, his uniform still garnered respect.

Lieutenant Fox crept behind the stables, and Emmett waited, but he didn't emerge on the other side. What could he be doing in the space between the edge of the stables and the fort's high wall?

Emmett walked along the side of the stable building until he reached the corner, and there he paused, listening. It was difficult to make out sounds over the noise of the horses, but he thought he heard voices. One was low and clipped, and the other sounded nasal and especially patronizing. He set down the barrel, slowly leaned forward to peek around to the rear of the building and then pulled quickly back.

In the shadows, Lieutenant Fox stood speaking to an Indian warrior, and from the quick glimpse, Emmett thought the two were performing an exchange of some sort.

He moved away, hurried along the building to the front and entered through the stable doors, grabbing the first tool he saw: a shovel. He acted as if it were the very reason he'd come into the stables in the first place, making a show of inspecting the handle and the blade. None of the stable workers even spared him a second glance.

As he studied the shovel, he saw a flash of red as Lieutenant Fox walked past the stable door. Emmett stepped outside, following behind at a distance.

In one hand, Lieutenant Fox carried a rough burlap bag with a large brownish stain on the bottom.

The apprehensive feeling Emmett had before grew as he imagined what might make a stain of that color, and what might be valuable enough for a lieutenant to make a secretive trade with an Indian brave.

Lieutenant Fox crossed the road and walked past a pen that housed two large hogs. He tossed the bag into the pen and continued on.

Emmett resumed his course, following from a distance and, when he reached the pen, used the shovel to pull the bag toward him. He held his breath, both from the smell of the hogs and the smell coming from the bag. Stomach clenched, he loosed the knot and looked inside. What he saw filled his stomach with lead.

The bag held dozens of human scalps.

Emmett dropped the bag, feeling ill. He leaned his elbows on the wooden rail of the fence and rubbed his eyes, knowing exactly where these scalps had come from. His men at Frenchtown.

Anger and utter despair stole his breath and made his chest hot. His hands were shaking. He'd feared this very thing when Lieutenant Fox had convinced General Procter to leave the city without guards. Tecumseh's Indian army didn't follow the same rules of war. They didn't accept a full surrender, trusting a gentleman's word of honor that the fighting had ended. And the lieutenant had *known* this would happen. He'd doomed injured and ill men to a horrific death and had even paid for the evidence.

Clenching his hands into fists, he turned his back toward the pen and, in doing so, glanced up the road. Lieutenant Fox stood in the doorway of a building, watching him. He dropped his eyes conspicuously to the bag. His brows rose, and then his lip curled up into a sneer.

Emmett started toward him, red fury filling his vision until the consequences of a prisoner of war attacking his captor didn't matter to him at all.

Lieutenant Fox called out an order, and soldiers rushed at Emmett.

He pushed through, straining to get to his enemy. Fueled by rage, he swung blindly, landing punches at the men in his way and cursing at the arrogant officer.

The shovel was wrested from Emmett's hands, and he bent over when a soldier used the handle to deliver a blow to the gut. For a moment he couldn't draw in a breath. Another blow hit his head, dazing him. Emmett looked up and locked eyes with Lieutenant Fox.

The man's mouth spread into a smile that looked more like a sneer. He motioned with a finger. "Take a walk with me, Captain Prescott."

Emmett had no choice but to obey; however, he didn't have to go willingly. He planted his feet and struggled to pull his arms free but was dragged forward.

The lieutenant didn't look back but moved along, head held high and arms swinging as if he was out for a leisurely stroll. When he reached a side alley between the buildings, he spun around and tilted his head back so, even though they were of similar height, he was looking down his nose at Emmett.

Two soldiers still held on to Emmett's arms, and another two stood close behind.

"Well, that was a bit of an overreaction," the lieutenant said. He raised his brows and shook his head, as if embarrassed for Emmett. "I imagine you are upset because of what you saw in that filthy sack." His nose wrinkled and he sniffed.

Emmett's fury spiked, sending a bolt of heat through him. "You did this." He fought to keep his voice calm but was not successful. "You killed those men."

The lieutenant brushed some imaginary lint off his sleeve then straightened the cuff. "We both know that is factually untrue."

"It was your action, or more precisely your inaction that is the cause. You allowed innocent men to be butchered." Emmett's anger made his words come out in a sputter.

The lieutenant merely gave a pleasant smile. "I did not only allow it but encouraged it, Captain."

Emmett had thought he would certainly deny it. The man's admission left him unable to answer. He just stared at the foppish Englishman.

Lieutenant Fox let out a sigh and studied his fingernails. "Let me tell you a bit about war, Captain. It is not all marching, training, and heroism in battles. There is also an element of psychology involved. Surely you must know this, although based on what I've seen, American military schools appear to be lacking when it comes to training their officers." He sniffed again, making the sound as patronizing as possible. "But as I was saying, if one is able to make the enemy fear, really *fear*, there is an automatic advantage. A person who is afraid makes decisions based on that fear. He second-guesses himself and forgets his training." His smile became more animated. "And right now, the most fearful weapon the British army has at its disposal isn't the cannons or even our highly trained troops. It is the Indians."

Lieutenant Fox clasped his hands as if he were telling a merry tale at a Christmas party. "Americans fear the Indian tribes, because they know they have mistreated them . . . pushed them off their lands, obliterated their villages, and so forth. The Indians were not a threat before, but now those very warriors have the backing of the strongest army in the world. And they want revenge." He flicked his fingers. "Their methods are, shall we say, grotesque, but the amount of fear a group of men in war paint with tomahawks is able to produce . . . well, one cannot put too fine a price on it."

"I cannot believe a man of honor is capable of such an atrocity," Emmett said. He felt sickened.

"Oh, I am entirely capable." The lieutenant shrugged.

"Those men had surrendered. They were sick and injured—" Emmett began.

"And can you imagine the hysteria it will cause once their fate is known?" Lieutenant Fox looked delighted. "I imagine the American militia enrollment will drop significantly."

Emmett knew the lieutenant was right. Fear would spread like a wave when people learned the infirmary patients had been massacred. He'd seen with his own eyes how the men in the battle completely panicked when the screaming, painted Indians ran at them brandishing knives and axes. And two things could come of it. Either people would be outraged and take up arms, or they would cower. He worried it would be the latter. Fort Detroit itself had been taken without a fight when the commander, General Hull, had seen an angry army of Indians reinforced by the British soldiers and his thoughts had gone directly to his daughter and granddaughter staying inside the fort with him. Against the advice of his officers, he'd snatched up a white tablecloth and hung it out the window before the armies had even taken their positions. Fear did strange things to a person's judgment.

Lieutenant Fox was watching Emmett's reaction. "I imagine you would like to kill me." He sighed dramatically. "I don't blame you. But know that I am not one you want for an enemy. Especially in your current circumstances."

Emmett clenched his fists. He had never felt such anger directed to one person in his entire life. "If given the chance, I will kill you, Lieutenant." He'd never imagined saying such words to anyone, but in that moment, the objective had become Emmett's highest priority.

The lieutenant gave a small shrug. "Very well. Then at your wish we shall be adversaries." His face remained impassive, but something inside his eyes grew hard. "But know this, Captain Emmett Prescott. I do not like to simply kill my foes. It is messy and unsatisfying. I prefer to break a man. Destroy his confidence, hurt people he cares about, leave him wondering when I might strike next, force him to question his own sanity." He patted Emmett's shoulder in a condescending manner. "Fair warning, sir. You'll not like me as an enemy."

"I cannot consider you anything else," Emmett ground out.

Lieutenant Fox gave a nod of acknowledgment and motioned to the soldiers. Emmett was returned unceremoniously to the prison camp.

That afternoon, Emmett sat in the barracks on his bunk. His insides were twisted up with anger and grief as he thought of the massacre at Frenchtown. Nothing in his training had prepared him for this feeling. He should have stopped it from happening. He had known, and he should have done something.

A voice inside his head told him there was nothing more he could have done, but that didn't dispel the wrenching guilt. His eyes burned as he imagined the men's last moments. He was angry with General Procter for not posting guards, General Winchester for ignoring warnings. He was angry with himself for not running faster, angry with Tecumseh's native confederacy for taking out their revenge on his men, but more than anything, he was angry with the vile Lieutenant Sebastian Fox. Thoughts of vengeance filled his mind, making his anger turn into something almost tangible.

He'd not told his fellow officers, but he would. He'd decided to do it after the evening call to quarters, so they'd have the night to process the information before they would be required to put on strong faces for their men in the morning.

His festering was interrupted by a knock. The door swung open, admitting a slender man with spectacles, followed by a guard.

Emmett stood.

The soldier stood to attention beside the door, and the bespectacled man crossed the room. "Captain Prescott?"

"Yes."

"I am Dr. William Tidwell. A pleasure to meet you." The doctor held Emmett's gaze a moment longer than was necessary, and Emmett recognized the shape and color of the man's eyes, though, in his opinion, they looked much lovelier on a woman.

"How do you do?" Emmett said.

The doctor sliced his eyes toward the soldier, and Emmett understood at once that they'd not be able to speak openly about his friendship with Abigail. Such a thing would put her in danger of being presumed a traitor. She had, after all, aided and abetted the enemy.

"An associate of mine told me you have some sutures needing to be removed. It was, in fact, the doctor who treated you, who sent me."

Emmett couldn't help but feel pleased at the man's words. He should have known, even after all that happened, that she'd not forget about his injuries. And since she could not come herself, she'd sent her father. Emmett smiled.

The man raised his brow, a miniscule movement that was accompanied by a twinkle in his eye. *He knows*, Emmett thought. And the knowledge felt comforting, like her father was a tie between himself and Abigail.

"If you'd please remove your shirt and sit just here." Dr. Tidwell motioned toward the bed then turned to the guard. "Corporal, would you bring the lantern closer?"

The man did so, and Dr. Tidwell pulled a chair beside Emmett.

"An arrow, was it?" Dr. Tidwell said.

"Yes."

"And here, a knife?" He pointed to Emmett's arm.

"I believe so," Emmett said. "It was dark, and the attack happened rather quickly."

Dr. Tidwell nodded. He leaned close to study the wounds, pushing up his spectacles, then touched his finger to the skin around the sutures, just like Abigail had done. "Fine work," he muttered.

"I had fine care," Emmett said.

The doctor glanced up, his brow twitched again, and then he reached into his bag for scissors and tweezers. "This may sting." He set to work, and Emmett sat still, twisting his head around to watch the procedure.

"Corporal," Dr. Tidwell said after a moment. "Have I told you about my daughter, Abigail?"

Emmett grew very still.

The corporal looked surprised, as if he wasn't used to being addressed during doctoring procedures. "No, you have not."

"She arrived just yesterday to assist in the sick bay. She's also serving as a midwife in town." He finished with Emmett's side and started on his arm, little strings of sutures making a small pile on a scrap of bandage he'd set out for the purpose.

"That is very . . . nice," the corporal said, sounding unsure of how to respond.

Dr. Tidwell nodded. "Very nice indeed. I am happy to have her, even though she can only stay a few weeks. And I was pleased that she made the journey safely. She had good people watching over her. I'm grateful to them for the care they took."

The corporal nodded, perhaps wondering why the doctor chose to share this. But Emmett knew why, and he was touched that the man would communicate this to him. Dr. Tidwell was very much like his daughter—clever and more compassionate than he could believe. Especially as pertaining to forgiveness. He wished he could see her, just for a moment. The wish became a longing, because he knew it was something that could not be. Especially with Lieutenant Fox and his spies watching Emmett's every move. For her own safety, he couldn't give any indication that anything existed between Abigail and him.

"There now, Captain." Dr. Tidwell wiped his tools and returned them to his bag. "You're healing well. Continue favoring this side as much as possible."

"Thank you, sir." Emmett hoped the man knew he wasn't just thanking him for removing the stitches. Knowing that Abigail was safe and happy and her father held no ill will for Emmett's actions had eased part of the heaviness he carried.

They bid farewell, and then the doctor departed, followed by the guard. Emmett turned back to the room, noticing a wad of bandages that Dr. Tidwell had left behind. The importance of keeping order in the barracks was instinctual. Meaning to dispose of them, Emmett picked up the bandages, and when he did, he felt something inside. Something small and very heavy.

When he uncovered it, he saw it was a chunk of iron. Hematite, he thought. A metal that appeared to be formed of iron bubbles. This wasn't one from his pouch. He wondered if Abigail had found it. He smiled at the thought. Only she would discover a rock with the ground covered in snow and know it was just the thing to tell him she was thinking of him. The rock was cold and smooth, and when he closed his hand around it, Emmett was filled with delicious warmth that seeped into his bones.

CHAPTER 15

ABIGAIL UNWRAPPED THE BANDAGES AND studied the marred flesh beneath. Her father had done his best work, repairing the gash on the soldier's face. It was so much improved from a week earlier that if she hadn't seen the man when he'd arrived, she'd not have believed it to be the same person. "Hardly any swelling, Corporal," she said, touching her fingers along his cheek and giving an encouraging smile.

The wound began at his hairline and ran down, across the bridge of Corporal Willard's nose, ending beneath his ear. In her entire life, Abigail had never seen a person recover from such a horrible injury.

"I'll have a scar, though, won't I, Miss Tidwell?" His voice even sounded normal—no longer nasally—as his nose healed. Beyond a doubt, her father was the best physician-surgeon in the entirety of the British Army.

"I suppose you will." She lifted her shoulder as if the scar would be of little consequence then leaned close, her eyes twinkling. "A scar lends an air of mystery, you know. I imagine it will only increase your popularity with the ladies."

Corporal Willard's face broke into a grin, and he laughed. A sound she'd heard precious little of in the hospital wards. "I'll take all the help I can get," he said.

She left his face unwrapped, thinking the wound had sealed enough that it would probably do well to let it have some air, and took her leave of the corporal. She had a few more patients to see before meeting her father for luncheon. As she stepped into the passageway between the wards, a soldier approached.

"Miss Tidwell?"

She turned, studying the young man, but he didn't look familiar. "Yes?"

"Private Matthews," he said, giving a succinct bow. "I bring an invitation from Lieutenant Fox, miss. He hopes you would be amenable to a visit this afternoon at two."

Abigail's chest twinged nervously at hearing the lieutenant's name. Something about the man made her extremely uncomfortable, and she could not quite figure out what it was. She hadn't appreciated his overly curious questions and rudeness when they'd first met after the battle or his arrogant manner when they'd chanced to meet during her week at the fort. And he'd so rudely dropped Emmett's rocks onto the ground.

She opened her mouth to give an apology but then remembered she'd overheard that Lieutenant Fox was one of the officers responsible for the prisoners. Abigail knew better than to ask directly, of course, but if she could compose some very innocent-sounding questions that would lead him to volunteer information about her friends . . .

"That would be very nice, Private."

"The lieutenant thought you might enjoy a walk outside."

Abigail wondered if the weather had changed in the past hours. Her quick walk to the hospital building this morning had been very cold indeed. But she figured a promenade was much more tolerable than a formal visit. "I would like that. Thank you."

Private Matthews gave another tight bow. "Very good, miss," he said and departed.

Lieutenant Fox arrived at the hospital building at exactly two o'clock. Abigail's father's eyes narrowed the smallest amount when he was announced. His reaction gave her another twinge of discomfort. Her father rarely disliked anyone, and never without reason.

"Do not worry. I will be back soon, Father," she said, patting his hand. She retrieved her cloak and bonnet from a closet near the hospital entrance.

At her approach, Lieutenant Fox bowed gracefully. "Miss Tidwell. A pleasure."

"Lieutenant." She dipped in a curtsy.

"You look very lovely indeed." He held her cloak courteously, settling it onto her shoulders. "I do appreciate your willingness to accompany me today."

She took his offered arm, and they stepped outside. The sun was hidden behind low clouds, and the day was gray and cold. Abigail shivered.

"If you're chilled, we can return inside," he said.

"I will warm up once I get moving," Abigail said, remembering having a similar conversation with Captain Prescott and what had followed. An ache rose inside her. She wished it were his arm she was holding.

"I've hardly seen you since you arrived at the fort, Miss Tidwell, and I decided such an oversight must be rectified at once."

His words were polite—overly so, but they didn't set Abigail at ease. Rather the opposite, as they led her to believe he was trying to gain her favor. Again she felt as if the visit contained a hidden motive. "I have been busy in the hospital," she said.

"Ah yes, you are a healer." His voice carried a hint of sarcasm that made Abigail clamp her teeth together. "Is that not what you told me at our first meeting?"

"Yes."

"A curious thing," he said, his words light, though she could hear an intonation in his words that indicated more than he was saying. "I still do not understand how you came to be in the company of two American soldiers so far from Detroit."

A cool wind blew along the street, lifting frozen flakes from the hard ground and sending them in flurries that stung her cheeks and hands. It was certainly not a pleasant day for a walk.

"I suppose I was just fortunate to find someone to accompany me," Abigail said. She clamped her teeth again, but this time to keep them from chattering. The lovely dress her father had bought was not designed to be worn out of doors on a cold day for an extended period of time, even with a cloak covering it.

"Yes, but—"

"How do you enjoy Fort Detroit, Lieutenant?" Abigail interrupted him, not caring that it was rude. She was not willing to submit to his interrogation and knew men like Lieutenant Fox could usually be distracted with a chance to talk about themselves. "I imagine it is quite different than your home in England."

He made a snorting sound. "That is an understatement indeed. Do you know my father is Lord Westing of Devereaux Park?"

"I did not know."

"Well, needless to say, a frontier fort in a freezing wilderness is the complete reverse of where I grew up." He brushed at something on his sleeve and gave her a haughty look. "There are few things that appeal to me less than tending to uncivilized prisoners in the back of beyond."

"Oh, come, Lieutenant." Abigail felt a bit insulted that he would so quickly dismiss the beautiful forested countryside. "It cannot be as bad as all that. Surely you'd not rather be fighting or marching."

He shook his head and raised a brow. "I'd prefer either one. At least I'd be doing something to bring His Majesty's army closer to finishing this pathetic war and returning home." Beneath her hand, his arm was tight, as were his words. He was quiet for an uncomfortably long moment.

Abigail looked around, just now realizing they were walking toward the fort's entrance. Ahead she could see the stables and beyond, the tents of the prisoner's camp. Did the lieutenant intend to take her from the fort? She was just about to question their route when he turned, leading her along the side of the stables, past a pen with a large hog.

"But we've strayed from the topic," Lieutenant Fox said, sounding much calmer. "I still would like an explanation of what brought you to Frenchtown. It is quite out of the way for a person traveling from Amherstburg to Detroit. I'd estimate nearly twenty miles out of the way."

Abigail didn't feel as if she owed him an explanation, but she didn't want the lieutenant to think she had something to hide. "I told you before, sir. I heard the cannons and thought my skills as a healer might be of use."

They were walking along the edge of the prison camp, and Abigail had to keep herself from looking too interested in the men they passed, even though she desperately wanted to study each face and find her friends. Especially . . .

The flap of one of the tents pulled aside, and a man stepped through carrying a sheaf of papers.

Emmett.

Her step faltered as Emmett's gaze met hers. Or more precisely as it rolled over hers and moved away without any change in his expression. He strode away without appearing as if he were aware of her at all.

Abigail's heartbeat refused to return to normal. Of course, her mind understood Emmett would not show any sign of recognition in front of Lieutenant Fox, but she couldn't completely convince her heart of it. The shock of seeing him and then seeing his apparent indifference put her off-balance, and it wasn't until she noticed the lieutenant looking at her that she realized he was waiting for her to elaborate.

What were we talking about? Had he asked another question? Or more concerning, had he noticed her reaction?

She attempted to speak as if nothing had happened. "I did not hear news of the patients who remained behind in Frenchtown. None of them have come to Detroit, and it has been more than a week. Do you know how they fared, Lieutenant? Were they taken care of?"

"I imagine so," he said, turning their course back toward the hospital building. "I imagine they have been taken care of." The edge of his mouth was twisted in a smirk, and the tone of his voice sent a chill over her skin. He looked at her with an expression of satisfaction, and she felt cold bands of foreboding closing around her lungs.

★ ★ ★

Two weeks later, Abigail held the baby to her chest, breathing in the smell of him. His soft hair brushed her cheek, and she smiled at the tickle. At Captain Lovell's request, she'd come every day for a week after the birth to make certain the child and his anxious mother were healthy and getting on well in their new roles. She'd spent most of the time reassuring the new parents that the infant was quite normal and his behavior typical of a seven-day-old baby.

"And his head shape, are you certain—"

"He's perfect, Mrs. Lovell," Abigail said, finding it harder to maintain the comforting tone after so many hours of listening to the same worries. "He squeezed his entire body through a small space only a few days ago. Soon, he'll plump up and be the beautiful baby you imagined." She laid the baby back into his mother's arms and touched the small head. "Truly, he's perfect." She smiled as the child yawned then lifted her gaze to the mother. Abigail wagged a finger. "Don't forget to rest yourself as well."

Abigail bid Captain and Mrs. Lovell farewell and stepped out into the cold air. She walked with quick steps through the now-familiar streets of Detroit, glancing up at the towering battleships as she passed the dockyard. Three weeks had passed since the Battle of Frenchtown, and the influx of new patients in the fort's hospital wards had diminished. Now that the Lovell's baby had finally come, Abigail didn't really have a reason to remain.

She felt sad at the thought of leaving her father, but of course they both knew she would need to return home eventually. Drawing near to the gates of the fort, she walked past a large boulder. In the space beneath it, shaded from the snow, was a patch of red dirt, indicating a rich oxide deposit. She thought back to her first days in Detroit, how her father had patiently waited while she investigated the patch of dirt, hoping the ground wasn't too frozen for her to discover a band of ore or an iron deposit. She'd not been disappointed, and when she unearthed the bit of hematite, she'd just known Emmett should have it.

Although Dr. Tidwell assured her that he'd delivered the hunk of metal, she hadn't had any indication that Emmett actually received it. Not that she expected a letter or a messenger. Of course he wouldn't attempt to contact her; it was dangerous for both of them. But she wished they'd had some interaction before the prisoners had been transferred from the fort. Now she supposed she'd never know what he'd thought of the gift. Or, if she were being completely truthful, she'd never know what he thought of *her*.

She sighed. Her thoughts had been down this path so many times that she was becoming impatient with herself.

Her mind was filled with doubts tainting the various scenarios of their interactions as if she were studying them through different lenses. The embrace on the

ice while she wept contrasted with the quick way Emmett had left her behind at
the camp in the forest. And how could she not think of the *kiss*? Just the memory,
weeks later, made her sigh and her heart melt a bit. But maybe his earth hadn't
utterly shifted on its axis as had hers. She felt naïve and silly, thinking that for him
a kiss may not have been any more than just . . . a kiss. Why had she believed she
was different than the thousands of women left behind with a kiss when a man
departed for war? Now that she was thinking clearly, the exchanges took on different meanings.

The longer she considered, the more foolish she felt. Emmett hadn't brought
her to the camp because he wished to spend more time with her; he'd needed her
to heal his friend. She'd been, if anything, an inconvenience for the company.
Thinking of her juvenile conversation and the fears she'd confided in him sent
a flush over her skin. She'd convinced herself that there'd been more to his
attentions than simply politeness. Her embarrassment deepened into humiliation
as she remembered Emmett's disinterested expression when he'd seen her walking
with Lieutenant Fox.

Abigail felt childish. What had she been thinking? She'd given the man a
rock, for heaven's sake.

When they took luncheon that afternoon, she told her father it was time
for her to return home.

He set down his fork and studied her. "Are you certain, Abigail?"

"There are so few patients, and I . . . I suppose my adventure has to come
to an end sometime." She spread the napkin flat on her lap and gave a small
smile. "Besides, Maggie will be tired of Mr. Kirby's grumbling."

Her father smiled in return, but she thought his gaze was a bit too scruti-
nizing. Finally he nodded. "I will miss you, my daughter."

"You will come home soon, won't you?"

He shrugged. "I hadn't planned to remain so long. But I will stay as long
as I'm needed."

Once the decision was made, it was only a matter of making travel arrange-
ments, packing her few clothes, and bidding her father farewell. The next afternoon, Abigail found herself accompanied by two soldiers, riding in a sleigh
toward home.

Her knee bumped into the old musket. Goodness knows how her father
had found it among the confiscated weapons, but they both felt safer knowing
she'd have it at home with her.

As they rode, she was surprised by a pang of sadness, thinking that she'd not
be treating patients or giving Mrs. Lovell advice. In Detroit she'd felt needed,

and she realized she'd felt that way ever since discovering a bleeding captain in her barn. Now she'd return to the life she'd always known. Abigail tried to convince herself that there were worse things than loneliness and boredom.

Once they reached the log house, she bid the soldiers farewell and entered through her front door. The house was just as she'd left it, comfortable and familiar. She hung her cloak in its spot and returned the musket to the pegs above the fireplace, making a list of the chores she must do in the coming days. Maggie would need to be retrieved from the Kirbys', and the house hadn't been swept or dusted in nearly a month. The woodbox was empty, bread must be baked, butter churned—well, once Maggie was back. There would always be plenty to do.

"I suppose my adventure is indeed over," she said to the empty house, and the sadness changed to resignation.

A thumping sound made her spin, and she let out a yelp.

"It's only us, Abigail." Barney emerged from the kitchen, his wide smile easing the jolt of fear.

"Barney, what are you—?" she began, but stopped when Jasper entered through the front door.

"Soldiers are gone," he said.

Murphy followed Barney from the kitchen, and Luke came down the stairs.

Abigail stood, one hand pressed to her breastbone, staring at the men with her mouth agape. She had no idea what to say. "You, all of you, you're here . . . Why are you here?" She fumbled with the words, her surprise making her sound completely witless.

"The English paroled the militia—sent us all home," Luke said.

"We've come because we need your help," Murphy said.

Abigail looked at each of the men in turn. They all appeared healthy. What could they possibly need from her? "My help?"

"Captain Prescott is in danger," Luke said.

"In danger? From what? Or whom?" Each of the men's declarations flabbergasted her more than the one before.

"A British officer," Murphy said. "Lieutenant Fox is the commander directing the prisoner transfer. In Fort Detroit, Captain Prescott confronted him about—" He stopped speaking abruptly, and his eyes darted to Jasper.

"Mistreatment of prisoners," Jasper finished for him.

Abigail looked between the men, trying to understand the strange exchange.

"The lieutenant's evil, Abigail," Barney said, motioning with his hands. "And he's set his sights on the captain."

"He'll kill him." Luke's brows were pulled together in worry.

Abigail had no doubt Lieutenant Fox was more than capable of making Emmett's life miserable. He was unpleasant, and she believed he could probably be quite spiteful. But killing anyone seemed rather a stretch for the foppish gentleman.

"Surely he'll not kill him," she said. "I know Lieutenant Fox. He's rude, certainly, and patronizing, but he's not a murderer."

"He purchased the scalps of the prisoners left behind at Frenchtown," Jasper said.

The others darted their gazes toward him as if he'd revealed something they'd agreed to keep secret.

Abigail squinted, trying to understand his words. "I don't . . . what do you mean?"

Murphy stepped across the room and took her arm. His expression was gentle, as if he was telling a young child something upsetting. "Abigail, the lieutenant had them killed, all of them. And he paid the Indians for the proof."

She shook her head, a bitter taste filling her mouth. Hardly noticing that Murphy led her to a chair, her mind tried to process what she'd heard. "I don't understand," she finally said. "The men were sick and wounded. They'd surrendered . . ."

She looked from face to face, but each of the men looked grim.

"You can see what kind of man he is," Jasper said. His face was even stonier than usual. "And what he's capable of."

The horrible truth sank in, and her nerves tingled in panic. *Emmett.* Abigail stood, knowing they should act but not sure exactly what course to take. "What can we do?"

Murphy gave her arm a soft squeeze. "The American officers and regular soldiers are being held in an outpost near the town of Byron."

"Byron is over a hundred miles away," she said. The desperate feeling of wanting to act was joined by a heavy dismay. They were all looking to her expectantly, but in this she was helpless. "And there is nothing I can do. I have no influence on His Majesty's army."

"The commander of the outpost is Major Isaac Tidwell," Jasper said.

"He's your brother, isn't he, Abigail?" Barney took a few steps closer.

Abigail clenched her hands into fists and gave a nod. Perhaps she was not utterly helpless after all. With her brother as the commander, nobody would question her being there. "Then we shall go to Byron."

CHAPTER 16

EMMETT LEFT THE PRISONER'S MESS room directly after the meal, deciding he'd spend the evening writing a letter to Lydia instead of playing cards with the other officers. He crossed the road to the wooden building, nodding to the guard, who unlocked the door and stepped aside to admit him. While he wouldn't consider them careless, the guards had become much more relaxed over the months as they'd attended their American prisoners. The duty was not difficult. The prisoners offered no resistance. They'd surrendered, given their parole, and in the two months as they'd been detained in two different forts and traveled more than a hundred miles, there had been no escape attempts. Obviously, the harsh terrain gave the captors an extra level of security. Byron was surrounded on three sides by hundreds of miles of snow-covered forests and a partially frozen lake on the other. Even if one did evade the guards, sentries, and pickets, survival would be nearly impossible in the hostile wilderness.

Once Major Tidwell had made the decision to keep the prisoners in Byron until the lake thawed and they could be transported to Halifax by ship, he'd ordered the temporary barracks built. Emmett and the other soldiers were deeply grateful for it. The wooden structures were primitive, but they were a vast improvement over living in a tent.

Emmett had a high regard for Major Tidwell. In the few weeks he'd known the man, he'd found the commander of the Byron way station to be an excellent leader. He was strict but fair. The men in his command respected him, and he treated the prisoners well. Emmett had tried not to stare when he'd noticed the major's particular gestures or facial expressions that reminded him of the man's younger sister. Each time, they'd caught Emmett off guard, and he'd been taken aback by how badly he missed her.

He wished he could write to her this evening instead of Lydia and receive a letter in return. Over the long hours, he'd composed hundreds of letters in his mind, thinking of puzzles that she might enjoy involving different chemical compounds, or stories she might find interesting. And he spent an equal amount of time wondering what she might write back to him. Sometimes thinking of her made him smile, or laugh inside, and other times, he felt an ache. Tonight he missed her, wished he knew what she was doing. Had she left Detroit? Was she home alone again in Amherstburg milking Maggie and reading one of her thick volumes about geological phenomena?

Emmett entered through the doorway of his small cell room then froze, his stomach tightening. The evening sun shining through the greased-paper window gave off a soft light. The room contained a desk and chair, a wooden chest, and four cots, and it was upon one of these that Emmett's gaze was fixated. Specifically on his own bunk, where a black-and-gray bird lay on the blanket, yellow feet curled up and its head twisted at an unnatural angle.

The sight sent a chill over him. He didn't cringe away from the sight of a dead bird. He'd certainly seen plenty of those, but for it to be placed just so on his bunk was unnerving. And unnerving was a sensation Emmett had become more than familiar with in the months since he'd confronted Lieutenant Sebastian Fox next to the hog's pen.

He lit the lantern and moved closer. Lieutenant Fox's harassments were escalating. They'd started out as pranks that were almost childish in nature, such as the evening Emmett had discovered his blanket missing and then found it on the stable roof. The antics had grown into tricks reminiscent of a schoolyard bully. A shove from one of the lieutenant's underlings as he passed or clumps of snow hitting the back of his head as they'd marched from Detroit. Emmett had ignored these pranks, thinking them not worth his effort, but he had started to become more aware of where Lieutenant Fox and his subordinates were whenever he was out in the drilling yard or moving around the camp.

This, however, was so much more sinister. And it was unsettling to know the lieutenant was aware of where he slept—that he or one of his men had been in the room while Emmett was absent.

He picked up the bird and tossed it outside then returned, checking that none of his other belongings had been tampered with.

He didn't fear Lieutenant Fox. A person that relied on juvenile tricks to intimidate was a coward. He didn't think the man would hurt him. But Emmett worried that, true to his word, the lieutenant would hurt a person Emmett cared about. It had been a relief when the militia were paroled and sent home before the prisoners had left Detroit. Now Lieutenant Fox wouldn't be able to use Barney or Jasper or any of his friends against him. Emmett had distanced himself from the other officers in the camp, not wanting to make any of them targets.

The one moment he'd felt actual fear was when he'd seen the lieutenant walking with Abigail in Fort Detroit. He'd thought it odd that he'd been sent to fetch the prisoner transfer papers precisely at 2:30, but when he came out of the tent and saw the pair, he'd known without a doubt that Lieutenant Fox had planned the encounter. Emmett had turned away, feigning disinterest, but not before he'd seen the triumph in the lieutenant's eyes at Abigail's reaction. The meeting was intended as a message. Not only did the lieutenant know a connection existed between the two, but he was reminding Emmett of his promise to harm the people he cared about. Ice-cold terror had poured into Emmett's gut, and he'd spent the remainder of his time in Fort Detroit terrified the man would follow through on his threat.

Emmett was tempted to return to the mess room with the others. His nerves were tense and he felt on edge, but he was certain this was precisely the sort of response the lieutenant intended. His tactic was intimidation, and Emmett promised himself he wouldn't allow himself to react. He moved to the small desk and sat with his back to the door, just as he'd have done if an unpleasant message had not been left on his bunk, and composed his letter.

Two days later, Emmett's company was assigned to firewood duty. A satisfying job, Emmett thought. One he'd never actually performed himself until joining the army, but it had become one of his favorites. He liked beginning with a large, seemingly indestructible tree and reducing it to a neat stack of uniform pieces that would fit into the fireplaces and kitchen stoves. Of course, for the wood to produce heat and burn slowly, it would need to be a dense hardwood, and that required more strength to cut to bits. With the amount of lumber needed to keep the camp supplied, wood was chopped year-round and stored in sheds to season before it could be burned, and so the duty was rotated regularly through the companies of prisoners. Spending months in a prison camp made the men restless, and they were glad for any excuse to exercise.

When they gathered at the far end of the camp, Emmett saw that some of the British soldiers who hung about Lieutenant Fox had joined the guards. Instead of showing any recognition, he moved away, making certain his men stood at attention and were ready to march. He watched the soldiers from the corner of his eye, wondering if any of them were the ones who had delivered the bird to his room.

Emmett and his men followed the guards into the forest, arriving in half an hour at the clearing designated for the purpose. Some men were assigned with axes to fell a large oak or maple farther in the woods, and others took their places at chopping blocks, with wedges and mauls to split the seasoned wood into useable sizes and move it into the sheds.

Throughout the day, the duties would rotate. Emmett began at the chopping block, even though as an officer he wasn't required to do the actual labor. There was something soothing about the repetition. He'd come to understand how different wood split; some, like oak, broke apart in the middle, while maple was easier to slice near the sides. Seeing the stack of logs turn into a stack of firewood was immensely satisfying, as was the physical exertion required while swinging the sledge.

He placed a section of wood onto the chopping block, set his feet in the snow, and swung, feeling the wood split with a gratifying crack. Even with the sounds of axes chopping, men grunting, and wood breaking, the forest felt peaceful, the cold wind refreshing.

After a few hours, the groups rotated. Emmett rolled his shoulders as he walked and opened and closed his blistered hands, knowing he'd be sore for the next few days. He listened to the men, smiling when he realized he didn't hear any complaining. After months as prisoners, any change to the routine was welcome at this point.

They came to an enormous oak with a trunk so broad three men could reach around it, unable to touch hands. The boughs were thick, twisted, and snow-covered, the missing limbs making it easy to see where the other group had left off stripping the branches from the trunk. Emmett gave orders, sending some of the men high into the tree and others to haul away the downed limbs. Instead of climbing into the tree himself, he stood with the guards, feeling it was more important to make certain none of his men were beneath the heavy branches when they fell.

In the dense forest, the tree had little space around it, and the men had to chop the large branches into smaller parts to drag them away. Between the men chopping, dragging, climbing, and guarding, the area was confusing, and one miscommunication could result in an accident. Emmett stepped as far back as he could, finding a spot where he could see the entire tree and the area beneath.

As he watched the scene, his eyes were drawn to a particularly broad-shouldered soldier. Corporal Reynolds came from a small lumber town in Pennsylvania. Both the British soldiers and the Americans understood the value of the man's expertise in this type of situation and relied heavily on his advice. Emmett had never seen a person climb a tree as quickly and as sure-footed as the man. The corporal directed others, telling them where to stand while they chopped and what branches to avoid.

At the moment, Corporal Reynolds sat high in the tree, legs wrapped around a branch as he chopped another. When it was near to falling, he called out, and the men beneath him cleared out of the way. He struck a few more sure blows, and the heavy limb crashed down through the branches beneath and hit the ground.

While some of the waiting men began cutting up the large limb, the corporal gave directions to another group about which branch should go next and then moved to a different position. Emmett was so caught up in watching Corporal Reynolds swing from branch to branch that his mind didn't register the warning shout until after his body reacted. He jumped, rolling out of the way just as a tree crashed to the ground exactly where he'd been standing.

Soldiers from both armies ran toward him, checking to make sure he was unhurt, wondering what had happened, and trying to figure out how the tree had fallen.

Emmett's heart raced, his mind coming to realize just how close he'd come to being crushed. He assured both the guards and his own frightened-faced men that he was unharmed then joined a group of officers as they studied the breaking point in the horizontal trunk and the ground around it. Hands shaking, he listened as the others attempted to recreate the chain of events.

"Wasn't an accident. The tree was cut," Lieutenant Devon said, pointing to the axe marks on the stump.

"By whom?" one of the British officers asked, his face pale and his brows creased in concern. "Did you see anything, Captain Prescott? Hear anything?"

Emmett shook his head. His attention had been focused on the activity in the larger tree. But how had he not heard the sound of an axe? Had the tree been cut nearly through before he arrived and needed only a push to send it over?

Lieutenant Devon brushed snow from Emmett's arm, giving him a pat on the shoulder. "It's fortunate you reacted so quickly, Captain. If not for your reflexes . . ." He glanced meaningfully at the place Emmett had been standing. "I'm glad you're unhurt, sir."

Emmett left the men to their discussion and sat heavily on a stump. How had he reacted so quickly? He tried to remember the moments before the tree fell. He'd heard something, a warning shout. And now that he was thinking clearly, he realized the voice had sounded like *Jasper*. Of course . . . He peered around, deeper into the woods.

Impossible.

In the panic of the moment, his mind must have conjured a false memory.

Rubbing his hands over his face, he remembered stories he'd heard of guardian angels. He wasn't an overly religious man, but in that moment, Emmett bowed his head and offered a prayer of thanks.

When he opened his eyes, he saw the two red-coated soldiers he'd noticed earlier—friends of Lieutenant Fox. They stepped from the forest, looking around as if hoping nobody had been aware of their absence. A flare of rage exploded behind Emmett's eyes. He rose quickly, startling the men.

"I imagine you're disappointed," he said in a loud voice, marching toward them.

The pair looked at each other, fear turning their faces pale, and they hurried toward the guards.

Emmett followed after them, stepping to the side to pass a guard who blocked his path.

The guard put out a hand. "Captain . . ." His voice carried a warning.

The other guards joined him, and Emmett was forced to stop.

"I want those two investigated," he said. "This was an attempt on my life, and those two men—"

One of the senior British officers put a hand on his sword. "Captain Prescott, we will of course look into this . . . incident . . . but at the moment we have no reason to believe it was any more than an accident." His expression looked almost bored, which made Emmett furious.

"An accident?" Emmett pointed to the broken stump of the tree. "Did the tree *accidentally* chop itself with an axe?" His hands were shaking again.

The two officers hurried away, and Emmett moved to follow them.

The guards shifted, blocking him again.

"Captain, I understand you suffered a fright, but an accusation of this nature is very serious," the officer said.

Emmett opened his mouth to deliver a scathing response, but a tug on his arm stopped him.

"Come, Captain," Lieutenant Devon said. He turned to the British officer. "Sir, if I may return Captain Prescott to the barracks? He should rest himself." The tug became stronger, jerking Emmett backwards.

The officer sniffed. "Yes, yes. See that he does."

Emmett planted his feet, ready to object, but another of his men grabbed on to his other arm, and his soles slid in the snow as the two pulled him away.

"Beg your pardon, Captain, but 'twon't do any good to argue," Lieutenant Devon said in a low voice. "And we'd rather you didn't hang, sir."

Emmett knew the man was right, but that did little to ease his anger. He stormed through the forest, the other two and a British guard walking quickly to keep up.

When they crossed the tree line, they came upon the two men who had fled, accompanied by a group of guards and Lieutenant Fox.

Emmett's insides flared with heat. He stopped, breathing hard and clenching his fists. The men with him each took an arm and tried to continue forward, but Emmett remained rooted to the spot.

"Captain!" Lieutenant Fox called in a cheerful voice. He and his friends strode forward. "I didn't expect to see you, sir." His brow lifted and a smirk twisted his lips.

"I wager you didn't, Lieutenant." Emmett lifted his chin and fought to keep his voice steady. He would not give the lieutenant the satisfaction of seeing any emotion.

Lieutenant Fox inclined his head and indicated for Emmett to walk beside him. "I am delighted to find you unharmed after your mishap."

"I doubt that is true." Emmett kept walking. His entire concentration was focused on restraint, keeping his emotions under control. Once he was in his room, he'd be able to think through the situation calmly. Come up with a strategy. Until today, he'd thought the lieutenant's torments to be mostly harmless, but now he realized something had to be done. He had to act, or he would die, and he refused to be killed by a pretentious monster in a prison camp.

"It *is* true, in light of recent events." The lieutenant's voice sounded almost giddy, which was unsettling. He walked next to Emmett, swinging his arms and smiling as if the two were out for a friendly stroll. "I have splendid news that simply could not wait," he said.

Something in his voice sent a chill over Emmett's skin. In spite of his plan to ignore the man's goading, he couldn't help but look at him.

Lieutenant Fox's face spread into an enormous smile, but his eyes were hard, cunning. "I've just now discovered that Miss Abigail Tidwell has come to Byron to visit her brother."

CHAPTER 17

AFTER MAKING THE APPROPRIATE INQUIRIES, Abigail was directed to her brother's residence in the town of Byron. A slender woman who Abigail assumed to be close to her sixtieth year sent word to Isaac and then showed her to a sitting room.

"I'll just stoke the fire then I'll fetch the tea." The woman spoke in a warm voice and gave Abigail a smile. She poked at the hearth and added a few logs.

"Thank you," Abigail said.

Once the woman left, she sat on the velvet-covered sofa. She had no idea her brother lived in such luxury when he was away from home. The Tidwells had never employed servants. Abigail let her gaze travel around the room with its fine furniture and thick rug on the floor.

Sunlight shone through gauzy curtains, making the wood in the room glow a golden color. It seemed ages since she'd been warm. And sitting reminded her of how sore she was. Her legs and back ached from days of hiking, and her feet were blistered. The two dresses she wore hadn't completely dried over the course of the journey, and Abigail didn't imagine the smell of her clothes and sweating would be of any help with making new friends.

She accepted tea from the housekeeper, whom she found was called Mrs. Bennett. Abigail's estimation of the woman rose as she tasted one of the little pastries that accompanied the tea. She felt a bit guilty indulging while her traveling companions were at this moment searching for a campsite and setting rabbit snares, but it was such a relief to finally be at the end of the journey.

Only a quarter of an hour passed before she heard noise in the entryway, and a moment later, Isaac burst into the room. "Abigail!" He rushed toward her, kneeling on the rug before her. He took her hands. "Is it Father? The farm? What has happened?"

She winced. Of course he would assume a catastrophe to be the reason for her making the journey. She should have anticipated it. "No, Father is fine. And the farm is just as it has always been. I am sorry to have worried you."

He sat on the sofa beside her and scratched his cheek in the way he did when thinking something through. "It goes without saying that I'm very happy to see you," he began then cleared his throat. "But your arrival is somewhat of a surprise. Did you send word ahead?"

"No, I'm sorry to come unannounced." She took his hand and gave the answer she'd prepared over the week-and-a-half-long journey. "I've missed you, Isaac. And with father gone, the farm's been quite lonely." She wasn't proud of employing guilt as a tactic, but she figured it wasn't truly a lie. She *had* been lonely, after all.

"But, how did you . . . surely you didn't travel alone?"

"Of course not. In Amherstburg, I met a group traveling this direction, and they offered to accompany me as far as Byron." She was pleased that the answer was entirely truthful.

He pulled his brows together. "Group? What group?"

"A group of travelers." She knew that wasn't the answer he was looking for, but she kept talking, hoping to redirect his line of questioning. "When I heard they were coming through Byron, I of course thought how much I'd love to see my brother, and also, I helped Father treat the American soldiers after the battle of Frenchtown, and I heard some of my former patients had been transferred here. I thought I'd check on them."

Isaac's eyes widened. "You were in Fort Detroit?"

"Yes." She offered him the plate of pastries. "Perhaps the doctor in town has need of assistance?"

Isaac took the plate from her without looking at it and set it on his lap. "I'm sure Dr. Baldwin would be grateful for any help you could give." He let the sentence hang in the air as if there were a "but" following.

"Well, it's settled, then." She jumped up and moved toward the fireplace, holding out her hands to warm them. If she kept talking and moving, she was certain she could distract him from probing too deeply.

Isaac rose as well. "Abigail . . ." His voice was uncertain. Her brother was not one who enjoyed having his routine interrupted, and she knew a surprise such as this would take him some time to come to terms with.

She turned and wrapped her arms around his waist, laying her cheek on his chest. "I am so happy to see you, Isaac." She pulled back and grinned. "Now, I'm certain my intruding without an appointment has put a wrinkle in your afternoon schedule." She could see the truth of it in his eyes. "Do not worry about me at all. I am quite tired, and I'd like some time to freshen up. Return to your duties, and later this evening or tomorrow, you can show me around town."

His expression relaxed. "Yes, of course." Opening the door to the passageway, he called for Mrs. Bennett and instructed her to prepare a room and a bath for Abigail.

"I am glad you are here, Abby-snail," he said. The teasing way he said her childhood nickname told her he was adjusting to the surprise. "Please, do not think me rude for my questioning. You caught me unawares."

"And I know how much you dislike being caught unawares."

"I'll return in a few hours," he said, fetching his hat from the table where he'd tossed it. "Please, make yourself at home."

"You know I will," she teased.

Isaac gave a theatrical sigh. "Yes, I do." He winked, pulled on his hat, and departed.

Abigail let out a sigh. She'd survived the first round of interrogations. And done it quite well, she thought, swallowing down a small surge of guilt. She didn't like deceiving her brother. But what was the alternative? She couldn't very well tell the commander of the camp that she'd arrived in the company of enemy soldiers with the goal of protecting their leader. How would he react? Isaac didn't see things the way her father did. His perceptions were black and white, right and wrong, and Emmett was the enemy.

She looked through the window at the forest beyond the town. Jasper and the others had promised to keep a close watch on her and Emmett. She hoped they were at this moment spying on the prison camp, making certain he was well.

As the group had sat around their campfire in the evenings, they'd told her more about Lieutenant Fox and discussed the best ways for Abigail to go about her mission. The first duty was to gather intelligence. Discover where Emmett was being held, make certain he was well, and attempt to determine the nature of the hostility between him and Lieutenant Fox. "It may have run its course," Murphy had said.

But Barney had shaken his head. "The lieutenant is wicked," he said, his face somber. "I knew a man like that before—you remember Abe Gustafson, don't you, Luke?"

Luke nodded, his face looking ill. "Liked to play games with people—cruel games meant to frighten."

"And he didn't stop," Barney said. "Just got worse."

"I won't let him hurt Emmett," Abigail told them. She'd spoken the words without thinking, and as soon as they'd left her mouth, she'd felt foolish. Did she actually believe herself capable of stopping a powerful man with a vendetta? Or think she was the one to protect an army captain?

But the others hadn't laughed or treated her vow with looks of patient indulgence as she'd expected.

"That's why we came for you," Jasper said. He gave a succinct nod of his head, his mouth pulled into a tight line.

The simple words made Abigail's heart feel light and her cheeks hot.

"If you please, Miss Tidwell, I've drawn your bath." Mrs. Bennett entered the room, pulling Abigail from her reminiscing. "And I'll have your dress laundered," she said, giving the dirty gown a disappointed look as Abigail imagined matronly women in fine houses often did. She gestured for Abigail to follow.

A bath sounded wonderful. "Thank you."

The next morning, after breakfast, Abigail wore the new gown her father had given her, and walked arm in arm with her brother through the small town of Byron, Ontario. The location was very remote, a few miles north of Lake Erie, along the main route from the larger cities of York and Kingston to the east. With the lake frozen, the road was the lifeline for supplies to the western settlements.

The main street consisted of a small inn and a few shops. Isaac told her about the various structures, and then they continued farther, out of the town toward the military buildings.

Abigail would have liked to visit the military area the day before, but of course a young woman wandering about a prison camp would have been inappropriate, and she'd forced herself to be patient.

Isaac showed her his office and pointed out the barracks, both those that housed the British soldiers and those housing the prisoners, and then he led her into the hospital building.

A slender young man with a large nose rose from a desk and hurried toward them, and Isaac introduced her to Dr. James Baldwin.

Abigail curtsied, and the doctor bowed awkwardly, as if he were not used to meeting new people.

"And how can I be of aid, Major Tidwell, Miss Tidwell? Not feeling ill, I hope, miss?"

"I hoped to offer my assistance here in the hospital."

Dr. Baldwin looked at Isaac, obviously thinking he was the more reasonable of the two.

"Abigail treated some of the prisoners after Frenchtown," Isaac said.

"Indeed?" Dr. Baldwin's eyes widened, and Abigail braced herself for the man's skepticism when it came to a woman working in what was typically a man's domain.

Isaac must have seen the doubt in the doctor's eyes as well. "She has worked closely with my father for many years, and she is quite skilled."

The doctor nodded politely, but didn't fully hide his disbelief. "I will be grateful for any help she can offer." He spoke the words as if he knew he was supposed to say them, but they were far from convincing. "Would you accompany me to the ward?"

He led them through a doorway to the large room beyond. The hospital ward's smell was a familiar combination of healing medications and bodily fluids. Abigail was used to the unpleasant aromas, but Isaac's hand flew to his nose at once. He dropped it quickly, but his nose was still wrinkled as if he felt nauseated.

Abigail stifled a smile at his reaction. Isaac had never been comfortable with illness of any sort.

Dr. Baldwin motioned with a wave of his arm to the few occupied beds. "Right now, we've only the typical camp maladies to contend with."

"Such as dysentery, leg sores, arthritis, and impetigo?" Abigail said.

"Yes." He glanced at her before continuing. "Regular colds, of course, and a few cases of fever, although I do not believe any to be typhus."

"No red-colored spots on the chest or abdomen, then," Abigail noted.

Dr. Baldwin glanced at her again and this time raised a brow.

"You see, Doctor Baldwin," Isaac said, restraining a smile. "Abigail is very capable."

"We shall see," the doctor muttered.

Abigail was used to people lacking confidence in her abilities. She would just have to prove herself. "In Detroit, I treated a Lieutenant Cartwright." Abigail studied the faces of the patients in the ward but didn't recognize any. "He had a leg full of shrapnel. Have you seen him?"

Dr. Baldwin nodded. "Had quite a difficult march, but he made it, and his wounds are healing well." He squinted. "You administered the sutures?"

"I did," Abigail said. "And another man . . . oh, what was his name?" She tapped her chin as if trying to remember and congratulated herself for a stupendous dramatic performance. "Captain Prescott? Yes, I believe that was it. He had an arrow in his side." She pointed at her arm. "And a laceration on his bicep."

"I've not attended a Captain Prescott," Dr. Baldwin said.

"I believe he was the man involved in the accident in the forest yesterday," Isaac said.

Abigail's insides clenched. "And was he hurt?" She gasped out the words.

"Fortunately, no one was injured," Isaac continued. He glanced nervously at a bowl filled with bloody bandages and did not seem to have noticed Abigail's response. She glanced at the doctor, hoping he'd not noticed either.

He appeared to be watching Isaac. Perhaps she should be glad the man seemed intent on ignoring her. In the future, she'd need to be more careful with her reactions, she thought, frustrated with how easily she'd slipped.

"Shall I leave you here, then?" Isaac said, glancing toward the door. "I've duties to attend to, but I'll return you home if you'd rather—"

"No. If Dr. Baldwin is in agreement, I'll stay." Abigail was disappointed she'd not get a closer look at the prison camp, but she thought the hospital was the surest place to meet the American prisoners and inquire discreetly about Emmett.

"Yes, very well. You'll find an apron in the cabinet." The doctor pointed to the other side of the room. "And, if you please, mix up a bread-and-milk poultice."

"Of course." She could tell Dr. Baldwin was testing her, hoping she would ask what exactly was a bread-and-milk poultice, and how did one make it? But she'd been treating ulcerations for more than a decade, and she thought she could probably do it with her eyes closed. As long as the hospital had the proper ingredients.

Isaac bid Dr. Baldwin farewell, and Abigail accompanied her brother to the door.

"I'll fetch you for luncheon, then?" he asked.

"If it's not an imposition."

"Of course it's not, Abby-snail." He kissed her cheek and tipped his hat. When he opened the door to leave, he drew back.

An officer stood outside, his hand outstretched as if he was about to open the door himself. Isaac had very nearly plowed him over. The man snapped to attention, his heels clicking together, and saluted the major.

"At ease, Private," Isaac said.

"Sir, if you please, I've a note for your sister."

Abigail blinked and looked closer at the man. His voice sounded familiar, and at once she knew exactly who he was. "Private Matthews," she said, recognizing him from Fort Detroit. He was Lieutenant Fox's assistant. "How nice to see you again."

"Miss Tidwell." He bowed. "Lieutenant Fox sent me to inquire after your health and to ask if you're amenable to joining him for tea tomorrow afternoon. He lifted his gaze to Isaac. "You are invited too, Major."

A muscle in Isaac's jaw twitched. The small movement spoke volumes to Abigail. He was apparently not an admirer of the lieutenant.

"If you like, Abigail," Isaac said. "I will happily join you. Though I'm certain the lieutenant will understand if you are still too fatigued from your travels."

Abigail smiled at her brother. She admired how gracious he was, agreeing to an engagement he clearly didn't care for and at the same time giving her an excuse if she chose to take it. She considered for a moment. Of course, Lieutenant Fox was the last person she wished to see—the very last. But if she was to find out anything about Emmett, the lieutenant was very likely the best place to start. "Meet the enemy head on," as the Irish poet said.

She reminded herself to be on her guard. Both Jasper and Murphy had speculated that her chance encounter with Emmett while walking with Lieutenant Fox in Detroit was very likely planned by the man in order to gauge her reaction.

"I would like that," she said. Or *lied* as the case was. "Tell Lieutenant Fox thank you for the thoughtful invitation."

"Very well, Miss Tidwell. Four o'clock tomorrow."

Isaac glanced at her but did not say anything as he and Private Matthews bowed and took their leave.

CHAPTER 18

EMMETT PACED BACK AND FORTH over the packed dirt floor of his cell room. In his entire life, he couldn't remember ever feeling such a lack of control. A shoulder-crushing mixture of frustration, fear, and anger. If Lieutenant Fox was to be believed—and Emmett's gut told him in this case the man was telling the truth—Abigail was here in Byron. Emmett had thought the one advantage of leaving Detroit had been getting the lieutenant away from her. But now she was here, within the man's reach, and again Emmett had no way of protecting her. He smacked a fist into his palm.

"Calm yourself, Captain," Major Graves said from the chair in front of the desk. "You're making the lot of us nervous." He set down a quill and turned. "Still unsettled about the incident in the forest yesterday?"

Emmett sat on the narrow shelf of his own bunk and didn't reply. *Unsettled?* Of course he was unsettled. An infernal tree chopped by two tea-sipping buffoons had nearly crushed him. And nobody was doing a thing about it. In this instance, Emmett had managed a narrow escape, but it was just a matter of time before Lieutenant Fox succeeded in catching him off guard. That worry, however, was secondary to Abigail's safety. He could only hope her brother's rank afforded her some measure of protection.

"You should be feeling fortunate instead of agitated." The major nodded as if dispensing sound advice. "A dangerous business, chopping trees. Accidents aren't uncommon."

"We're probably all safer here as prisoners than out there with the battles and the Indians," Lieutenant Devon said. He set aside the letter he was reading and stood, carefully placing the miniature portrait of his beloved on a ledge on the uneven boards of the wall. He crossed the small room and poured a cup from the water pitcher, offering it to Emmett.

Emmett shook his head, turning down the drink. He didn't explain his real concerns. Didn't want to give the others reason to worry about him or their own safety. He scooted back, leaning against the wall and picked up the bit of hematite from the ledge beside his own bunk. He'd found rubbing his fingers over the bumps of the cool metal to be extremely soothing. "I trust all is well at home, Lieutenant?" He nodded toward the letter, glad to have something else to think about.

Lieutenant Devon looked toward the miniature portrait and smiled. "Yes. All is well. Georgiana is complaining of the naval blockades and the shortage of fashionable gowns and bonnets in Boston. But she and her family are safe and healthy."

"I'm glad to hear it." Emmett noticed the way the man's eyes shone when he spoke of his beloved. He set the rock back on the ledge.

"I'll just be happy when this infernal war is finished." Lieutenant Devon raised the cup in a salute and downed the contents, grimacing. "The well water tastes worse every day."

"The lake should thaw soon," Major Graves said. "A month at the latest. Then we'll at least enjoy a change of sce—"

The cup dropped from Lieutenant Devon's fingers, hitting with a thud. He pressed a hand to his throat then doubled over, clutching his stomach as he fell to the floor.

Emmett jumped from his bunk and crouched beside him. "Lieutenant?"

The lieutenant groaned and pressed his arms tighter against his middle.

Emmett looked up at the major.

"I'll send for the doctor." Major Graves hurried to the door.

"Lieutenant." Emmett patted his back. "Can you speak?"

"Going dark." The man spoke through clenched teeth, the sound hardly more than a grunt.

Lieutenant Devon wore no coat, and his shirt was quickly soaking through with sweat. He groaned and pulled into a tighter ball.

Emmett retrieved the cup and poured some more water, kneeling down to help the lieutenant drink. But he stopped. He lifted it to his nose and sniffed. The water had a strange smell. Emmett touched it to his tongue and frowned at the bitter taste. The tip of his tongue started to burn then went numb.

This reaction was certainly not the result of stale well water. Had the lieutenant been poisoned? He looked up at the pitcher and felt a wave of nausea as realization hit. The poison had been meant for *him*.

Dread clenched his chest tight. As long as Lieutenant Fox continued his vendetta, Emmett put anyone close to him in danger.

He heard footsteps in the passageway, and Major Graves rushed into the room followed by a guard and *Abigail*. Emmett's heart caught at the sight of her, and in the next moment, his stomach turned hard. He forced a neutral expression, hoping the conflicting emotions hadn't shown on his face.

Abigail held Emmett's gaze for a split second then dropped her medical bag and knelt beside him. "What has happened?"

If he'd thought a hunk of rock to be comforting, it was nothing to the sensation of having her here next to him. It took every ounce of his self-control not to reach for her. "He took a drink and immediately fell, holding his stomach and saying that everything was going dark."

She touched the lieutenant's neck, right below the jaw, feeling for his heartbeat. "Sir, can you hear me?"

A groan was the only response.

She pressed her palm to his forehead then his cheek. "What is his name?" she asked Emmett.

"Devon. Lieutenant Devon."

"Lieutenant Devon?" Abigail leaned close, shaking his shoulder. "Can you tell me where you are hurting?"

"Stomach." He groaned again.

Abigail rose, motioning to Emmett and the guard. "If you please, can you get him to a bed?"

Emmett grabbed beneath the lieutenant's arms and hefted while the guard lifted his feet, moving him up onto his bunk.

Abigail opened her bag, taking out a few bottles and looking at the labels. "Now, what did he drink?"

Emmett jerked up his chin toward the pitcher. He handed her the cup. "I think he may have been poisoned."

Abigail sniffed the water then touched it to the tip of her tongue just as Emmett had a moment earlier. Her face darkened, and she spit. "Monkshood." She looked at the pitcher and then at Emmett. Her eyes opened wide.

A thin man with a pronounced nose hurried into the room. He looked at the patient then at Abigail, and his nostrils flared. "Ah, Miss Tidwell, I see you've beat me to it."

"The lieutenant's ingested monkshood." She chose a bottle and moved to the bedside. "If you please," she said to the guard. "A bucket. And some clean water."

"We cannot treat him here," the thin man said. "Bring him to the hospi—"

"Doctor, there is no time. We must expel the poison immediately." Abigail reached past him and took the bucket from the guard. "His heart rate is slow, and his sight is darkening."

The doctor looked as if he would argue but thought better of it. He stood near, scowling as Abigail poured some of the syrup into the patient's mouth.

"Now, this won't be pleasant, Lieutenant Devon. I'm sorry. Captain, please, can you help me turn him on his side?"

The next moments were extremely unpleasant for all involved as Lieutenant Devon expelled the contents of his stomach with violent force. After each spasm passed, he would collapse onto the bunk, trembling.

Emmett felt extremely sorry for the younger man.

Abigail rubbed the lieutenant's arm and spoke to him softly, occasionally brushing back a damp lock of hair or wiping his mouth with a cloth.

And Emmett felt a bit less sorry for him.

Finally, the vomiting ended. The lieutenant lay back, breathing shallowly. His skin was as gray as the dirty snow outside.

"There, Lieutenant," Abigail said in a gentle tone. She mopped his brow with the cloth. "Rest now."

"Miss, am I going to die?" Lieutenant Devon's voice shook. He glanced toward the miniature portrait on the ledge.

"Not if I can help it," Abigail said, giving his arm a pat. She pulled down the picture and studied it. "Lovely. What is her name?"

"Georgiana." His eyes were drooping.

Abigail put the picture into his hand. "Rest now, Lieutenant," she said and took a step back.

The doctor must have seen this as his signal to take charge. He ordered some men to bring in a stretcher, and for a few minutes, the small room filled with confusion as too many people got in one another's way as they maneuvered the patient through the doorway.

The chaos moved down the hall, and Emmett and Abigail were alone.

When he turned to her, he saw her gaze upon the piece of hematite beside his bunk. She smiled, and a small blush colored her cheeks.

"You have to leave Byron," Emmett said, with no time for preamble.

Abigail's smile dropped away. She blinked. "Emmett, you're in danger." Her eyes darted to the door.

"I know. But you must leave. Return home immediately." He held her arm and looked directly into her eyes. "You must. Promise me, Abigail."

She shook her head, her brows pulling together above her nose. "I will not. Not while you—"

Footsteps sounded in the passageway, and she moved away from him to the lieutenant's bunk, packing the bottles into her bag.

The guard stepped into the room. "Anything else, miss?"

"No, I think I have everything. Thank you."

He nodded and stood aside to allow her to pass.

She met Emmett's gaze just for an instant as she left the room, and his heart dropped. Her face was set in a mask of determination.

The guard picked up the bucket and followed her.

Well, if nothing else, this time Emmett had evidence. Absolute proof of Lieutenant Fox's attempts on his life. The British officers would have to take the threat seriously now.

But when Emmett turned to the desk, the offending pitcher was gone.

CHAPTER 19

ABIGAIL COUNTED THE HEARTBEATS BENEATH her fingers, keeping her gaze fixed on the hands of the clock in the hospital ward. Satisfied, she released Lieutenant Devon's wrist and sat back onto the chair at his bedside. "Much better, Lieutenant," she said. "Your pulse rate has returned to normal. How do you feel now?" Nearly six hours had passed since she'd found the man writhing on the floor of the prison barracks. And during that time, there had been moments when she'd been fearful that he'd not survive.

"Better," he said. His breathing still seemed shallow. "My mouth and face have still not regained full sensation, and I've some pain in my stomach, but it has eased significantly." He glanced toward the small portrait on the table next to the bed. "I am going to recover, aren't I?" Abigail heard hope where before there had only been fear.

"Yes, Lieutenant," Abigail said. "I believe you will."

His lids lowered in a look of relief, and he sighed. "Thank you, Miss Tidwell."

"You are very welcome." Abigail felt like sighing herself. She patted his arm and poured a fresh cup of water, helping him sit up to drink. She was tempted to ask the man any number of questions. Had he seen anyone suspicious in the barracks? Who had filled the water pitcher? Had Emmett mentioned any young ladies? But she knew now wasn't the time for an inquisition. "You should rest."

Lieutenant Devon closed his eyes and lay back on the pillow.

Abigail adjusted the blankets around him then glanced at the clock again, just now registering the time that was displayed. Nearly four o'clock. She'd have to hurry or she'd be late to her tea appointment. Abigail had quite a few questions for Lieutenant Fox, and she'd had an entire day tending to a man who had very nearly died to come up with them. As far as she was concerned, in this case, it *was* time for an inquisition. Knowing Isaac would be there eased her fear significantly, and today she would do what she'd come here for—she'd figure out how to keep Emmett safe.

She informed Dr. Baldwin she was leaving, removed her apron, hanging it in the hospital cupboard, and fastened on her cloak and bonnet.

The winter air did little to cool her anger. She thought she could actually feel flames on her cheeks spreading to heat her ears. Only a very small amount of Monkshood was required to kill a man, and the poison was known for the horrifically painful death it produced. If the pitcher had contained less water, if the lieutenant had taken a bigger gulp, if she hadn't arrived in time, if Emmett had been the one to drink it . . . Each *if* made her clench her fists tighter, and she had to remind herself to be cautious lest her anger show.

She marched toward the row of houses where the officers lived. And to the one Isaac had pointed out as the house shared by the lieutenants.

As she walked, she remembered Emmett's words when they were alone in the barrack room. If she were to be honest, they'd stung a bit. He hadn't looked delighted to see her, but unhappy, angry even. Of course, he'd just seen his friend collapse after drinking poison. But a month had passed since they'd seen one another—nearly two since they'd spoken—and his only words were a request for her to go away?

He must know the gravity of his situation and fear her safety was in jeopardy, she reasoned. But of course his worries were foolish.

Her brother was the commander of the town, and Lieutenant Fox, while unpleasant, didn't harbor any antipathy toward her. She was the safe one, while Emmett was in grave peril, and her relationship with the enemy was such that any help she could offer must be done in secret or risk causing him further trouble, as well as her brother.

She let her mind wander, wondering what Emmett might have said to her under different circumstances if she'd recently arrived in a town where he lived. She imagined he might greet her with a smile and a bow, perhaps even a gentle tease about a shared experience in hopes of making her laugh. He might request a visit or meet her at a party. Maybe he'd reveal a new rock he'd found or tell her of a particular geological anomaly just outside of town.

Would he not? An uncomfortable resurgence of her doubts itched at the back of her mind. If there were no war, how *would* Emmett treat her? Had the things they'd shared been a result of their forced circumstances? Or was there something more? Were her feelings reciprocated?

She reached the door and lifted her hand to knock but paused and shook her head, as if sending her doubts flying. No matter the depths of his affection,

Emmett was her friend, and she'd promised Jasper, Barney, Luke, and Murphy that she'd help him. That was all there was to it.

Straightening her shoulders, she knocked. A servant woman opened the door, took Abigail's cloak and bonnet, and admitted her to a small parlor beside the entry hall. The servant informed her that Lieutenant Fox was in a meeting but would join her shortly. Isaac had sent word that he'd been detained but would arrive soon.

She thanked the servant, and once the woman excused herself, Abigail sat on a sofa to wait. The room was well appointed with fine furniture and a shelf filled with books. Dark stain was the color of choice for the wooden tables. Paintings of landscapes and foxhunts adorned the walls, and the sofa was covered in a deep burgundy velvet. The smell of cigars and brandy and masculinity permeated the room.

Aside from the homey crackle of the fire, the only other sound was the murmur of men's voices. Abigail noticed a door on the other side of the room was slightly ajar, and it was from the small crack between the doorjamb and the door that she heard the lieutenant's nasally voice. She strained her ears and finally moved closer, pretending to study an oil painting should someone come in and discover her eavesdropping.

". . . have been thwarted at every attempt," Lieutenant Fox was saying. "How does one man consistently possess such an abundance of luck?"

They couldn't be speaking about Emmett, could they? It was too great a coincidence, but Abigail crept closer to the door just the same.

"The tree wasn't our fault," said a voice that sounded quite a lot like Private Matthews. "He was warned and moved at the last second."

"And the poison," another said. "We'd no way of knowing who would drink it."

Abigail's heart beat so noisily, she was having difficulty hearing over it. Her breathing even sounded loud, and she put her hand over her mouth to make certain she'd not give herself away.

"It must be tonight," Lieutenant Fox said. "I grow weary of waiting. Tonight we will act directly and leave no room for error. Now, if you will excuse me, I am taking tea . . ."

Abigail didn't wait to hear more. Her thoughts were folding in on her and her legs weakening. She had to get away, had to think, to devise a plan. Tonight? It was four o'clock in the afternoon. She had hardly time to come up with any strategy, but she must. Emmett's life depended on it.

She ran from the room, startling the servant in the entry hall as she rushed past. "I'm sorry. I must go."

The woman chased after her down the pathway with her cloak and bonnet. Abigail grabbed them, gave a hasty thank you, and kept running, not even bothering to put them on. She reached Isaac's house and flew up the stairs to her bedchamber.

What do I do? She repeated the question over and over as she paced across the room, twisting her hands together. Her insides felt hollow, yet she could scarcely draw a breath. *What do I do?* Her thoughts were filled with such fear and disbelief that she couldn't organize them into coherence. It was one thing to hear others accuse the lieutenant, but to hear the man himself . . . It was all true. He intended to kill Emmett.

She stopped, willing herself to calm. Enough panicking. The time had come to think.

Leaning her back against the door, she slid down, clasping her arms around her legs and resting her cheek on her knees.

She needed Jasper to devise a plan, but how could she get word to him? Before parting, they'd arranged a spot, a crooked fence post at the north end of town, where she would go if she needed help. After a few hours of surveillance when they arrived, Jasper had determined the pickets were lighter north of the town where there was no road, thicker forest, and less of a chance for a surprise attack. The Americans would check the spot at regular intervals throughout the day and night. But she had no way of knowing what time they would be there.

And she couldn't very well stand out at the edge of town alone in the middle of the day without raising suspicion. Perhaps she could find somewhere to hide as she waited. But no, hours could pass, and time was not something she had in excess. Could she leave a note? But how would she get a reply? There was no time to go to the spot twice.

What she needed to do was get word to Emmett. But how?

A knock sounded behind her. "Abigail?" Isaac asked through the door. "Are you ill?"

She stood and stepped lightly across the room toward the bed, not wishing to reply from directly beside the door. "A headache. Nothing to be concerned about."

"What shall I do? Shall I send for Dr. Baldwin?"

"That won't be necessary." She opened the door and saw his face tight with worry. "I just need to rest."

"You are very pale. I will tell Mrs. Bennett to look in on you."

Abigail put a hand to her head. She didn't try to still the trembling that lingered. "In a few hours."

Isaac nodded and rubbed her arm gently. "Sleep then, and recover." He bid her farewell and departed.

A fresh rush of guilt burned Abigail's throat. She was deceiving her brother again. But what was the other choice? He would never believe one of his men to be a villain.

She sat at the small desk and thought for a long while before composing a short note to Emmett. She explained that it was imperative that he leave this evening. After some thought, she decided his primary obstacle was the guard outside the barracks entrance, and she told him she would cause a distraction at precisely half past nine.

Abigail thought that was a particularly good time, because it would be full dark, and the people of the town as well as the soldiers would be finished with their supper and hopefully in for the night. Emmett would have less chance of being seen as he made his escape.

And she reasoned Lieutenant Fox would wait to set his plan into motion. He'd act late when the town was asleep, not when he'd possibly be missed. At least, she hoped that was the case. She continued with the letter, describing the broken fencepost north of town where he could meet Jasper and the others, in case she did not get a chance to tell him herself.

She read over the letter a few more times, hoping she'd not overlooked anything. The plan was simple, to be sure, but she reasoned fewer factors left less room for error.

Her next challenge would be getting the letter to him. Then she'd need to come up with a plan to draw the guard's attention from the barracks. Abigail pushed those other problems to the back of her thoughts, only focusing on one step at a time, lest she become overwhelmed with the enormity of what she was doing. Performing small tasks was much easier than looking at the entire undertaking.

In the cell room, she'd determined the bit of hematite indicated which bunk belonged to Emmett. But if she slipped the note beneath his blanket, he may not notice it until much later. And if she left it sitting on his pillow, someone else might find it. The problem was now how to make him discover the note without drawing any unwanted attention. And of course, she needed a way to get into the room in the first place. But that, at least, seemed possible.

She changed into her homespun dress, thinking it would be warmer for walking about in the evening, and drew on her cloak and bonnet. Emmett's rock pouch lay on the bedside table, and she picked it up, smelling the soft leather. She'd miss this reminder of him.

Tipping it, she poured out the native copper nugget and slipped it into her pocket. The copper was her favorite, and she trusted he wouldn't mind parting with it. She'd also brought the blue fluorite Emmett had so admired, thinking he might like to see it again. Now, she hoped he would wish to keep it as a remembrance of her. Before she cinched the drawstrings, she slipped the letter inside.

She took a small glass bottle from her dressing table and hurried out the door.

Abigail glanced up and down the street before starting toward the prison barracks. She worried she might chance upon her brother or Lieutenant Fox or even someone who would mention to one of them that they'd encountered her, so she took a different path through the small town, staying in the evening shadows as much as possible. The air smelled of woodsmoke as dinners were being cooked in the houses around her. Windows glowed, shining yellow on the snow.

She'd learned that because of the wind's direction over the lake, the farther east one journeyed along Lake Erie, the deeper the snow, and walking along the less-traveled roads took longer than she'd expected.

When she arrived at the barracks, she stopped on the other side of the road in an alley between two buildings, shaking the snow from the bottom of her skirts. Only one guard stood outside the door. The man was young, with a round stomach that pushed out the middle of his redcoat. He stood at attention, musket at his side, eyes straight ahead.

She crossed the road. "I beg your pardon. I'm Abigail Tidwell, Major Tidwell's sister."

The guard dipped forward his head. "Private Ferland. At yer service, miss." Seeing him up close, she thought he couldn't be older than eighteen. Black spaces shone where teeth were missing, and his heavy accent indicated he was from the lower class of London society.

"I hoped you might be able to help me, Private. I was called here earlier today when a man took ill, and I believe in my haste, I left behind a bottle of witch hazel. Might I fetch it?"

"Aye. O' course." He took a key from his belt, opened the door, and followed her inside. "It were Lieutenant Devon's cell?"

"Yes, I believe that was his name." Abigail attempted to act indifferent as she tried to devise a way to get the key. She could think of nothing. Perhaps tonight she'd need to convince the guard to open the door first and then distract him, or she'd get the key once they returned outside. The plan was not coming together as well as she'd like, but she'd worry about one step at a time.

The guard took a lantern from a peg inside the door and lit it, spreading a sphere of light over the wooden walls of the passageway. "Third door on yer right. Prisoners are eatin' supper now, so not to worry about anyone bothering ya." His voice was loud in the narrow corridor.

Even though she didn't expect anyone to be inside the cell, she still knocked before opening the door. Private Ferland stood behind her in the doorway as she entered.

"I wonder where that witch hazel has gone to . . ." She tapped her lip and made a show of turning around, sweeping her eyes over the desk and other places a bottle might be, and then she leaned over and peered behind the trunk.

"Perhaps it rolled underneath one of the bunks," the guard suggested, holding the lantern higher to send light behind the trunk.

"A good suggestion," she said. "Shall we check?"

He set the lantern on the ground then crawled beneath Lieutenant Devon's bed, poking into the corners. "Nothin' 'ere," he grunted.

Abigail moved quickly while he wasn't looking and placed the pouch on Emmett's bunk, leaning it against the wall where she hoped the shadows would conceal it from the guard's notice. She moved to the space beneath the desk and stood up at the same moment he did, holding the bottle in her hand. "Oh, look here, I've found it!"

"Right ya did, miss." He gave her a smile as if he was proud that she'd solved a complicated mystery.

Another twinge of guilt poked at her, and she felt sad for involving such a kind person in her scheme. But if all went well, there would be no reason for the private or anyone else to suspect she was responsible for Captain Prescott's escape. The entire plan had gone much easier than she'd expected, and her shoulders relaxed. "Thank you for your help, Private Ferland," Abigail said, moving past him into the hallway. She wanted to leave quickly before he or anyone else noticed the pouch with the note.

However, when she turned toward the exit, she nearly collided with a person who'd approached without her notice.

"Miss Tidwell."

Abigail's insides froze as she heard the nasally voice. How had he known she was here? A look at the smirk on his face sent cold spreading down her spine, freezing away the confidence she'd felt earlier. The truth struck her like a blow. The partially open door, the blatant conversation from outside the drawing room . . . he'd intended her to hear it all along.

"I was so disappointed you missed our tea." Lieutenant Fox's voice carried an undercurrent of malice that shocked her. He clasped her arm and motioned with a flick of his fingers. Two men pushed past them into the cell room.

She choked, trying to keep her voice steady. "If you'll excuse me, Lieutenant. I was just leaving."

His hand tightened.

One of the men emerged with the pouch and her letter. He unfolded the paper and handed it to Lieutenant Fox.

"Bring that lantern, Private," the lieutenant said.

"Release me at once, Lieutenant Fox." Abigail jerked, trying to pull her arm away. Her heart pounded so loudly she could hardly hear the noises around her. "I need to return to my brother." Her voice wavered as her hopes of saving Emmett crumbled.

The smirk spread over Lieutenant Fox's face, sending a chill across her skin as he looked up from the letter. "A fine idea. Why don't we all pay a call on the major?"

CHAPTER 20

"Captain Prescott?"

Emmett looked up from his supper and swiveled around on the bench, surprised to see two guards standing behind him. After the morning's incident with Lieutenant Devon, he'd been so deep in thought he'd not even noticed their approach. Not a good policy for a man whose life was under threat, he thought.

"You're to accompany us, sir," one of the guards said.

A warning signal went off in Emmett's mind. He looked around the room, suddenly alert. This scenario felt contrived, as if Lieutenant Fox was somehow behind it. "What is this about, gentlemen? Can't you see I'm in the middle of supper?"

"Our orders are to bring you immediately to Major Tidwell's office, sir." The guards didn't act at all suspiciously—their manner was that of regular soldiers doing their duty—but that did not mean Lieutenant Fox hadn't sent them.

Emmett rose warily and followed them from the mess hall with his nerves on alert. They crossed the prison yard and entered a building of offices. He followed them through a passageway then one of the guards opened a door and stood aside, indicating for Emmett to enter.

When he stepped through the doorway, his gaze locked with Lieutenant Fox's. The man's expression was even more smug than usual and held a look that Emmett could only describe as triumphant. Emmett's skin tightened against the sense of foreboding.

He looked away, glancing at the others in the room. Beside the empty desk stood the two cronies who always lurked near the lieutenant, the young night guard from the prison barracks, two soldiers, and upon a chair in the corner . . . *Abigail.*

Her face was pale, her cheeks were wet with tears, and her shoulders slumped forward as she visibly shook, arms wrapped around her middle.

When his eyes met hers, he started, and his worry turned to panic. "Somebody tell me the meaning of this." He barked out the order, even though as a prisoner, he had no right to demand information. His eyes moved over her quickly, assessing. She was terrified. Anger swelled up inside him, and it took all of his will not to rush toward her. Had she been hurt? When he found out what had happened, Lieutenant Fox would wish he'd never heard of Emmett Prescott or the United States Army.

He pulled his gaze from Abigail, knowing his reaction at seeing her must have been obvious to all in the room. "Lieutenant, I demand you tell me what is going on." He ground out the words through clenched teeth, surprised that in his anger he'd managed to speak them without cursing or yelling.

Lieutenant Fox gave no verbal reply, but the smirk twisted his mouth, and his eyes sparkled with a glee that made Emmett's hands tighten into fists. The other soldiers stepped forward. Apparently, Emmett hadn't concealed his desire to strike his enemy as well as he'd thought.

Footsteps sounded in the passageway, the sound of boot heels clicking together indicated the guards outside the door snapped to attention, and a moment later, the door was thrown open.

Major Tidwell stormed through. His eyes swept the room, his expression becoming more confused, but no less angry as he looked from person to person. When he saw Abigail, his eyes widened in alarm, and he strode toward her, kneeling beside her chair. He placed a hand on her arm and leaned closer, whispering something the others could not hear.

She shook her head and covered her mouth to stifle a sob.

The major's expression darkened, and he stood, facing the others, his face like a thundercloud. "Explain this at once."

Lieutenant Fox stepped forward. "Sir, I have uncovered a conspiracy."

Major Tidwell's eyes narrowed, and he leveled his gaze at the lieutenant. Emmett could see true loathing in the glance. "Lieutenant Fox, you had better provide a very convincing reason for dragging me from my supper. My sister is ill, and I do not appreciate—"

"Your sister is guilty of treason." Lieutenant Fox's voice hung in the silence after he'd spoken.

Emmett's mouth went dry.

The major looked more furious than Emmett would have thought possible. Not only had a subordinate just interrupted him but he'd accused his sister of a crime punishable by death. He took a step toward the lieutenant and flung out his arm, pointing toward the door. "Get out."

Lieutenant Fox's pleased smirk did not waver. "I have proof." He pulled a piece of paper from inside his coat and unfolded it with a dramatic flourish.

"Impossible," Major Tidwell said. He snatched the paper from the lieutenant and glanced at it. Then he stepped around the desk and took a pair of spectacles from a drawer and put them on. As he read, the major's face paled. His eyes moved to the top of the page and he read again then again.

Finally, he lowered the page. "Abigail, is this . . . this cannot be true." The sound was no longer the booming voice of a man used to shouting orders, but that of a worried brother. And at that moment, nothing could have frightened Emmett more.

Abigail nodded, and another sob escaped.

No. Emmett's stomach turned to lead. He could think of only one reason Abigail would take such a risk. What had she done?

"The note was concealed in a bag of pebbles," Lieutenant Fox said, tossing Emmett's pouch onto the major's desk. It landed with a thud, and Emmett heard the familiar sound of the rocks inside shifting. The sight of his pouch—the pouch he'd given to Abigail months earlier—made the entire situation seem all the more real.

When Emmett looked back at the major, he saw the man's eyes boring into him. His gaze was dark and the muscles in his face tight as he pulled off the spectacles. "What is the nature of your relationship with my sister, Captain?" Major Tidwell snapped each word precisely, as if he were fighting to keep himself under control.

"She is my friend, sir."

Lieutenant Fox snorted, and his companions snickered.

"That is enough." Major Tidwell's voice was a whip, silencing the room immediately. He held Emmett's gaze. "How do you know Abigail, Captain Prescott? And I warn you, do not lie to me, sir."

Emmett could see barely restrained fury in the man's gaze. Surely all this would be sorted out once the major knew the entire story. Nothing inappropriate had happened between the two of them, and at this point, he wouldn't be revealing any classified information that would give away his regiment's position. There was nothing to be lost by telling the truth, and he hoped it would help instead of hurt Abigail's case. He nodded and took a breath. "Two months ago, I was leading a small company on a reconnaissance mission in the area around Fort Malden, when we were ambushed. I was gravely injured with an arrow in my side and, when Miss Tidwell came upon me, nearly dead. She tended my wounds and those of another in the company, a young militiaman of only seventeen. She saved both our lives, sir."

Major Tidwell's chin dipped in a small nod, but his expression did not soften. "And why would she attempt to help you escape from Byron? Why would she assume you were in danger?"

Emmett felt sick as his fears were confirmed. The letter had been intended for him. "I do not know, sir. I can only assume the men of my company, once they realized her relation to the commander, implored her to come here on my behalf."

Major Tidwell studied Emmett a moment longer then turned toward his sister. "Abigail, what led you to believe Captain Prescott was in danger? Did he or the American soldiers deceive you?"

She stared down at her clasped hands.

"Answer truthfully, Abigail," Major Tidwell said. "You have no need to fear any of them here."

"I am not afraid of the Americans." She spoke in a soft voice, twisting her fingers. "I overheard the lieutenant today before tea." She darted a quick glance toward Lieutenant Fox and his companions. "He spoke about how the tree and the poison had failed, but tonight, he would make certain to do it right." She looked up at her brother, and her chin trembled. "I couldn't let them kill him, Isaac."

"Why would they do this?" Major Tidwell's expression was utterly bewildered. He turned toward Emmett. "Captain, tell me why your men would assume you to be in danger when you'd given your parole and were being detained peacefully as an officer."

And now for the moment of truth. Emmett could feel Lieutenant Fox's gaze on him as he organized his thoughts, searching for the words to convince an enemy commander that one of his men had violated the regulations for the humane treatment of soldiers. Not to mention, the man he was accusing was a nobleman, an officer of the king's army.

"The lieutenant and I had a . . . dispute . . . after the Battle of Frenchtown," Emmett began. "A heated dispute that has led to enmity between us."

"A dispute over what?" Major Tidwell said.

Emmett glanced at the lieutenant and saw his smirk was still firmly fixed to his smug mouth, but the skin around his eyes was tight. He was worried. Perhaps he had assumed the major simply wouldn't bother to ask the American for his side of the story. "I found evidence that the lieutenant had conspired with Indians to attack those injured men left behind after the battle."

"Yes. I heard about this. A tragedy indeed. But the army had left Frenchtown long before the Indians attacked. It is a heavy accusation you make against one of my officers, sir."

"It is. And I would not have made it if I had not seen with my own eyes." He drew in a breath. "In Fort Detroit, I witnessed Lieutenant Fox giving money to an Indian brave in exchange for proof that the deed had been done."

"What sort of proof?" Major Tidwell asked.

Emmett paused and glanced at Abigail. He didn't want to discuss this in front of her. He'd seen her tending to the injured after the battle. The murdered men had been her patients.

"What proof, Captain?" The major's voice was impatient.

"Scalps," Emmett finally said. "The Indian brave delivered a bag of scalps."

Abigail did not react with surprise. She closed her eyes, breathing out a sad sigh. Emmett realized she must have already known.

"Is this true, Lieutenant?" Major Tidwell asked.

Lieutenant Fox shrugged. "The Indians had their chance for revenge, the enemy's morale is lowered, Fort Detroit and all of Upper Canada are safe. The deuced Americans are too frightened to attempt another attack." He flicked away an invisible bit of lint from his sleeve. "A win for all involved. Well, except for the Americans. I deserve a commendation, not censure from a prisoner."

Major Tidwell looked at Lieutenant Fox for a long moment. He sat heavily onto his chair, rubbed a palm over his cheek, then drew it across his mouth. He stared at the letter then his gaze moved to Abigail, Emmett, Lieutenant Fox, and back to his sister. Someone's feet shuffled, a throat cleared, but the major remained quiet.

The silence in the room sounded loud to Emmett's ears. He thought through the implications of what had happened. There was no doubt in his mind that Lieutenant Fox had made certain Abigail would overhear the conversation. He'd known, given only a few hours, that she'd act rashly, and he must have been watching, just waiting, to amass the evidence to implicate her.

But causing an innocent young woman to commit *treason*. A crime for which there was but one punishment, and for the satisfaction of revenge; such an action was more deplorable than he'd ever have imagined the lieutenant capable of.

Finally, the major rubbed his eyes. "Abigail, why didn't you tell me any of this?"

She looked surprised, as if the idea of enlisting her brother's help hadn't crossed her mind.

"I . . . I don't know."

"Did you think I would allow an innocent man's life to be endangered when he is under my protection?"

She didn't answer, but another tear slipped from her eye.

"Abby," the major's voice sounded choked as his control slipped for the first time. "Do you know what you've done?"

"I'm so sorry, Isaac," she whispered.

Emmett's heart pounded. Major Tidwell couldn't allow his own sister to be charged for a crime she'd committed under deception.

"She'll hang, obviously." Lieutenant Fox's sneer could be heard in his voice. "We've evidence and two witnesses. Men have gone to the gallows with much less."

Major Tidwell rose slowly and planted his hands on his desk. "Lieutenant Fox, in your thirst for revenge, you violated the Code of Conduct by threatening the life of a prisoner who'd given his surrender. You tricked a young woman into committing an act of treason, and I imagine if I were to ask your companions, they'd provide me with additional information about your dealings with the injured prisoners at Frenchtown."

He leaned forward. "When a military career is at stake and a court-martial is on the horizon, men will give up a great deal of information." He looked between the two men flanking the lieutenant. "Private Matthews, Corporal Henry, I assure you, you've much more to fear from me than the lieutenant."

Both men's faces paled, but Lieutenant Fox's face was so white Emmett wondered if he might swoon. His smirk was completely gone, and instead of a smug aristocrat, he looked like a frightened adolescent.

Major Tidwell's face was hard. "Guards, remove these men to separate cells and allow no communication between them."

Lieutenant Fox began to argue, but Major Tidwell gave the guards permission to use force if necessary, and he quieted down straightaway, allowing himself to be led from the room.

Emmett thought he should have felt some sort of vindication seeing his enemy receive the consequence he deserved, but no bit of triumph could erase the dreaded uncertainty of Abigail's fate. Even a major in His Majesty's Royal Army had no power in this case. The air in the room felt thick and hot.

"And you, Private?" Major Tidwell said, looking to the young private with the round belly.

"Ferland, sir. I was the guard at the prisoner barracks when . . ." He winced, and his cheeks reddened as he glanced at Abigail.

Major Tidwell nodded, looking tired. "Yes. Return to your duty."

The private saluted and hurried from the room, leaving only Abigail, Emmett, and the two guards he had arrived with.

Major Tidwell rubbed his eyes, and his shoulders drooped in exhaustion, as if maintaining a strong appearance had completely worn him out. Emmett thought in only an hour the man had aged quite a lot. "Abby-snail." He held out his arms, and his sister moved into his embrace.

"I'm so sorry, Isaac," she said.

"You will be given a trial, but the lieutenant was correct. With witnesses and evidence . . ." His voice choked.

Emmett would have given anything in that moment to be able to hold her and reassure her, and he felt deeply grateful that her brother treated her with care instead of anger.

"Captain Prescott is not to blame," she said. "He had no knowledge of . . . any of this. And also Private Ferland. He was not negligent in his duty. I deceived him into allowing me into the barracks."

The major glanced at Emmett, his face pained as he allowed his sister to weep. Then, kissing her cheek, he sent her away with one of the guards, promising to visit her soon.

Abigail glanced once at Emmett as she left the room, her expression filled with apology, and the heaviness that had pressed down on him since that morning when Lieutenant Devon was poisoned became so weighty that he hurt. His heart felt like it was being crushed, and hovering over all of it was a sense of desperation to fix this. Abigail could not hang—just thinking the words made his throat constrict, and panic set his nerves humming.

"Sit, Captain Prescott." Major Tidwell jerked up his chin, pointing to a chair on the far side of the room.

Emmett sat.

Major Tidwell rested his elbows on his desk and his chin on his knuckles. He stared at the note. Moments passed. The major continued to stare, Emmett continued to fret, and the guard stood quietly beside the door as if he could not feel the two men's despair.

The major reached for the pouch and tipped it, spilling out some of the rocks. Emmett recognized his own, and the fluorite from Abigail's collection. The ache inside him grew.

Major Tidwell's jaw tightened. He returned the rocks to the pouch and rose, pulling the cord tight and setting it back onto his desk. His face took on a determined look as he crossed the room toward Emmett.

Before Emmett had a chance to react, the major's fist connected with his jaw and his head hit the wall, sending a burst of pain that made the edges of his sight flash. Emmett blinked as his sluggish thoughts caught up with what had happened.

The major hauled him up by his coat lapels and, just for an instant, his expression changed. His eyes were wide and pleading. "Your friends are north of town," he whispered. "Please, save her."

Emmett felt something cold and heavy slide into his shirt pocket as the major shoved him back into his chair.

Major Tidwell whirled toward the guard. "Return him to his cell," he ordered and stormed from the room.

CHAPTER 21

ABIGAIL SAT ON THE SMALL cot in her cell. Hours had passed, and she assumed it was past midnight, but she was unable to sleep. Pulling the scratchy blanket tight around her shoulders, she leaned back against the wall and wept as she'd done since the evening before in Isaac's office. She'd never have believed herself capable of so many tears.

Accompanied by a guard, Isaac had come late last night and explained what would take place the following day. Since he considered himself incapable of impartiality, he'd assigned three lieutenants to decide Abigail's case.

Isaac had full trust in the men, he'd told her. He was convinced they'd make the correct decision, but he also warned they could not overlook the law. With the witnesses and the letter as evidence, he feared they would find her guilty of treachery against the Crown.

"If there is anything else, Abby," he'd said. "If you were tricked or threatened or somehow did not understand what you were doing, perhaps—"

She shook her head. "I knew full well the risk."

Isaac sighed. "You are too intelligent not to." He pinched the bridge of his nose and swallowed, fighting away tears.

Seeing his struggle made Abigail's eyes burn, but she forced herself to be calm for his sake. She glanced at the guard, wishing she and Isaac had a moment of privacy, but under the circumstance it was impossible. Trying to ignore the man, she took her brother's hand. "If I'd have known I'd hurt you so badly, I'd never . . ." Her voice trailed off. She couldn't bring herself to finish the sentence, because it wasn't true. She'd have done anything necessary to save her friend's life, even at risk to her own. And she knew that Isaac knew it too.

"That reminds me." He pulled out the rock pouch from his pocket. "I thought you might want these."

"Thank you." The leather of the pouch smelled and felt familiar, the weight sturdy and comforting in her hands.

"If you trust Captain Prescott with your rocks, he must be worth trusting." Isaac gave a sad smile.

She could read the unsaid words in his expression. *But is this person really worth dying for?*

"I love you, Isaac."

"I love you too, Abby-snail."

He embraced her and departed, taking the guard and the lantern with him and leaving her in darkness.

The moment the door closed behind him, she fell to pieces.

And even now, hours later, she still could not stop her tears. Abigail pulled up her feet onto the bunk, wrapping the blanket tighter, and rested her cheek on her knees. What would her father say? Thinking of his kind eyes, knowing she'd never assist him with a surgery or hear his voice again, started a fresh bout of weeping.

Would Father be ashamed of her? News would reach Amherstburg in just a few weeks. Would the residents seek out a different doctor instead of trusting a man whose daughter was a turncoat?

And Isaac. She'd never seen such disappointment and sorrow. And no matter what she did, there was no way to make it right.

She sniffed and wiped her cheeks with the corner of the blanket. She reached along the straw mattress until she found the pouch and pulled it close, feeling the different shapes through the leather.

Holding the pouch, she could not help but think of Emmett. And the thoughts brought a heap of regret. She'd never have a chance to explain herself, to apologize and to reassure him that she didn't consider any of this to be his fault. She wondered what would happen to Jasper, Murphy, Luke, and Barney. Would they leave Ontario now that Emmett was safe? She had full confidence that Isaac would prevent any further threat from Lieutenant Fox. Would Emmett eventually be part of a prisoner exchange and return to Baltimore? Would he continue on with his life and forget he ever met a woman named Abigail Tidwell?

At the bugle call, she jerked awake, realizing she must have dozed. Soft light glowed through the greased paper in the high window. Outside she could hear the noises of a waking military camp: voices, doors opening and closing. She imagined Isaac was on inspection, supervising the drills, or meeting with the officers as he did in the early morning hours.

Would he come this morning? Or would she not see him until her hearing? With no hearth and only one blanket, the morning was cold. She pulled the blanket more tightly around her shoulders and closed her eyes, hoping for a bit more sleep.

As her mind wandered, something changed in the noises outside, though she could not quite tell what it was. The sounds seemed less orderly. Calls had become yells, and the voices were louder. She listened closer and heard shouting. *Fire!*

Abigail sat upright. Fire. Where was the fire? She wondered if anyone had been hurt. Would Dr. Baldwin need help treating burns? She listened closer but couldn't discern any details from the muffled voices that reached her.

A key grated in the lock and turned with a click. The door swung inward. Emmett stepped inside. "Abigail." He closed the door and crossed the room.

She stared. "Emmett?"

He took her hand, bringing her to her feet. His eyes held hers as he moved a strand of hair from her forehead. "You've been weeping." His fingertips brushed down her cheek. "Everything is all right now."

She glanced at the door, terrified he'd be discovered. "What are you doing here?"

"No time. We must go, now." He flung her cloak around her shoulders. "Your boots. Quickly."

Abigail bent down and fastened her laces with shaking fingers.

Emmett folded the blanket and tucked it under his arm. He put the rock pouch into his pocket then stood to the side of the door and peeked into the hallway.

"Emmett, we can't." Her heart pounded. If they were caught, there would be no trial for Emmett. He'd be shot on sight, and she . . . she'd be back in the cell before she could blink, awaiting a trial from a much less sympathetic group of lieutenants. She hesitated.

"Luke is waiting." Emmett winked and flashed a smile that did nothing to slow her heart's frantic pace. He slipped through the door, and Abigail hesitated then followed.

They hurried through the passageway and down a flight of stairs then out into the morning cold. The sounds of shouts and running feet were much louder outside. Smoke hung in the air.

Abigail saw no guard. She followed Emmett around the corner of the building. Luke met them in the alleyway, a bound and gagged soldier unconscious at his feet.

She gasped and crouched down, but Emmett pulled on her arm, drawing her back into the shadows. "Just a small bump on the head, Doctor," he whispered.

"Hello, Abigail," Luke said. She assumed the unconscious man at his feet was the reason the young man's chest puffed out as he smiled.

She smiled back but couldn't help glancing down at the guard.

Emmett crept to the other end of the alley, keeping in the shadows, and beckoned them toward him. "All clear."

They hurried across a road and ducked into another alley. "We must hurry before the guard is discovered," Emmett muttered. "But not so quickly as to draw notice."

They needn't have worried. Chaos was everywhere. Men running with buckets, horses galloping through the street, women hurrying past with worried faces and pulling children behind. Shouts, cries, hoof beats, all of it beneath billows of gray smoke.

Not a glance was spared for the three as they stepped quickly along the main road and up the first lane they came to. When they reached the north end of town, Emmett grabbed on to Abigail's hand. "Now we run."

They darted across the open farmland toward the forest. Abigail's muscles were tight, and she ducked her head, thinking any moment they'd hear a call to halt or, worse, a gunshot. But the town was too occupied with the fire to notice the fugitives. The snow was wet and melting, leaving her boots and the bottom of her skirts wet. When they entered the forest, they moved quickly through the areas where trees had been cut, but before long, they were forced to slow, scale over logs, duck beneath limbs, and move around underbrush.

Emmett didn't release her hand, pulling her to move quicker in spite of the more difficult terrain. Luke followed behind.

After a quarter of an hour, Emmett stopped. All three of them were breathing heavily, their cold breath coming out in white puffs under the shadow of the trees. He turned as if he'd say something but stopped when Jasper stepped from the trees.

The Kentuckian's lips pulled to the side in what Abigail understood to be his replication of a smile.

"Burning down the town?" Emmett said. "Don't you think that was rather dramatic?"

Jasper shrugged. "You said a distraction." He turned. "And it was the army's livery, not the whole town." He jerked his head to the side, motioning for them to follow. "Won't be long before they notice you're gone."

He led them to the east, following a winding depression Abigail thought must be a creek bed when the ground wasn't frozen. Walking along the smooth rocks was difficult, and she stumbled often, but Emmett had her hand and didn't allow her to fall.

"Maybe we should find a different path," she huffed as her foot slid off another rock.

"The rocks conceal our footprints," Emmett said, gesturing behind them.

Abigail glanced back at their path and saw the truth in his words. Where the pristine snow around them would have been blemished by their passage, their footprints were nearly indiscernible in the rocks and the lumpy snow of the creek bed.

When she turned back, she started. A dark bruise showed on Emmett's jaw. She hadn't seen him in the sunlight until now. "Emmett, your face." She moved to take a closer look, touching the tips of her fingers to the purple mark. "This is new."

"Last night." He nodded, taking her hand again and continuing. "Your brother gave me that."

She pulled back. "Isaac *hit* you?"

He turned and faced her directly. "Had to. With all the guards around, he needed a reason to get close enough to give me this." He held up an iron key.

She stared at it then at him. "Isaac helped you? Us? He helped us to escape?" Her throat squeezed as she thought of her brother and what he'd risked.

"Not a bad fellow, Major Tidwell." Emmett gave her the key. "In different circumstances, the two of us might have been friends."

Abigail looked down at the key in her hand. She closed her fist around it, and her eyes grew misty as tenderness filled her chest. Of course Isaac would help her.

"Knows how to land a decent facer," Emmett muttered as he tugged her forward.

"We're nearly there, Abigail," Luke said.

A few moments later, they stopped at a steep hill. Luke walked directly up to a large snow-covered clump of bushes and reached behind them. Abigail was surprised to hear the hollow sound of wood when he knocked.

The bushes swung outward.

"A springhouse," she said. A perfect hiding place. Nobody used the structures during the winter, and the door to this one was so well concealed, she didn't think there was any chance of discovery.

Luke entered, followed by Emmett.

Jasper stood beside the opening, waiting for her to follow the others. "I knew you'd succeed," he said, his voice hardly more than a mumble.

"It was hardly a success," Abigail said. "I acted foolishly."

"You acted bravely." His eyes held hers. "Sometimes it is the same thing."

She felt pleased at the compliment, knowing Jasper did not give praise lightly.

He started back down the creek bed, and Abigail smiled at his abrupt manner of ending the conversation.

She entered the cave-like room and shivered. Just like the springhouse at home, a creek ran beneath this stone building, keeping the inside cool during the warmer months. A single lantern sat on the floor, illuminating bedrolls, blankets, and provisions, arranged tidily as befitted soldiers.

"Abigail!" Barney scooped her up in an embrace. "I am so glad you didn't hang."

She smiled at his candor. "I am as well."

He released her and stepped back, a grin on his round face. "And you saved the captain."

"Well, to be precise, the captain saved *me*," she said.

"My masculine honor thanks you for the clarification, Miss Tidwell." Emmett swooped his hand and gave an exaggerated bow.

"Glad to see you safe, miss." Murphy stepped forward. He put an arm around her shoulders and offered a mug of warm broth, which she gladly accepted.

Jasper came into the room and closed the door. "Our tracks are covered and, so far, no sign of pursuers, but they'll be about soon enough."

The moment of happy reunion ended as they were reminded of the peril of their circumstances. Abigail sighed, dismayed. "I've placed you all in danger."

Emmett took the cup from her shaking hand and slid his arm around her waist.

"It's the nature of war, miss," Murphy said. "We all knew what we were getting into when we enlisted."

"And we've been in worse danger from eating Barney's cooking," Luke said.

The others laughed, but to her ears it sounded forced.

She smiled at the attempt to ease the tension, but the reality was, they were a small group in enemy territory. And soon, the forest would be crawling with redcoats searching for them. They'd get no mercy if they were captured again.

"We're in much better shape now that our captain is here to make a plan," Murphy said.

They sat on the bedrolls around the edge of the small room, with the lantern in the center, much like they'd done at camp around the fire.

Emmett draped the blanket from the prison cell around Abigail's shoulders, and she pulled it tight against the chill of the stones.

He bent forward, arms resting on his knees. "We haven't a map, but I believe Byron to be near the center of Lake Erie, more than a hundred miles from

Detroit in the West and Niagara in the East." He moved his finger over the ground as if drawing a diagram on the stones.

"They'll be expecting us to go south. Cross the lake into New York," Jasper said.

"Can we cross?" Emmett asked. "Is the lake still frozen?"

Murphy nodded, tapping his finger on his chin. "Maybe, but it's at least thirty miles to the other side. We'd need a sledge."

"We'd do better farther east where the lake is shallower and guaranteed to be frozen through," Emmett said. "And a shorter crossing."

Abigail felt a burst of panic at the thought of leaving Ontario permanently. She drew in a quick breath.

As if he could sense her fear, Emmett slipped his arm around her shoulders, drawing her against his side.

She leaned her head onto his chest.

"I agree that east is our best choice," Jasper said. "But it's imperative that we stay hidden by moving deep into the forest. The road—the supply line—is well-guarded."

Emmett scratched his fingers through his hair. "And if we get too close to Queenstown, we run the risk of being discovered by the British force stationed on the Niagara."

The more they spoke, the more helpless Abigail felt. Was there no safe path?

"Can we ask the natives for help?" Luke asked.

"Do you know which are friendly?" Murphy said. "I'm not approaching an unknown Indian camp without an entire army behind me. Not after Frenchtown."

"The Oneida are friendly," Abigail said.

The men didn't look convinced.

Emmett made a frustrated sigh. "Well, gentlemen, we can't remain here. And I'm certain Jasper will agree, our best chance of escaping Byron and evading the pickets is to go by night."

"New moon tonight," Jasper said. "Darkness is our surest ally."

"Then it is decided," Emmett said. "We leave tonight."

The others drifted away into their own conversations. Murphy laid down to rest, Barney and Luke gathered the cups and plates, and Jasper stood beside the door, peeking out through a crack.

"You're shaking," Emmett said to her in a low voice.

"I'm afraid," Abigail admitted.

"You're with me, with us. We'll keep you safe."

She twisted, moving her shoulder out from beneath his and sat up, facing him. In the lantern light, shadows made the hollows beneath his cheekbones dark, and his curls cast shadows on the wall behind them. "Emmett, I'll never go home again. Never see my father." Tears filled her eyes. "I don't know what it's like in New York. Everything before me is unknown."

He brushed away a tear with his thumb and cupped her cheek in his palm. "The war won't last forever, Abigail. You'll see your father again."

She shook her head. His words were those a person would give a child to comfort them, but she didn't believe him. The war would end eventually, but if the British were victorious, she would always be a fugitive, always hiding, and never safe.

Emmett brushed away more tears. "Fear of the unknown is the most frightening. It leaves a person feeling powerless. Terrified."

Abigail closed her eyes.

"That is how I've felt ever since Detroit."

She opened her eyes. "You were afraid Lieutenant Fox would harm you?"

He shook his head. "I was afraid he'd harm someone I care about. Afraid he'd harm *you*." He cupped her other cheek, holding her face as he leaned closer to rest his forehead against hers. "When I learned you were in Byron, and last night when I realized what you'd done . . . Nothing has ever frightened me more. Not fighting off an army at Frenchtown with no reinforcements or escaping from a prison or hiding out in the forest hunted by the enemy." He tipped his head to the side and whispered against her lips. "Nothing frightens me more than losing you."

CHAPTER 22

EMMETT AND JASPER CREPT TO the top of the hill, careful not to disturb the heavy-laden branches or dislodge clumps of snow that might slide down and reveal their location. They took cover behind underbrush and snow-covered boulders, moving slowly upward until they could see the valley below.

Long, low wood-framed structures with coils of smoke snaking from chimneys dotted the space surrounding an open gathering area. On the edges of the village were fields, their tidy rows visible beneath the snow. Dark-haired people moved between the long houses, going about their daily chores. Some wore thick skirts and others leather tunics. Feathers poked out from hairstyles and babies were bound to their mothers' backs with strips of cloth and leather.

Emmett raised his eyes, looking past the Indian settlement to the lake beyond dotted with villagers fishing through the ice. "We'll never cross without being seen," he muttered.

Jasper nodded.

Over the course of their two-week journey, they'd debated the dilemma countless times. If they continued west, past the Oneida Village, they ran the risk of encountering British soldiers stationed at Fort Niagara. But farther east, the lake was too wide. Crossing it would take days, and a longer crossing brought with it dangers of its own. With spring coming, the change in temperature would cause cracks in the ice and air pockets in the center of the lake. Not to mention they risked exposure with no place to conceal themselves from the weather or enemies. They'd searched along the coast but always arrived at the same conclusion. This was the safest place to cross.

As far as Emmett was concerned, none of the options were satisfactory. And he'd not risk their lives unnecessarily, not with Abigail. He looked back at the village. Abigail had claimed the Oneida tribe was friendly, and watching children play and women talking together as they worked, he could almost believe it to be true. But when he remembered Frenchtown—the war paint, the braves wielding tomahawks, the soldiers dead and dying with their scalps torn from their heads—he couldn't bring himself to take the chance.

The journey from Byron had been slow as they followed the curve of Lake Erie. And as anxious as Emmett was to get to the safety of the American side of the lake, he knew one hasty move would get them captured. They spent a good part of every day scouting out the safest routes then moved cautiously through the thickest parts of the forest, taking hours to hike only a few miles in the deep snow.

Finally, a week earlier, they'd halted and spent nearly an entire day crafting snowshoes from pliable branches. The contraptions were clumsy and difficult to maneuver at first, but once they got used to taking sliding steps, walking on top of the snow became easier, and they covered more ground.

Abigail had chatted as they wove frozen branches together, telling stories of her father wearing snowshoes and pulling her on a sled as a young girl. She had a way of keeping the men's morale up with her cheerful nature. Emmett supposed having a woman in the camp reminded the men of home, of the mothers and sisters and sweethearts they'd left behind.

She somehow knew just the thing to lift a man's spirits, talking to Luke about his plans to attend university or Barney about the woman he hoped to marry. She asked Murphy about his family and even managed to persuade the silent Jasper to tell about his home in Kentucky.

In the evenings, it made him happy to see the men all gathered, eating the sparse meals together, their temperaments pleasant in spite of the arduous walking and the cold. Abigail's grandmother's colorful stockings hung from branches over the fire, and she tended blisters and rolled ankles and checked each of the men's hands, feet, and ears for frost burn.

But by far, the favorite part of Emmett's day was when the others rolled into their blankets for sleep or left the camp to keep watch. Abigail would pull the prison blanket around her shoulders and snuggle close to him. The two would whisper into the night, sometimes teasing or talking about nonsensical things, and other times they'd mutter soft confessions, speaking of personal matters that required trust to reveal.

After a while, Abigail's words would become slow, sometimes making no sense at all as she fought to keep herself awake. Emmett cherished those moments with her cheek on his shoulder, his head resting on hers. Once he was certain she'd fallen into a deep sleep, he'd move her to lie closer to the fire, resting her head on his pack. He'd watch the light flicker over her face then settle himself down to sleep as well, but not before he brushed a kiss—

"If you don't mind my saying, Captain . . ."

Jasper's words pulled him from his thoughts. What had they been talking about? Emmett cleared his throat. "Yes, go ahead, Corporal."

Jasper gave a strange look before continuing, and Emmett wondered if his thoughts had been evident on his face. His ears heated.

"Every day brings us closer to capture," Jasper said. "Either by those pursuing or those ahead. Your fate and Miss Tidwell's are sealed if we're taken by the British. And the longer we remain in Upper Canada, the slimmer our chance for escape."

"If we wait until the lake thaws . . ." Emmett began but quickly saw the danger in the idea. He sighed. "We risk discovery. Once the water is passable, the lake will be so full of warships and merchants, we'll be seen for sure." He was speaking more to himself than his companion, but he hoped that by going over the problem again and again, another solution would present itself.

"With the Indians, there's at least a chance," Jasper said.

"A chance," Emmett muttered. "I wish I had more to offer all of you."

"We knew the risk, Captain."

Emmett clasped his friend's shoulder. "Then it is decided." He nodded and looked back toward the village once again. "Let's go tell the others."

When they arrived back at the camp, Murphy was stirring rabbit soup over the fire. Abigail and Luke sat visiting on a cleared flat rock. When she saw Emmett, she smiled.

He grinned in return. It was a sight he'd never tire of.

Luke jumped to his feet, offering Emmett the spot beside Abigail.

Emmett sat and, with Jasper, explained their decision to approach the Oneida Indians and cross the lake from the shore near their village.

The men looked nervous at the proposition but agreed, as he knew they would.

Abigail slipped her arm through his. "You are worried."

"I am."

Instead of offering a trite bit of advice or telling him there was no reason for concern, she leaned her head onto his shoulder and stayed silent, offering comfort.

The soldiers talked through the plan, deciding to rest for the remainder of the day and approach the village in the evening. Once they explained their peaceful intentions to the villagers and received their permission, they'd cross the lake by moonlight.

Emmett drummed his fingers on his knee, wishing he could foresee the outcome of their gamble. But all he could do was pray and hope. He hoped no

British patrols came this far west. He hoped the Oneida would recognize that they meant no harm. He hoped he could protect his men and Abigail. They'd all placed their trust in him, and all he had was hope. Was it enough?

"You've grown tense." Abigail's voice was soft, meant only for him. She squeezed his arm as if to illustrate. When he didn't respond, she sat up and pulled the rock pouch from her skirt pocket. "Shall I distract you with this fine collection of minerals?" She poured the rocks into her lap. "Oh, what's this?"

The surprise in her voice made him turn.

She was untying a small scroll, similar in size to a short cigar. "I hadn't seen this before," she said. When she unrolled the papers and laid them flat, Emmett saw they weren't papers at all, but bills. British currency, which retained its value better than did its American counterpart. Abigail stared at the money. "Isaac delivered the pouch to me in the prison. He must have . . ."

Emmett was again impressed by her brother's innovation. He'd secretly aided in their escape and provided the funds to help his sister on her journey, all without endangering his position or his country. "Like I said before, your brother is a fine man."

"Here, you should take this." She held the roll toward him. "Perhaps we can hire a carriage or some horses. At least buy food."

He closed his hand around hers and the bills. "Your brother meant this for you."

"But it might help us."

"Keep it safe. It will do no good with the Oneida today."

Abigail agreed and slipped the bills into her pocket.

Emmett felt the weight of his responsibility all over again. He was Abigail's guardian. Her brother had entrusted her to his care. Approaching the Indians . . . the plan did not sit well with him. He scratched his cheek, wishing he could come up with an alternative. When he set his hand back onto his knee, Abigail slipped a rock into it.

"Now, don't look, but guess what it is."

He turned the stone over in his fingers, feeling the rough edges. It was lightweight, with two smooth planes. One side felt as if it were coming apart in sheets. "Mica," he said.

"That was too easy."

He smiled at the reminder of the first time they'd engaged in a contest of mineral knowledge, and her attempt to distract him from his worries. "Now your turn. Close your eyes."

She did as he asked, holding her hand out. "No cheating."

"Cheating?" Emmett pretended to be offended. "How would I cheat?"

"By giving me a rock from the ground or a clump of snow." Her lips parted just the slightest bit.

Emmett kissed them.

Abigail started, but she did not move away.

When he pulled back, she opened her eyes and smiled. "You did cheat."

Emmett laughed. "I only added a further dimension to the game. But if you'd rather stick to guessing stones . . ."

Abigail's cheeks turned pink, and she glanced at the other men.

They'd all suddenly found a reason to move away from the fireside. Jasper had disappeared, and the others were taking an extreme interest in a nearby tree. She looked down at the rocks in her lap. "I like your game better."

Emmett did not need another invitation. He slipped a hand beneath her ear, drawing her toward him. This time, Abigail wasn't taken by surprise. She kissed him back, a sigh escaping her soft lips, the sound making his worries fall away.

He kissed the corner of her lips and along her jawline.

Abigail tilted her head, nestling against him.

"Just think," he said. "After tomorrow, we'll be in America, and we won't have to scout or stand watch or hide away in the daytime."

She snuggled closer against him. "It sounds perfect."

He leaned his head on hers and tightened his arm around her shoulders. "I'll take you to Rosefield Park, far away from the war. You'll love it there." Abigail grew very still, and he thought she must be nervous about the lake crossing and unsure about her future. It was understandable. "The plantation is beautiful in the spring. You and Lydia will attend garden parties and teas with the other ladies." She still did not move, so he kept speaking in an effort to ease her concerns. "And of course, she'll insist that you accompany her to shop for gowns. Once we cross the lake, you'll not have to worry about the war again."

Abigail didn't respond.

That evening, the small band approached the village, taking no efforts to conceal themselves. They had only one weapon between them, Abigail's father's old musket. And Jasper held it low with one hand in as unthreatening a manner as possible.

They walked at a steady pace, neither too rushed in a way that might be considered aggressive, nor too slowly, which might give the impression that they were sneaking up on the village.

The moment they stepped into the valley, a group of warriors joined them. The men didn't speak or make any effort to communicate other than walking alongside them, accompanying them to the village. Even though they were not outright threatening, the men's manner left Emmett in no doubt that he and his band were their prisoners.

Abigail's hand slipped into Emmett's—whether to give him courage or because she herself was afraid, he did not know.

They reached the gathering space in the center of the village and were escorted through the silent crowd. From the side of his eye, he saw curiosity in the villager's faces, but not fear. A few pointed to Jasper's head covering.

They stopped when they reached a group of five people arranged in a semicircle. Four men who Emmett assumed were the elders of the tribe sat, two on either side of a woman.

The woman was past middle-aged. Wrinkles crisscrossed her sunken cheeks and lined her mouth, but she sat tall, hands folded calmly in her lap, regarding them with intelligent eyes. Her hair was parted in the middle, and a beaded tiara of sorts encircled her head above her brow.

Emmett could see the woman was in charge. She's the one they'd need to convince if they were to leave peacefully. He wished he knew what approach to take with her. Would she respond to charm? Or should he try to gain her pity?

The woman studied the group, and then her eyes moved to Emmett, realizing he was the leader. She nodded her head, waiting.

Emmett stepped forward, but Abigail tugged on his hand. She stood on tiptoe to whisper into his ear, "Say *she-kú*. It is a greeting."

"*She-kú*." Emmett gave the woman a gentlemanly bow and his most charming smile.

"*She-kú*." The woman returned the greeting but not the smile.

"My name is Captain Emmett Prescott." He laid his hand on his chest and spoke slowly, unsure if any of those gathered understood what he said. "My friends and I mean you no harm. We simply wish to cross the lake." He motioned toward the shore behind them.

The woman regarded him for a long moment. Emmett clasped his hands behind his back and regarded her in return. He waited patiently, not wanting to seem intimidated.

Finally, she leaned to the right and spoke to the man beside her.

"Soldier?" the man asked, nodding at Emmett's uniform coat.

"Yes, I am a soldier."

The woman said something else, and the man listened then translated.

"But not a red soldier."

"No, I am an American soldier." A burst of panic flared in his chest. If they wished to, the Oneida could easily turn them over to the British force stationed in Niagara. They would probably be paid a reward. He had no way of knowing the nature of the groups' association. Were they allies? Neutrally friendly? Enemies? He clenched his hands behind him to still their trembling.

The woman spoke and pointed to Abigail.

"What is your name?" the translator asked.

"Abigail Tidwell."

"You are the soldier's wife?"

"No," Abigail said.

The woman scowled at Emmett.

He didn't like the implication in her expression. "I hope she will be soon," he said. He glanced at Abigail and smiled.

She returned the smile, looking shy in front of the crowd.

His words were translated, and Emmett's reassurance seemed to please the councilwoman, or at least make her less angry.

"Why do you wish to cross the lake?"

"We want to go home. We are in danger here." His heart pounded as he said it, but he thought the truth was the wisest course. The council, and especially the woman at its head, didn't appear as if they would tolerate lies or half-truths.

"In danger?"

"From the British—the red soldiers."

When the translator finished speaking, the woman sat quietly. Whispers sounded from the crowd around them, but the council didn't discuss. They sat in silence, waiting, and Emmett realized they were waiting for the woman to give her verdict.

She sat still as a statue, except for the beads on her forehead blowing in the cool evening breeze. Her expression betrayed nothing.

Barney and Luke fidgeted, Jasper stood stoically, Murphy coughed, and still the head of the council watched them, her deep-brown eyes piercing each of them in turn.

"We have a gift," Abigail said after the silence had stretched past the point of discomfort. She stepped forward and handed the woman the pouch of rocks. "Some are valuable, but most are just pretty." She spoke as if apologizing, a sad quality to her voice as she turned over her treasures.

The woman poured out the rocks, studying each in turn then dropping them back into the pouch. She took her time, methodically examining the various specimens. The rest of the council watched her movements, as did the gathered crowd.

Emmett observed Abigail instead, seeing her eyes follow the rocks as if she were hoping the woman could see the same value she saw in them. He took her hand and squeezed her fingers.

Once she'd returned the rocks to the pouch, the woman stood. She swept her arm in a wide arc in front of her, saying something in a loud voice.

The crowd broke apart, the warriors moved away, and women came forward, leading them toward a long house. Emmett held on tightly to Abigail's hand through the bustle. Murphy, Luke, and Barney glanced around with panicked eyes as they were pulled forward. Jasper walked calmly.

Once they entered the building, the women showed with gestures that they were meant to sit on the thick skins scattered over the floor. Children brought wooden plates of cornbread and bowls of venison stew.

Emmett's men accepted the food warily but, at his nod, tucked in. It was the most delicious food they'd eaten in weeks. Warm vegetables, fresh meat.

"*Yawe'-kó*," Abigail said, accepting a bowl of stew. She smiled at the young girl who'd brought it.

"*Yawe'-kó*?" Emmett asked.

"Thank you," Abigail replied.

"Abigail, you never fail to surprise me."

"I know two words in the Oneida language, Emmett. It isn't as much of an accomplishment as one might think."

"Do you remember what I said as I was leaving to warn the army at Frenchtown?"

"I remember you compared me to a hydrated amorphous form of silica with an internal structure that refracts light." She smirked.

Emmett laughed aloud, drawing strange looks from the Indian people as well as his own men. "Exactly," he said and winked. The relief of their success with the Indians made him jovial. "Today, your quick thinking saved us." He bit into a warm piece of cornbread.

She blushed and looked down, moving the spoon around inside her bowl. "Women like beautiful gifts. I did nothing extraordinary."

He wouldn't allow her to be modest. "It was your most valued possession and sentimentally precious as well. And you gave it away to save your friends." He bumped his finger beneath her chin, tipping her face upward. "Abigail, that is *not* nothing extraordinary."

"They are just rocks." She shrugged, though he could see she was pleased. "I'll find more. But I should have asked before I gave away yours."

"They weren't mine. They were *ours*. As it should be. I promise, when we reach America, we will find a church and get married right away. The next time an Indian council asks, I want to be able to say that yes, you are my wife."

Abigail smiled at his joke, but the expression didn't light up her face as it usually did. She turned to say something to Luke and waved at the young girl who brought their food.

Emmett couldn't understand what had changed. This was the second time she'd become distant when he'd mentioned marriage. Was she feeling sad that her father and Isaac wouldn't attend her wedding? Uncertain about what her life would be like in Virginia? She loved him, didn't she? Doubts flooded his thoughts. Was Abigail unsure about *him*?

CHAPTER 23

THEY CAME UPON THE ROAD rather abruptly. Abigail was surprised. One minute they'd been following a forest path that only Jasper could see, and the next, they were standing on a muddy thoroughfare rutted by the passage of wagons. She let out a heavy breath, her heart hurting. She'd hoped for more time.

The six turned, facing one another. The time for farewell had come. Barney and Luke would accompany Murphy west to Pittsburgh and then continue onward to their farm near Cincinnati, while Emmett, Jasper, and Abigail turned east to meet the stagecoach in Williamsport.

Tears welled in her eyes, and she pulled Luke into an embrace. "Please write to me. I want to hear everything about your schooling."

He patted her back. "I promise, Abigail."

"And don't exert your arm. You should still treat it gently."

He grinned, and Barney grabbed her, nearly crushing her ribs as he enfolded her in his arms. "Thank you for rescuing the captain and for saving my brother," he said. "And for the socks."

She wiped tears from her cheeks. "Winifred Morgan is a lucky woman, Barney. Please give her my best."

Murphy was, as usual, more reserved. He took Abigail's hand and bent to kiss her fingers. "I enjoyed traveling with you, miss."

She clutched his hand between both of hers. "Farewell, Murphy." She tried to smile. "Take care of your lungs. Rest when you can, especially when you're out of breath. And try to avoid smoke."

He nodded. "I'll do that."

The men shook hands, bidding one another farewell, and then Abigail watched her three friends walk away. Barney turned at a bend in the road and waved, a grin on his round face. Then they were gone.

Emmett put an arm around her shoulder.

She sniffed, her lips pulling downward, and she tried to keep from breaking down into sobs as she lost another piece of her life. For the past weeks, she felt like she was hanging over a chasm, and the ropes holding her up—her family, her home, her friends—broke away one by one. She was falling, with nothing to cling to and no way to make it stop.

They turned east, and she walked between the men with her head down. Emmett squeezed his arm around her shoulder, pulling her toward him. Of course, she had Emmett. Reassuring, steady Emmett. She loved him, and he wished to marry her, but even that brought no peace. Because soon, even Emmett would be gone.

Why am I always left behind?

She'd remained home while her father attended medical lectures at universities in America and Britain. She'd lived alone for months when Isaac and her father were needed to support the war effort. And now, she was heading toward a future of staying behind, living in an unknown place with strangers while Emmett returned to the war.

She'd acquiesced before because she'd no other options, but now things felt different. She'd tended wounded men in a hospital tent on a battlefield and performed minor surgery in a forest. She'd diagnosed and treated a man who was poisoned and delivered a baby for a naval captain's wife. For the past months, Abigail had felt valued, needed, and after this, how could she go back to staying behind while others did what she should be doing?

She imagined garden parties and gown shopping to be amusing, enjoyable even, but with men being wounded in battle and diseases ravaging camps, sipping tea and engaging in small talk felt frivolous.

"Feeling better now?" Emmett asked, taking back his handkerchief.

She didn't remember him giving it to her. And suddenly, she felt terrible. Emmett adored her, cared for her, wanted nothing more than to keep her safe, and all she could think of is how unimportant she'd feel. Her thoughts were selfish. Emmett loved her, and she loved him in return. That was what mattered, wasn't it?

Then why did it feel like it wasn't enough?

"Yes. I'm feeling better. Thank you." The words felt hollow.

"We still have Jasper for a few more days. Then, within a fortnight, we'll be at Rosefield Park. And all of this cold and mud and marching will be behind us."

"Behind me."

"Pardon?" He tipped his head to the side.

"All of this will be behind *me*," she said. "You intend to leave me at your family's plantation in Virginia and return to lead troops to battle."

"Well, yes, of course. I must." His voice was tentative, as if unsure of what answer she expected. "You'll be safe at Rosefield. And I'll return as soon as I can. Surely you don't expect me to take you along?"

She shrugged and continued walking.

Jasper remained behind at a polite distance, maybe sensing they were having a personal discussion.

Emmett pulled on her arm, stopping her. "Abigail, what is it?"

His blue eyes were wide, brows pulled together. He looked so worried, and her guilty feeling swelled, making her feel ill.

"I'm sorry, Emmett. Nothing is the matter. I'm just sad to see our friends leave."

His concerned expression softened, melting into sympathy. He held her close against him, and she nestled into his embrace, seeking reassurance from his closeness.

That is enough, Abigail, she thought. Her selfish thoughts were going to hurt the man she loved. She put them behind her and determined to look ahead to her future with an optimistic attitude.

"Come. We should reach Williamsport before nightfall," he said.

She took his offered hand and squeezed. "I love you, Emmett."

He grinned and lifted her fingers to his lips. "No words could ever make me happier."

They continued east along the winding road, weaving through forestland and the occasional farm.

In the past week as they'd journeyed southward, spring had come to Pennsylvania. The majority of the snow had melted, leaving the ground muddy but making walking easier. Trees were budding with leaves or blossoms that were ready to burst open. White flowers of the chickweed and the bright-yellow buttercup grew in clumps. She studied the plants they passed, keeping a watchful eye for healing herbs.

Abigail was glad for the change of season. Winters in Ontario were always long, but this one had seemed especially extended, as she'd spent most of it outside. The spring sunshine could not help but lift her spirits. Birds sang and carried twigs and clumps of dried grass off to build spring nests. Squirrels and chipmunks chattered and scurried about, appearing cheerful and busy as they celebrated the arrival of warmer weather.

Coming around a bend in the road, Abigail and Emmett encountered a child. The boy was young—in Abigail's estimation, no older than six.

"Hello." She waved.

They drew nearer, and she saw he'd been crying. He rubbed his eye with a fist. "Please. My ma needs help."

"Of course we'll help," Abigail said. "Where is your mother?"

At that moment, Jasper rounded the bend. When the boy saw him, he cried out and ran.

"No, wait." Abigail hurried after him. "Don't be afraid." She caught up to him and took his arm gently to stop him. She crouched down to his level. "We won't hurt you."

"He has a bear head." The boy looked behind her, eyes wide with fright.

"It's only a hat," she said.

He squinted, studying Jasper skeptically. "Where did he get that hat?"

"You'll have to ask him," Abigail said. "It's a very thrilling story. But first, tell me, where is your mother? You said she needs help."

"In her bed. She can't get up."

Abigail winced. Was the mother injured? Ill? Did the boy have anyone else to care for him? She looked past him and up the hill to the farmhouse then held out her hand. "Take me to her."

The boy held her hand, and they started up the hill.

Emmett and Jasper followed.

"What is your name?" she asked.

"George Holmes," he said.

She smiled, thinking a good portion of Americans she'd met had been named after the country's first president. This child, as well as the other Georges, had quite a legacy to live up to. "My name is Abigail."

When she stepped into the farmhouse, the smell of sickness filled her nose. George led her through the main room to a smaller chamber at the side of the house. The smell grew worse, and she stopped in the doorway.

A woman lay in the bed. When they approached, she raised her head. "Is that you, Georgie?"

"Yes, Ma."

"And you brought the cat inside."

Georgie wrinkled his nose, confused, and looked up at Abigail.

Abigail turned back to Emmett and Jasper in the main room. "Stay here," she said. "And don't touch anything. The illness might be contagious." She didn't tell them her worry that George's mother had contracted typhus fever. The woman's confusion worried her. It was a symptom of the disease, but it could also just be attributed to fever madness. She stepped toward the bedside. "Mrs. Holmes? My name is Abigail. How are you feeling?"

"Marianne, how nice to see you." Mrs. Holmes's eyes were unfocussed. "And did you ride all this way in the rain?"

"My name is Abigail," she said. "I'm a healer."

"I feel so tired," the woman said.

"Yes, I know. And do you have any pain?"

"My stomach is ill."

Abigail touched the woman's forehead, noting the high fever. "Have you noticed any spots?" Abigail asked. "Perhaps on your torso?"

The woman allowed her to check, and Abigail frowned when she saw the rose-colored splotches. She pressed gently on her abdomen, and Mrs. Holmes gasped when Abigail touched her right side.

She straightened. There was no need to examine her further. Mrs. Holmes was suffering from typhus. Abigail left the room and joined Emmett and Jasper. "She needs immediate medical care. Will you fetch a doctor from the town?"

"What is the matter with her?" Emmett asked, glancing past her to the woman's bedchamber. George stood in the doorway, watching them.

"Typhus." Abigail whispered the word, not wanting to frighten the boy.

Emmett's eyes went wide. "Abigail, you shouldn't—"

"I must help."

He pressed his lips tight, as if stopping himself from arguing. He wasn't pleased; she could see that. And she could see he was worried. He wiped his hands unconsciously on his trouser legs as if to keep the disease from getting on him. "Jasper can go for the doctor."

"You should both go. The less you are in this house, the better."

Emmett's brows rose.

She could read the meaning in his expression. He didn't want her close to Mrs. Holmes either. But she could not afford to worry about herself. She'd already touched the sick woman, and it wasn't the first time she'd tended to a person suffering from this malady. She wouldn't argue with Emmett. There wasn't time.

Abigail turned to the boy. "Georgie, do you have relatives nearby? Someone who could watch over you while your mother recovers?" She didn't like the idea of sending the boy to another house when he was possibly contaminated himself, but she couldn't leave him alone with a sick mother.

He wrinkled his brow. "Mrs. Langstrom is a neighbor. She bakes gingerbread."

Abigail nodded. "Once the doctor arrives, we'll speak to him about Mrs. Langstrom helping you."

"Abigail." Emmett touched her arm.

"I'll be all right," she said. "You must make haste. I've no medicine to give her aside from the herbs I've gathered the last few days."

He gave a tight nod, brushed a kiss over her lips, and left with Jasper.

Abigail moved to the kitchen. "George, does your mother keep any remedies? Herbs?"

He showed her a cupboard containing small jars, and Abigail looked through them, pulling out any that might be useful.

"Are you going to bake something?" George asked.

She wondered how long it had been since the boy had eaten. How long had his mother been ill? "If you like. Are you hungry?"

As if in answer, his stomach growled, and he nodded, rubbing it.

"I'll make you something to eat, but first, let's make a tonic for your mother."

"A tonic?"

"It will help her body even out her fluids. Would you like to help me?"

He nodded.

"Bicarbonate of soda, sugar . . ." she muttered, remembering the recipe her father used to keep a fevered patient from becoming dehydrated. She measured ingredients to George, and he poured them into a bowl. Once it was mixed, she administered it to Mrs. Holmes, followed by a tea made from yarrow, hoping to reduce the fever.

She searched through the pantry and root cellar and found ingredients to make a soup and biscuits.

Mrs. Holmes continued her incoherent rambling, and Abigail wished she had laudanum or something to help the woman sleep. She found alcohol far back in the cupboard and poured some onto strips of cloth then set them on the woman's forehead and wrists. It was an archaic treatment, but her father had thought it to be effective for treating fevers when no other remedies were available.

With George's help, she swept out the farmhouse and wiped down the surfaces. Typhus grew in unsanitary conditions, and the spring thaw was often a catalyst, bringing flies into the house from animal manure and outhouses.

Hours passed, and finally a knock sounded at the door. Emmett and Jasper entered, accompanied by an older man with a round belly.

"Abigail Tidwell, this is Dr. Wright."

The doctor removed his hat and gave a bow in greeting. "A pleasure, Miss Tidwell. And Georgie Holmes, how's your mother?" He ruffled the boy's hair.

"Ill, Doctor. She thought Abigail was a cat."

The doctor gave a tired smile.

Abigail led him into Mrs. Holmes's bedroom. "It's typhus fever. She has spots on her chest, and her abdomen is distended. The right lower quadrant is painful, and I can hear rattling in her breathing."

The doctor's brows rose. He held Mrs. Holmes's wrist, feeling her pulse. "And what treatment have you given?"

She explained how she'd cared for the woman with her limited medicinal resources, and the doctor's brows rose higher. "I wonder that you sent for me at all. You seem to have the situation well in hand."

"I am just passing through town, Doctor, meeting the stagecoach in the morning for Baltimore. I can't stay and give this patient the extended care she needs. And of course, there's George. He can't be left alone, and I did not want to send him to a neighbor for care if you recommended against it."

The doctor rubbed his already red eyes. "In the last weeks, I've treated similar cases all over town. You know how an outbreak like this spreads."

Abigail could see the toll the exertion had taken on the doctor. His skin was dull, and his shoulders drooped.

"You must take care of yourself, Doctor, or you'll become ill yourself. Surely you have help."

He blew out a heavy breath and sat on a chair next to the bed. "Many of the men have gone, marching against the British, and aside from the midwife, there is no one with any medical knowledge for miles around. I've considered sending to the medical college in Philadelphia for help." He leveled a steady gaze at her. "Someone with your skill would—"

Abigail felt a fluttery feeling in her stomach. She started pacing. "Like I said before, I'm just here for a day."

"Miss Tidwell, I'm a man of science, but I still believe in divine providence. Do you imagine it coincidence that your arrival coincides with the worst outbreak of typhus fever Williamsport has seen in decades?"

The fluttering grew frantic, and she pressed a hand to her stomach, trying to smash the feeling away. Her mind was spinning.

"If you could see your way to stay even for a few weeks . . ." He ran a hand over his thinning hair. "You and I both know young George runs the risk of contaminating another household if he is sent elsewhere. His mother needs care, along with many others. Care that one man is not sufficient to provide." He leaned forward, fixing her again with his gaze. "Miss Abigail Tidwell, you are needed here."

His words hung in the air, feeling significant, as if they'd been spoken from a pulpit. The idea of remaining in Williamsport terrified her. She knew nobody in this town. She wasn't even certain she could find it on a map. She had only her clothes, a few herbs . . . and, she remembered, the money from Isaac. She wasn't completely without resources. And being able to help George and his mother, Dr. Wright, the town. It is what her father would do. And it felt . . . right.

But, Emmett. She closed her eyes, swallowing hard through the painful tightness in her throat. He couldn't stay. How could she remain without him?

She stood in the doorway, watching as Emmett and Jasper tossed straw over the fence of the horse's pen and hauled water from the well. George followed behind, seeming much less afraid of Jasper now.

Emmett looked toward the house, and when he saw her, he jogged across the farmyard. He reached her and flashed a smile, holding out his hand. "Ready to leave?"

Everything inside Abigail hurt. Everything. She pressed her arms tightly around her waist, trying to contain the pain, but it pushed outward, growing so large that she thought it would surely crack her into pieces.

"Emmett, I can't go."

He glanced past her. "The doctor's here now."

"Infection is all over the town."

His hand was still reached toward her. "All the more reason for us to leave. I don't want you—"

She held up a hand. "I have to stay."

"I must report to Fort Henry as soon as possible. Abigail, we cannot tarry."

"Emmett, they need me here." Her voice shook, but in spite of the pain inside her, she felt certain she was doing the right thing.

His eyes squinted, and he shook his head as if unable to understand her words.

"They need me," she whispered again, willing him to understand.

"*I* need you." He furrowed his brows over wide eyes. "Abigail—"

She pushed a hand against her breastbone. "You love me. I know it is true. But you don't *need* me."

His eyes shone, and his chin quivered. "How can you say that? After everything, after all we've been through. How can you think—?"

"I have to stay."

"Please?" The word choked out of his throat.

"I am sorry, Emmett."

He rubbed his hands over his face, and when he removed them, his expression hardened. He spun, calling for Jasper.

Jasper hesitated, giving her a questioning look, but turned and followed.

"Emmett, I'm sorry," she whispered, knowing nobody could hear.

He strode away, his steps quick, but his shoulders drooped.

Abigail's heart cracked, and the pain made her gasp. She squeezed her eyes shut, holding herself tight.

After a moment, she felt a tug on her skirt and looked down to see George watching her. She pushed down her pain, locking it away, and took his hand.

CHAPTER 24

A MONTH LATER, EMMETT STOOD at the entrance to an assembly hall in Baltimore's fashionable district, holding in his hand a delicate goblet of champagne and on his face, an artificial smile. In spite of Emmett's protests, his father would not hear of his son missing one of these gatherings, and this week alone, he'd attended three. Or was it four?

The British naval blockades had nearly crippled the state's economy, plantations and coastal cities were being raided daily, and still, the upper crust of Baltimore society continued on, donning their fanciest clothes and jewels, eating expensive food, and pretending the world outside wasn't filled with battles, poverty, and refugees.

He felt an urgency to go, to do something, to return to his command. And luckily, he had only to wait a few more days before leading his new battalion north to Fort George on the Niagara.

From the far side of the room, Beauregard Prescott spotted his son and waved him over.

His father, looking much younger than his fifty-seven years, stood straight-backed, his chin raised and head tipped in a manner particular to a person possessing both extreme wealth and extreme self-confidence. His waistcoat was new and of the latest fashion, his jacket immaculately tailored. But his most handsome accessory was the woman, twenty years his junior, who stood beside him, adorned in equally lavish fashion.

"Good evening, Father, Emeline." He kissed his stepmother's cheek.

She curtsied and gave a refined smile.

"Come, there are people I wish to introduce you to." Beauregard spoke excitedly. He extended his arm to his wife and laid a hand on Emmett's back, guiding—or rather pushing him—toward a finely dressed cluster of ladies and gentlemen.

The group parted as they neared. Of course, as one of the foremost landowners in Virginia, Beauregard garnered esteem from his peers. Emmett was used to people deferring to the man when he approached.

"Good evening, Governor Barbour." Beauregard bowed to a gentleman with dark curls and extremely thick black eyebrows.

"Prescott." Governor Barbour shook Beauregard's hand. "And the lovely Mrs. Prescott. Always a pleasure." He bent and kissed the backs of Emeline's fingers.

She smiled politely, inclined her head, and dipped in a curtsy, the motions smooth, as if she'd performed them countless times, which she had.

Beauregard turned his shoulders, lifting his hand toward Emmett. "Governor, have you met my son, Major Emmett Prescott?"

The sound of his advanced rank was still new, the promotion made official only a week earlier. Emmett couldn't help but stand taller.

The governor's eyes flashed in recognition. "An honor, Major." He shook Emmett's hand.

Beauregard gave the group a charming smile. "I'm sure you've heard Major Prescott is a recipient of the congressional gold medal for gallantry in action."

"Very impressive." The governor gave a crisp nod.

"He was a hero at Frenchtown, you know," Emmett's father continued. "And commended personally by both President Madison and Secretary Armstrong. Who knows how many more lives would have been lost if not for his daring action?"

Emmett's ears were hot. "Well, of course I was not the only one who—"

One of the women stepped forward, a young woman with pouty lips, large green eyes, and a ruby necklace that sparkled in the candlelight. He noticed the color saturation of the corundum was very deep, nearly crimson. Shaking his head, he stopped all thoughts of the mineral compound of the woman's jewelry nearly as soon as they'd started. Reminders of Abigail were still too painful.

"Is it true, Major, that Tecumseh's Confederacy outnumbered the American forces two to one?" She blinked, opening her eyes wide, and laid a hand on his arm.

Emmett cleared his throat, shocked by the woman's boldness. "No, not exactly, miss. Combined, the British and Native Confederacy forces were close to fifteen hundred while General Winchester commanded approximately one thousand."

"I beg your pardon, Major," Governor Barbour said, glancing at the woman. "I have neglected to introduce you. If you please, this is Charlotte Benedict from Philadelphia."

"A pleasure." He bent over her hand and released it quickly.

"Likewise," she said.

"Excuse us, please," Beauregard said abruptly. His gaze was already on someone else.

Emmett didn't mind his father's rudeness. He wished to be away from Charlotte Benedict before he had to think of anything further to say to the woman.

"Of course," she said.

Emmett's father nodded politely to the governor. Emeline curtsied again. Emmett bowed, and they hurried away. Beauregard introduced them to a senator this time.

And the evening progressed in the same manner. Emmett bowed and smiled and made pleasant conversation with influential people his father eagerly introduced him to. He answered questions, recounting his small part in a small battle as ladies fanned themselves, pretending to be distressed, and gentlemen nodded gravely, pretending to be concerned. And all the while his father beamed, reminding his acquaintances of the medal and the presidential decoration.

Emmett's cheeks grew tired of forcing a smile, and after so many evenings repeating the same conversation for hours on end, he was feeling rather like a show pony. And it was . . . humiliating.

Seeing Lydia across the room, he excused himself. As he walked away, he heard his father's voice behind him. ". . . the congressional gold medal for gallantry in action . . ."

His sister sat on a sofa between two young men who were vying for her attention. Another man approached, handing her a glass of champagne.

She rewarded him with her stunning smile and a flutter of lashes.

One of the men on the sofa said something to regain her attention, and she giggled, tapping him playfully with the edge of her fan and putting to good use the largest blue eyes in the state of Virginia.

The young man's cheeks flared red. He was smitten.

When Emmett approached, Lydia jumped up, nearly spilling her drink and practically knocking over another young man who'd devised a reason to come speak to her. She flounced away from the lot of them with a wave of her fingers.

They watched her go with covetous gazes.

"Well, hello, Major." She smacked Emmett on the chest with her fan, much as she'd done to the young man a moment earlier. "Growing tired of your adoring fans?"

Lydia was one to talk. He glanced back at her flock of admirers then turned toward the veranda doors and offered his arm. "I am rather tired of being displayed."

She took his arm happily, and they strolled out into the night.

"And what is the matter, Brother?" she asked. "I thought you were enjoying the attention. Father has been singing your praises for weeks now."

She was right. For twenty-eight years he'd sought this very thing—his father's approval—but after being paraded around and shown off to his father's friends, the pride he'd felt at his father's praise was becoming dulled by repetition. And as the days went on and faces blended together, he realized his father was not boasting of his son at all, but of a medal and a title.

"He is not singing my praises."

She tipped her head to the side, making her curls bounce. A thoughtful gaze that she seldom bothered with entered her expression. "You think he's only acting this way because of that round piece of metal."

He shrugged. "Well, it's not as if he's ever showed interest before." He knew he sounded like he was pouting, but Lydia understood his history with his father. Emmett wasn't simply searching for reassurance. He spoke the truth. Beauregard Prescott had not shown the tiniest bit of pride in his second son for Emmett's entire life, and now that he did, Emmett was embarrassed by how much he longed for it.

He thought of the medal. Lydia was right—it was just a piece of copper with a raised profile of George Washington, but when President Madison had given it to him, announcing that he'd earned it by good conduct and gallantry in action, he didn't think he'd ever felt so proud. Few men received such a commendation, and of those, most were senior officers. But Father hadn't seen the battle, hadn't even asked what he'd done to earn the medal. He saw the token and not the deeds, nor the man behind them.

Lydia pointed to a wrought-iron bench on the edge of the veranda. She sat and pulled him down beside her. All traces of the giggling southern debutante had left her face, and she looked at him seriously.

"Em, remember when we were children and we found a kitten stranded on a branch in the middle of the creek?"

He thought back. The story sounded vaguely familiar. "I . . . yes, I think so."

"I was four, and you were fourteen. We heard the cries, and of course we knew there was nothing to be done. The water was moving too fast."

"Yes, I remember now."

"You found an old rope and tied it to a tree then jumped into the water. I remember how it pulled at you, dragging you downstream. Sometimes you'd go all the way beneath the water for moments at a time, and I was certain you'd drowned. But you held on, swimming out to the kitten, holding onto him, and pulling yourself hand over hand back to the shore."

"The infernal animal scratched my arms to ribbons." He smiled at the memory.

"Em, you've always been a hero to me. Not because you wear a uniform and everybody has to salute you and call you 'sir.' Because you fight for those who cannot defend themselves. You care to the point of risking your very life. That is why you are a good soldier. And that is why you are a hero. And I don't need a medal to tell me that."

She opened her eyes wide, leaning toward him, as if daring him to disagree.

He stared at his sister, shocked at her insight, and so moved that his eyes were itching and his throat becoming narrow. He'd never known her to be so considerate. "Lydia, I don't know what to say. I . . ."

She flicked her hand as if shooing a fly. "Oh, hush now, or you'll ruin the moment." Her mouth twisted in a teasing smirk.

He grinned, sliding his arm across the back of the bench and leaning back. He'd only had one other person call him a hero. His throat tightened further as he thought back to that first morning at the bivouac camp. What had Abigail said?

You're a hero, Emmett. No matter what anyone tells you. They don't give those gold shoulder decorations to just anyone, you know.

He closed his eyes against the surge of emotion the memory evoked.

Lydia leaned back against him, playing with her fan. "You've been different since you returned, sad maybe." When he didn't answer, she continued. "I suppose being in a war changes a person. But I hope it hasn't changed you too much."

Emmett had no answer. He knew he was changed. And the battle was part of it, but nothing could have prepared him for the pain of losing the woman he loved. Especially when he couldn't fully understand why. What had changed? Why hadn't Abigail wanted him? Thinking of her was so painful his lungs wouldn't take in a full breath. He needed to change the topic. "What about you?"

"What about me?" She sat up and twisted, looking delighted that the conversation had moved to her favorite topic.

"Tell me about those young men. Is there one in particular you fancy?"

She glanced back to the veranda door and wrinkled her nose. "One of *them*?" She blew out her breath in a very unladylike puff that lifted her curls from her forehead.

Emmett laughed at her absurd reaction. "What's wrong with them? They all seemed to be gentlemanly, well-mannered—"

"None of those men care about me." She looked at him as if this were obvious. "They just like to make me laugh and see me blush at their teasing. It is only a game."

"Father will be wanting you to choose one, and I imagine soon. You are eighteen, after all."

"Well, I shan't choose one of them. They are just looking for a pretty bauble to hang on their arm and show off to their friends." She rolled her eyes. "I do not just want to be a man's ornament."

Emmett thought of Emeline and the way his father treated her. An ornament was a good description.

"Then, who?"

"Who what?" She blinked and opened her eyes wide.

"Who will you choose for a husband?"

"Well, I don't know him yet, do I? Or I would be hopelessly in love."

He furrowed his brow, smiling. He'd never had a conversation like this with his sister and found it bemusing and rather fascinating.

Lydia leaned close, her hands clasped together. "The man I will love shall know me as no one else does. He'll see what makes me different from all the other young ladies, and instead of being bothered by my differences, they will be what he loves most about me."

He stared at her, again surprised by the depth his sister was capable of when she took the opportunity to use her mind. "He'll know what you need," Emmett said slowly.

"Yes, that's right." She nodded, making her curls bounce.

His heartbeat thumped against his ribs as the realization hit him. "And make you feel important," he said.

"Obviously." She looked at him with half-lidded eyes. She picked up her fan and spread it open, waving it before her and giving her most flirty smile. "And a gift of jewelry wouldn't be unwelcome."

"Lydia." He pushed down the fan. This was no time for banter. "I need your help."

She shrugged and opened her mouth as if she'd give a playful response but looked at him, and her face turned serious. "What is it, Emmett? You've gone pale. Are you ill? Or in trouble?"

"There is a woman." He rubbed his forehead. "She . . . I love her."

Lydia's concern vanished, and her face lit up with a smile. "Oh, I am so glad."

"But I've spoiled everything."

She nodded. "Of course you have."

He felt desperate. He'd never asked his sister for advice before, but suddenly she seemed the most clear-thinking person on the topic. "I must apologize, convince her that I love her, but I don't know how. Will you help me?"

She took his hands and held his gaze steadily, showing a composure he'd never seen in her. "Em, calm yourself, and tell me everything."

CHAPTER 25

ABIGAIL TOOK DR. WRIGHT'S HAND and climbed down from the wagon. "Thank you, Doctor."

"Good work today, Miss Tidwell." He handed out her medical bag then clicked the reins, and the wagon lurched forward, leaving behind a cloud of dust.

Abigail started up the pathway to the boardinghouse, inhaling the smell of supper. *Meat pies*, she thought, her stomach rumbling appreciatively. Mrs. Simmons, the owner of the house, made the best meat pies she'd ever tasted. She reached for the door handle.

A throat cleared behind her, and she turned.

"Good evening, Jasper." She smiled, still not used to seeing him without his bear head covering. "I didn't expect to see you this evening. Is everything all right? Caroline? Molly?"

"They're well," he said, his face softening as it did when he talked about his wife and her young daughter.

It delighted Abigail to no end that Jasper had married the shy widow who tended the counter at the grocer's. When Emmett had left nearly six weeks earlier, Jasper had stayed behind. He claimed to have nothing to return to in Kentucky, but she knew he'd remained to keep an eye on her. At first, seeing him was so painful, she could hardly bear it. Those first weeks, she'd immersed herself in her work, caring for patients long into the night and waking early to begin again. As long as she was busy, she could keep herself from remembering and keep her heart from hurting.

Now, however, Jasper's presence was a reminder of a happy time. A reminder that she'd been in love, and the pain of losing Emmett had dulled to an ache laced with remorse.

She set the medical bag inside the door and joined him on the porch.

Jasper, as usual, was quiet, but she sensed there was something he wanted to say.

"What brings you into town today?" she asked, knowing he'd need a little prodding.

He glanced up the street toward the row of shops. "Molly's birthday," he muttered.

"And you wish to buy her a gift?"

He nodded. "Thought you might help me."

"I'd be delighted to." She walked beside him up the road. "Molly is four?"

"Five."

"Maybe she would like a new bonnet or a hair ribbon?"

Jasper rubbed the back of his neck. "I thought . . . I've heard young girls are fond of dolls."

Abigail couldn't hold back her grin. She thought of the first time she'd seen Jasper. He'd terrified her. Who would have guessed beneath the buckskin and bear hide, he was so softhearted? "A doll is a perfect gift."

A quarter of an hour later, they emerged from the dry goods store with a small package. Jasper had purchased not only a doll but a hair ribbon for Molly in the same color as the doll's dress. He held the sack carefully in one arm as they walked back to the boardinghouse.

"She is going to be very happy with her gift, Jasper," Abigail said. She remembered her own father bringing home her doll from Philadelphia. Abigail had imitated her father as she'd seen him treat patients, listening to the doll's heartbeat and feeling its porcelain head for fever. Sometimes, she wrapped its arms or legs in cloth, pretending the doll had suffered a broken bone. A different ache stung inside her as she thought of her father.

She swallowed, and a melancholy descended over her, but she kept her smile for her friend's sake.

They reached the porch of the boardinghouse, and she bid Jasper farewell, turning to go inside.

"Abigail?"

She turned back to Jasper.

"The typhus outbreak is contained now."

"Yes, I am glad of it." She wasn't sure what he was getting at.

"Perhaps now you'd want to continue on to Baltimore? Caroline and I will accompany you if you don't wish to travel alone."

Abigail didn't think she'd ever heard Jasper say so much in the entire time she'd known him. She'd never had such a loyal friend, and he was loyal to Emmett too. She knew he wanted the two of them to be happy, to be together. But it wasn't as easy as traveling to his house in the city and knocking on the door. "I can't. I can't be what he wants me to be. I'm meant to help people." She twisted her fingers together, lowering her head. "I don't think he'd wish to see me even if I did go. When he left"—she glanced up—"he was very angry."

Jasper shook his head. "He was hurt, and hurt looks a lot like anger when a man's pride is involved."

She wiped away a tear. "Jasper, I wish it were different. That I were different, or . . . I don't know. But I miss him."

He nodded, reaching out and tentatively patting her arm, which for him was an extreme display of affection. "I know."

A week later, Abigail returned from the church service and climbed the steps to her room. She tossed her bonnet onto the desk and pushed open her window, a late spring breeze billowing the flowered curtains.

She stretched out on her bed, feeling lavish sleeping in the middle of the day. But as she had no farm to manage and no patients to tend . . . she'd indulge herself.

A knock came at the door. "Miss Tidwell," Mrs. Simmons called. "A gentleman is here to see you. He's in the parlor."

"Thank you, Mrs. Simmons. I'll be just a moment."

Jasper must have come to tell her about Molly's birthday. Her rest could wait. She hurried down the stairs and into the parlor. "Jasper, how did Molly—"

Emmett rose from the settee.

Abigail gasped. The shock of seeing him disoriented her, sending a flush of adrenaline tingling her nerves.

He crossed his arm in front of his waist and bowed. "Hello, Abigail."

"Emmett, what are you doing here?" She blinked at her own rudeness, feeling confused. "I'm sorry, I'm being a terrible hostess, you just surprised . . ." She curtsied. "How nice to see you. Please, won't you sit down?"

He grinned and waited for her to sit before joining her on the settee.

The sight of him was so familiar, his smell, his uneven grin, she could scarcely put two thoughts together.

"To answer your question, I'm traveling north to a new command in Fort George. The battalion is quartered in Williamsport for a week at least, to replenish supplies and wait for another regiment to join us from Ohio."

"Oh," was all she could think to say.

He smiled, apparently enjoying her awkward reaction. "I've come today in hopes that you might help me."

She smoothed down her skirts, composing herself. "Yes, of course."

He nodded. "I've received a promotion, and now—"

"Oh, congratulations! Emmett, that's wonderful." She looked at the insignias on his shoulder. "You are *Major* Prescott now."

"Yes, thank you. And you see, my new rank presents me with a problem. I'm responsible for staffing my battalion, and we still lack a doctor." He held an envelope toward her.

Abigail studied him for a moment, not sure what exactly he was getting at. His face was hard to read. He acted confident, but the skin beneath his eyes was tight. Was he nervous?

He waved the envelope. "Go on, open it."

The letter was addressed to her. She broke the wax seal and slipped out the paper. Unfolding it, she saw the emblem of the United States Army at the top of the stationery and read a formal request to hire her services as an army surgeon.

She stared at the letter, tracing the outline of her name: *Abigail Tidwell (doctor)*. Her hands shook, and a fluttering started in her belly. "Emmett, do you really mean . . ."

He swung around to kneel on the rug before her. "I was wrong, Abigail. Please forgive me for taking so long to realize that loving a person means loving who they are, all of them." He took her hand. "All of you. Abigail, the thing you want most is to be needed. To be able to help others. And I tried to change you. I was only concerned with what I want most—to keep you from harm." His brow wrinkled. "I hope in time I can figure out how to do both, but for now . . ." He motioned toward the letter.

She set it aside and placed her hands on his shoulders. She held his gaze, wanting him to see how grateful she was. "Thank you, Emmett. You've made me so happy."

He glanced at the letter. "We may need to change the wording."

Abigail tilted her head. "Why? I don't . . ."

He shrugged, one side of his mouth lifting. "I hoped to be able to hire a Mrs. Abigail Prescott." He pulled a small wrapped box from his pocket and set it in her hand. "If she will consent."

Tears clogged her throat. "Emmett . . ."

"Go on, open it," he said again. He moved back to sit beside her.

Abigail tore off the paper and opened the wooden box. "Oh," she breathed. "I have never actually seen . . . It's more beautiful than I dreamed." She held up a chain with a black opal affixed to it, watching the light diffract, making bursts of color. Even with her understanding of the mineral properties, she could find no words to describe the splendor of the gem.

She fastened the clasp around her neck, holding up the pendant, unable to stop admiring the magnificent gift. "I don't know what to say, I—"

"Say you'll marry me." Emmett took her face in his hands. "Say I won't ever have to leave you again." His eyes pleaded.

"I will," Abigail whispered. The words had hardly left her mouth before they were lost in his kiss. His lips were hot on hers, his fingers tangling into her hair. Abigail grasped on to his lapels, pulling him closer, feeling as if he could never be close enough. He'd said what she wanted was to be needed, to help others, but in reality, the only thing that made her whole was this man. Emmett had given friendship when she was alone, courage when she was afraid, and a purpose when she was lost. He wanted her to succeed and believed her aspirations to be as valuable as his own.

"I missed you," he whispered against her lips, his breath sending tingles over her skin.

She nestled beneath his arm as she had so often as they'd sat beside a campfire in a snow-covered forest. "Don't leave me again," she said.

He pulled her tighter against him. "I have one more thing for you."

"Emmett, you don't need . . ."

He reached down beside the settee and lifted a wooden bucket, setting it into her lap. Inside was a small, handheld pickaxe.

She looked at the bucket and then at him, bewilderment making her scowl. "What is this?" Was he ruining their romantic moment with a joke?

"I told you, the army is stationed here for a week, so I hoped we might honeymoon in Fredericksburg."

Abigail still didn't understand what a bucket and a pickaxe had to do with getting married or a honeymoon, or anything for that matter. After his other two gifts, this was somewhat disappointing.

He placed the bucket onto the floor then set the tool in her hand, closing her fingers around it. "Three miles north of Fredericksburg, there is a fossil bed where we can hunt for trilobites." He kissed her again, and the pickaxe transformed into the most romantic gift she could conceive.

"You know, once we're married, you'll be an American," Emmett said. "Or, as you so eloquently put it the first day we met, a *cursed* American."

"I suppose there are worse things than marrying one's enemy," Abigail said, and she pulled him close for another kiss.

ABOUT THE AUTHOR

JENNIFER MOORE IS A PASSIONATE reader and writer of all things romance due to the need to balance the rest of her world, which includes a perpetually traveling husband and four active sons who create heaps of laundry that are anything but romantic. Jennifer has a BA in linguistics from the University of Utah and is a Guitar Hero champion. She lives in northern Utah with her family. You can learn more about her at authorjmoore.com.